MW00978525

BILLY BUNTER'S
BANKNOTE

THAT STARTLING QUESTION CAUSED EVERY EYE
IN THE JUNIOR DAY-ROOM TO TURN UPON HIM

BILLY BUNTER'S
BANKNOTE

By
FRANK RICHARDS

Illustrated by
R. J. MACDONALD

First published by Charles Skilton in 1948

This edition published 1992 by:
HAWK BOOKS LTD
Suite 309
Canalot Studios
222 Kensal Road
London W10 5BN

Copyright © 1992 Una Hamilton-Wright

ISBN 0 948248 68 8

*All rights reserved. No part of this publication may be
reproduced, stored in a retrieval system, or transmitted in
any form or by any means, electronic, mechanical,
photocopying, recording or otherwise without prior
written permission of the copyright holder.*

Printed in England by Redwood Press Ltd.

CONTENTS

Contents

Chapter I

CAKE FOR ONE !

" I SAY, you fellows ! "

Harry Wharton and Frank Nugent, in No. 1 Study in the Greyfriars Remove, glanced round, as a fat voice squeaked in the doorway.

Billy Bunter, his ample proportions almost filling the doorway from side to side, blinked in through his big spectacles.

" Oh, here you are ! " said Bunter, " I've been looking for you."

" Now go and look for somebody else ! " suggested Harry Wharton.

" Oh, really, Wharton——."

"And shut the door after you ! " said Nugent.

" Oh, really, Nugent——."

"Buzz off ! " said both the juniors together: and they turned back to the occupation that Billy Bunter's arrival had interrupted.

It was tea-time ! There was a parcel on the study table. It was not a large parcel; but evidently it contained supplies for tea: and Billy Bunter's eyes, and spectacles, lingered on it covetously.

Wharton and Nugent were getting tea. They expected Bob Cherry, Johnny Bull, and Hurree Singh, to tea: and did not expect Billy Bunter. Neither did they seem happy to see him. Attractive fellow as Bunter knew himself to be, fellows never did seem exhilarated to see him at tea-time. Bunter was too quick a worker to be welcomed at the festive board when supplies were short.

Nevertheless, had Bunter rolled in, no doubt he

1

would have been allowed to remain, and annex his share—or rather more than his share—of what was going. But, to the surprise of the chums of the Remove, Bunter did not roll in.

"If you fellows think I've come to tea——!" said Bunter.

"Eh! Haven't you?"

"No!" roared Bunter, "Think I want a whack in your measly two-bob cake? Fat lot there would be to go round! Besides, I never knew you had a cake. Thank goodness I'm not always thinking about grub, like some fellows."

"Oh, my hat!"

"I'm going to tea with Mauly!" yapped Bunter.

"Poor old Mauly!"

"Yah!"

"Well, if you haven't come to tea, what have you come for?" asked Frank, "Not just to spoil the view, I suppose?"

"You fellows are for it!" said Bunter, impressively, "You're up for a row, and I jolly well know why. I saw you knock Coker's hat off in the quad after class."

Harry Wharton laughed.

"Coker can come up and see us about it, if he likes," he said.

"'Tain't Coker! It's the Head! The Head wants to see you in his study. I fancy he saw you knock Coker's hat off. Anyhow, he wants you. That's why I've come up—not after your measly two-bob cake!" added Bunter, scornfully, "Head's study at once—and you'd better pack some exercise books in your bags—he looked waxy!"

And with that, William George Bunter revolved on his axis, rolled out of the study doorway, and disappeared up the Remove passage.

Harry Wharton and Frank Nugent looked at

one another, across the table, in dismay. They did
not want Bunter to tea—but Bunter to tea would
have been better than a summons to the head-
master's study.

"Oh, rotten!" said Harry.

"Putrid!" agreed Nugent.

"I suppose he must have seen us from his
study window!" grunted the captain of the
Remove. "Blow! What does Coker's silly hat
matter anyhow?"

"Bother Coker and his hat!"

"Blow Coker!"

It really was hard luck. Knocking off a Fifth-
form man's hat in the quad was regarded, in the
Remove, merely as a harmless and necessary
relaxation. Neither Horace Coker nor his hat
mattered a boiled bean. Both were trifles light as
air, from the point of view of the Remove. But if
Dr. Locke had witnessed that trifling incident from
his study window, it had a more serious aspect.
Head-masters did not see eye to eye with juniors
of the Lower School in such matters.

"I suppose we'd better go!" grunted Wharton.

"Sort of!" grinned Nugent, "Beaks don't like
Lower-Fourth fellows to keep them waiting!
Only a jaw, I expect—the Old Man wouldn't whop
for that!"

And the captain of the Remove and his chum
left the study, and went down the passage to the
stairs.

From the door of No. 7 Study, further up the
passage, a pair of little round eyes, and a pair of
big round spectacles, watched them go.

As Wharton and Nugent disappeared across
the Remove landing, Billy Bunter rolled out of No.
7, grinning from ear to ear. He rolled into No. 1
Study. Billy Bunter's movements were generally
slow: but on this occasion he rolled, like Iser in the

poem, rapidly.

"He, he, he!" chuckled Bunter, as two fat clutching hands closed on the parcel on the study table.

Bunter had said that he did not want a whack in a two-bob cake. Bunter was not always veracious: but that statement was true. He didn't want a whack in that cake. He wanted it all.

Wharton had already untied the string of the parcel. Bunter proceeded to unwrap it. His happy grin grew more expansive as the cake was revealed.

Bunter gloated over that cake. He was hungry. He had had tea in Hall, to make sure of something to go on with. He was going to have tea with Lord Mauleverer—if Mauly couldn't help it. But there was plenty of room for the cake. He blinked round for a knife to cut it, found one in the table drawer, and was about to begin operations, when he gave a sudden jump.

" Hallo, hallo, hallo! " came a cheery roar in the doorway.

" Oh! " gasped Bunter.

He spun round in alarm. In his keen concentration on the cake, he had not heard Bob Cherry coming. He blinked at a cheery face under a mop of flaxen hair in the doorway. Behind Bob was another Remove fellow, with a dusky smiling face and a flash of white teeth.

" Beast! " gasped Bunter. " Making a fellow jump! I—I say, you fellows, I—I was just coming up the passage to tell you—you're wanted in the Head's study. Knocking Coker's hat off——."

"I didn't knock Coker's hat off. I only kicked it after Wharton had knocked it off! " answered Bob, cheerily. " And I don't suppose the Head cares a hoot about Coker and his hat."

" Well, I fancy it's that," said Bunter, shaking

his head. "Anyhow he sent me up to tell you. Wharton and Nugent have gone already. You'd better cut off. The Beak's always worse if you keep him waiting—and he's waiting now!"

"Oh, blow!" said Bob. "Come on, Inky. If there's going to be a row about Coker's silly hat, we're all in it. Blow!"

"The blowfulness is terrific!" said Hurree Jamset Ram Singh, dismally. And the two juniors, instead of coming into No. 1 Study, trailed off down the passage to the two stairs.

Billy Bunter grinned again when they were gone. A large slice was sliced off the cake, and the most active jaws at Greyfriars School opened wide. There was a sound of champing in No. 1 Study. It was a large slice, and a solid slice, but it did not last Bunter long. It disappeared rapidly on the downward path; and a fat hand grabbed the knife to cut another. But at that point there was once more an interruption.

"You've started, I see!" said a sarcastic voice in the doorway. "Where are the fellows?"

Billy Bunter whirled round, and blinked in great exasperation at Johnny Bull of the Remove. Really, these interruptions were very annoying.

"Oh! They've gone to the Head!" gasped Bunter. "You're wanted too, Bull. I've been looking for you to tell you——."

"You didn't look in my study, or you'd have found me."

"I—I was just coming, but Wharton asked me to unpack this parcel for him while he was gone. The Head wants the whole lot of you, for knocking Coker's hat off—he saw you from his window——. He's waiting for you."

Snort from Johnny Bull.

"Blow Coker, and blow his hat!" he said, crossly: and he went down the passage with his heavy tread, much to Bunter's relief.

Bunter's attention returned to the cake. All the Famous Five were gone to the Head's study now, and the coast was clear at last.

Billy Bunter sliced the cake, and settled down to enjoy life.

He did not fear any more interruptions: Harry Wharton and Co. were not likely to come back yet. Fellows sent for to the Head's study had to wait, if the Head was not there—and Bunter was aware that the Head was not there, having seen him go out!

They would wait a quarter of an hour, at least, Bunter considered, before they gave it up. That was more than ample time for Bunter.

Once more there was a sound of champing in No. 1 Study—and a happy fat Owl finished the cake to the last crumb and the last plum.

Chapter II

IN THE HEAD'S STUDY

" BOTHER ! " said Harry Wharton.

" Blow ! " said Frank Nugent.

It was really disconcerting. Having tapped respectfully at the door of the Head's study, and entered that apartment, they naturally expected to find the Head there—as he had sent for them. But the Head was not there. It had not occurred to them that Billy Bunter, with felonious designs on the cake, had invented that message from the Head.

" Wait, I suppose," grunted Wharton.

" I suppose so ! " agreed Nugent.

And they waited.

Tap !

The study door opened again, and they looked round, as Bob Cherry came in, followed by Hurree Jamset Ram Singh. They came in with the meek and respectful air proper to juniors entering the presence of their head-master : which, as soon as they saw that the Head was not present, dropped from them like a cloak.

" Hallo, hallo, hallo ! " exclaimed Bob. " Where's the jolly old beak ? "

" Goodness knows ! We're waiting for him."

" The esteemed and idiotic Bunter told us that the Head was waiting for us," remarked Hurree Jamset Ram Singh.

" We're waiting for him instead."

" Oh, blow ! " said Bob, " I want my tea."

" Same here ! "

" The samefulness is terrific."

" Bit cheeky of the Old Man to keep fellows hanging about at tea-time," remarked Bob. "Can't tell him so, I suppose, when he comes in."

" Better not," said Harry Wharton, laughing. " He can't be long, anyhow, as he told Bunter to send us here. Stepped out to speak to Quelch, perhaps."

Tap!

Johnny Bull came into the study. He stared at the Head's writing table and empty chair, and then at the waiting juniors.

" Bunter said——," he began.

" Join the queue," said Bob. " Wharton and Nugent were here first, so they're entitled to the first whops when the Head blows in. You come last."

Johnny Bull chuckled.

" I shan't push for a front place," he remarked. " What a rotten fuss to make about knocking Coker's hat off. Wouldn't have mattered much if we'd knocked his head off, so far as I can see. Nothing in it."

Bob Cherry sat on the edge of the Head's writing table, and swung his long legs. Wharton gave him a warning look.

" Better not let the Head see you there when he comes in!" he said.

" Oh, blow," answered Bob, " The Beak can't expect a fellow to stand around on his hind legs waiting for him. What the thump is he keeping us waiting like this for? If it's a whopping, a fellow wants to get it over. Dash it all, a head-master ought to keep an appointment when he makes one. Can't have forgotten sending for us, I suppose? If the jolly old beak is losing his jolly old memory——."

Bob Cherry broke off, suddenly, as the study door opened—without a tap this time!

"Oh!" gasped Bob.

He fairly bounded off the writing-table. Obviously his words must have been heard as the door opened, and what their effect might be on Dr. Locke, the venerable Head of Greyfriars School, was alarming to contemplate. All the juniors spun round towards the door, expecting to see Dr. Locke.

But it was not the Head who entered.

It was a little gentleman with fluffy hair, a pale complexion, a receding chin, and a pair of watery eyes that blinked through rimless pince-nez.

"Oh!" gasped Bob again, in great relief. "Only Twiss."

It was Mr. Twiss, the head-master's secretary.

Mr. Twiss was a newcomer at the school, having entered the Head's service only that term. The juniors had seen little of him: and were not interested in him: but Bob, at least, was glad to see him now—instead of his head-master!

Mr. Twiss gave Bob a rather severe glance. Then he looked round the little crowd of juniors, evidently surprised to find them collected in the head-master's study.

"What are you boys doing here?" he exclaimed, "You have no right to enter this study in your head-master's absence."

"We've been sent for, Mr. Twiss," explained Harry Wharton. "We're waiting for Dr. Locke."

"If you have come here to play some foolish trick in your head-master's study——." Mr. Twiss seemed suspicious.

"I've told you that Dr. Locke sent for us to come here," answered Wharton, curtly.

"Dr. Locke has certainly done nothing of the kind," retorted Mr. Twiss. "Dr. Locke is dining with Sir Hilton Popper, at Popper Court, this evening, and he left the school an hour ago."

"Wha-a-at?" ejaculated the five juniors, in startled chorus.

Mr. Twiss set the door wide open.

"You had better go," he said, drily. "If I find anything amiss in this study, I shall have no alternative but to report you to Dr. Locke in the morning."

"We were told to come here——!" stammered Nugent.

"Nonsense!"

Snort from Johnny Bull.

"Can't you take a fellow's word?" he demanded. "We were told by a fellow in our form that the Head had sent for us——."

"Dr. Locke certainly did not send for you, and the sooner you go, the better," snapped Mr. Twiss. "If you have done anything here——."

"We've done nothing!" growled Bob, "We came here because Bunter told us——."

"Please leave this study at once. I have work to do here."

Harry Wharton and Co. looked at one another. Evidently, if the Head had gone to dine at Popper Court, he couldn't be expecting to see five members of the Lower Fourth Form in his study. Equally evidently, he couldn't have sent for them, and no doubt he knew nothing whatever about the misadventures of Coker's hat!

"That fat villain Bunter——!" breathed Bob Cherry.

"Pulling our leg!" said Johnny Bull, with a deep breath.

"By gum! I'll——."

"Will you please go?" snapped Mr. Twiss, impatiently. "Whether you came here to play some disrespectful trick, or whether some foolish boy has deluded you, you have no business here. Go away at once." He was standing with his hand on the door. "Leave this study, please."

The juniors left the study, and Mr. Twiss closed the door after them with a snap.

In the corridor, they looked at one another again.

"Suspicious little beast!" said Bob. "He thinks we were up to something in the beak's study——."

"Oh, bother Twiss," grunted Johnny Bull. "He can think what he likes, and be blowed to him! But that fat villain Bunter—what the thump did the fat Owl play this idiotic trick for——? We might have waited an hour in that study if Twiss hadn't come in——."

"Lucky he did come in," said Harry. "If this is Bunter's idea of a joke, it's time he learned not to be so funny. He said he was going to tea with Mauly—we'll burst him all over Mauly's study ——."

"He was in your study when I saw him," grunted Johnny Bull, "scoffing cake."

"Cake!" repeated Nugent, "Oh, my hat! That's why!"

"The whyfulness is terrific!"

"Oh!" exclaimed Harry. He understood at last. While the Famous Five were wasting time in the Head's study, Bunter was not wasting time in No. 1 Study in the Remove—he was dealing with the cake!

"Come on!" roared Bob.

Five wrathful juniors ran for the stairs. They rushed up the staircase. They had not, after all, had to wait so long in the Head's study as Bunter had happily calculated. They came across the Remove landing with a rush. It was just ill-luck that Herbert Vernon-Smith was coming out of the Remove passage as they rushed into it. They did not even see him till they crashed. There was a yell from Smithy as he was strewn in the passage.

"Oh! Ow! Wharrer you up to?" The Bounder sat up and spluttered. "You silly asses —you mad chumps—you blithering maniacs—you burbling cuckoos—what the thump do you think you're up to?"

But the Famous Five had no time to waste on Smithy. They left him to splutter, and rushed on to No. 1 Study.

Chapter III

WHO HAD THE CAKE ?

BILLY BUNTER jumped.

He spun round from the study cupboard in No.
1, with a squeak of alarm.

Bunter had finished the cake. Not a crumb or
a plum remained—not the ghost of a crumb or a
plum. It was—or had been—a nice cake. Bunter
had enjoyed it. Added to tea in Hall, it had taken
the keen edge off his appetite.

But he was not finished in Wharton's study.
Like Alexander of old, he was not satisfied with
his plunder, and sighed for fresh worlds to
conquer. It stood to reason, Bunter thought, that
something more than a cake must have been provided for tea for five fellows. So there was Bunter,
standing at the open study cupboard, blinking into
it, in search of the something more. He had lots
of time—those fellows might wait an hour, at least
half-an-hour, for the Head. But a change came
o'er the spirit of his dream, as the poet puts it, as
there was a rush of feet in the passage, and five
fellows in a bunch burst into the study. It seemed
that they had not, after all, waited very long for
the Head!

"Oh!" gasped Bunter, " I—I say, you fellows
——."

"Here he is!"

"Where's that cake?"

"The wherefulness is terrific."

"You fat brigand——."

"You podgy pirate——!"

"I—I say, haven't you been to the Head?"

gasped Bunter. " I—I say, you had to wait if he
wasn't in his study. You'll get into an awful row
if you don't wait for him in his study——."

" So you knew he wasn't there, you fat fraud."

" Oh! No! I never saw him go out before I
came up to the studies—so far as I know, he hasn't
gone out in the car, and I never heard him tell the
chauffeur to drive to Popper Court——."

" Where's that cake? "

" Eh! What cake? " asked Bunter. " Did you
fellows have a cake? I never saw a cake——."

" You never saw the cake you were bolting
when I looked in? " asked Johnny Bull.

" I—I wasn't bolting it! I only had a slice—
just a teeny-weeny slice—just a taste! If you
fellows are going to make a fuss about a fellow
having a teeny-weeny slice of cake——."

" We won't make a fuss about a teeny-weeny
slice—where's the rest? "

" The—the rest? " stammered Bunter. " Oh!
I—I——."

" You fat villain," said Harry Wharton. " You
sent us to wait for the Head in his study, when
you knew he'd gone to Popper Court——."

" He, he, he! "

" And you scoffed the cake while we were
gone——."

" I didn't! " roared Bunter, in alarm, " I—I
haven't had the cake. The—the fact is——."

" Collar him! "

" Scrag him! "

" I say, you fellows." Bunter dodged actively
round the study table, " I say, do listen to a chap!
I never had the cake—another fellow had it. I—
I'd have stopped him, if I could—but—but Coker
was too big for me to tackle, and so—so I had to
let him walk off with the cake."

" Coker! " repeated the Famous Five, with one

voice.

"Yes! He—he came into the study, after—after you were gone!" gasped Bunter. "He—he collared the cake. I—I expect he did it because you knocked his hat off, you know. In fact, he said so. He said, 'Tell Wharton I'm bagging his cake for knocking my hat off!' Those very words."

"Oh, my hat!" ejaculated Bob Cherry, "Ananias was a fool to that chap! George Washington wasn't in the same street with him."

"If you fellows don't believe me——!"

"Believe you! Oh, crumbs!"

"Well, you jolly well go to Coker's study in the Fifth," said Bunter. "You'll find him and Potter and Greene scoffing that cake."

Harry Wharton and Co. gazed at William George Bunter. They were not likely to believe that Coker of the Fifth had raided that cake. Coker of the Fifth was the man to come up to the Remove studies for a row—especially after his hat had suffered from the playful attentions of the chums of the Remove. But the idea of a Fifth-form senior snooping a cake in a junior study was a little too steep. If Billy Bunter hoped to get by with that, it showed that Billy Bunter was an optimist.

"You fellows go and see Coker about it," urged Bunter, with a longing blink at the door. "I'd jolly well rag him for it, if I were you. He called you names, too, while—while he was snooping the cake. He—he said you were a stuck-up young ass, Wharton."

"Did he?" gasped Harry Wharton.

"Yes, and he said you were an obstreperous rhinoceros, Bob. He—he said you were a coal-black nigger, Inky! I—I'd jolly well go after him," said Bunter.

"O.K.," said Bob. "We'll go after him——."

" That's right! " gasped Bunter, in great relief.

" And we'll take you with us——."

" Eh! "

" As a witness that he had the cake," said Bob. " Come on! "

" Oh! " gasped Bunter, "I—I'd rather not go and see Coker, old chap. I—I've got to see a chap up the passage—Mauly's expecting me——."

" Take hold of his ears," said Bob. " Plenty of room to take hold——."

Billy Bunter executed a backward jump, as actively as a kangaroo.

" I—I say, you fellows, it—it wasn't Coker! Now—now I come to think of it, it—it wasn't Coker at all! "

" I rather thought it wasn't," agreed Bob.

" I mean, it was the cat——."

" The cat! " yelled the Famous Five.

" Yes, Mrs. Kebble's cat! That cat's always nosing into the studies," gasped Bunter. " She had Smithy's sardines the other day! Now—now she's had your cake."

" Oh, Christopher Columbus! " said Bob Cherry. " I can sort of see Mrs. Kebble's cat walking off with a cake! "

" Ha, ha, ha! "

" She—she didn't exactly walk it off! " stammered Bunter, " she—she ate it on the table. I—I'd have stopped her, only—only I—I could see the poor thing was hungry, you know. Cats don't get much these days. I—I was sorry for her, you know—you know I'm fond of animals——."

" We know you're fond of one animal," agreed Bob. " A fat animal named Bunter."

" Oh, really, Cherry——."

" And now, where's that cake? " demanded Johnny Bull.

" I've told you," hooted Bunter, "Coker of the Fifth—I mean Mrs. Kebble's cat—he ate it—I mean she ate it. I wouldn't make all this fuss about a measly two-bob cake—it wasn't much of a cake —hardly any plums in it———."

" He never ate it, but he knows there were hardly any plums in it," said Bob. " Coker had it —and Mrs. Kebble's cat had it—and it's inside Bunter all the time."

" Ha, ha, ha!"

" Cough it up, Bunter."

" Oh, really, you know———."

" We shall never see that cake again, without an X-ray outfit," said Bob, " unless we shake it out of Bunter. What about up-ending him and shaking it out?"

" Good egg!"

" Hear, hear!"

" Collar him!"

Billy Bunter made another backward jump. But it booted not. Five pairs of hands grasped Bunter. The fat Owl of the Remove was swept off his feet.

A frantic yell awoke all the echoes of No. 1 Study and the Remove passage outside.

" Yarooh! Leggo! Beasts! I say—— whooop!"

" Is he heavy?" gasped Bob Cherry, as Bunter whirled.

" Ha, ha, ha!"

" Ow! Leggo! You'll make my specs fall off— wow!—if they get busted you'll have to pay for them—yow-ow-ow!—— Leggo! Oh, crikey! Oooogh!"

Even five sturdy fellows did not find it easy to handle Billy Bunter's uncommon weight. But they handled it, with combined efforts. Billy Bunter's feet went into the air, and his fat head tapped on the floor of the study. The study walls seemed to whirl round Bunter, as he blinked dizzily, upside down, through his spectacles.

"Oooooogh!" spluttered Bunter.

"Shake it out of him," said Bob.

"Ow! Oh, crumbs! Help! I say, you fellows —yaroop! Oh, crikey! Gurrrrgh! I say— urrrrrrggh!"

"Ha, ha, ha!"

"Gurrrrggh!" spluttered Bunter. "Oooch! Leggo! Wooooh!"

Shake! shake! shake!

"Urrrrggh!"

"Is that cake coming?" asked Bob.

"Ha, ha, ha!"

"Ooogh! Leggo! I say, you fellows, I'll pay for the cake, if you like!" gurgled Bunter. "I'm expecting a postal-order to-morrow, and I'll pip-pip-pay for the kik-kik-cake! Oooogh! Leggo my legs, you beasts."

Shake! shake!

"Oh, crikey! Oh, scissors! Will you leggo my legs?" shrieked Bunter.

"It's not coming!" said Bob. "After all, I don't think I should care much for it now, if it did ——."

"Ha, ha, ha!"

"Leggo my legs! If you don't leggo my legs, I'll yell for a prefect! I'll get Wingate up here, and say——Yarooooooh!"

Bunter's fat legs were suddenly released. The plumpest form at Greyfriars School landed on the floor, with a bump that shook the study. Billy Bunter rolled and roared.

"Now," said Bob, "stand round him, you fellows, and jump on him. When I say three, all jump together!"

Billy Bunter sat up.

"Look here——!" he gasped.

" One! " said Bob.

" I say, you fellows——! "

" Two! "

Bob Cherry did not get to " three." Billy Bunter made one bound to his feet, and another to the doorway. He vanished into the passage.

Bob Cherry chuckled.

" Gone! " he said. " I wonder if Bunter fancied we were going to jump on him! "

" Ha, ha, ha! "

Harry Wharton shut the door after the fleeing fat Owl, and the chums of the Remove sorted a rather sparse tea out of the study cupboard. The cake that was to have graced the festive board was gone—with Bunter: but they supposed that they were done with Bunter, at all events.

But that was a little error. They were not quite done with Bunter. Five minutes later the door was cautiously opened from without, and a fat face and a big pair of spectacles blinked cautiously in.

" I say, you fellows——."

There was a half-loaf of bread on the table. Bob Cherry picked it up—and Bunter eyed him warily.

" I say, no larks, you know," urged Bunter. " I say, Mauly's gone out, and I can't find anything in his study. I say, have you got sardines? Good! I say, I never had that cake—it was Catter of the Fifth—I mean, Coker of the cat—I mean——."

Whiz!

It is said proverbially that half a loaf is better than no bread. But it did not seem so to Bunter, as that half-loaf landed on a fat chin. There was a howl in the Remove passage, and Billy Bunter vanished again. This time he stayed vanished.

Chapter IV

BUNTER WRITES HOME !

" HOW many K's in ' succeeded,' Toddy? "

" Eh? "

Peter Todd, of the Remove, looked up from his prep, and stared across the table at his fat study-mate, William George Bunter. He seemed rather surprised by Bunter's question.

Prep was on in the Remove. All the Lower Fourth were in their studies, hard at work—more or less. In No. 7, Peter Todd and Tom Dutton were giving their attention to the section of the Æneid which Mr. Quelch had set his form to prepare. Billy Bunter, as often happened, was giving prep a miss, " chancing it " with Quelch in the morning. Mr. Quelch really was not a form-master with whom it was safe to " chance it ": still, there was always a hope, in a numerous form, that a fellow might not be called on for " con ": and the fat Owl hoped for the best. Often did Billy Bunter adorn the study armchair with his fat person, while Toddy and Dutton did their prep. But on this occasion it was not laziness that had supervened. Bunter was busy—though not with prep.

" How many whatter in which? " asked Peter.

" K's in ' succeeded '," said Bunter. " I'm writing home, Toddy, and I want to be particularly careful about the spelling in this letter. The pater wasn't awfully pleased with my last report——."

" Must be hard to please! " remarked Toddy, with a deep sarcasm that was wholly and entirely lost on Bunter.

" Well, Quelch wasn't very nice about it," said

Bunter. "He rather runs me down, you know. He actually used the word 'lazy——'."

"Lazy! Now what could have put that into Quelch's head?" asked Peter, still sarcastic, and still wasting his sarcasm.

"He's prejudiced," explained Bunter. "Why, he even said 'untruthful.' Me, you know! That's the sort of justice we get here."

"Oh, crumbs!" said Toddy.

"So I want to make this letter jolly good, just to impress the pater," said Bunter. "You can't be too careful when you're writing home for money, can you? I don't want any mistakes in spelling, to begin with. Not that you can spell better than I can, of course. I could spell your head off. Still, a fellow wants to be sure—and I've forgotten, just for the moment, how many K's there are in 'succeeded.' Are there one or two, Toddy?"

Peter Todd chuckled.

"I shouldn't put any, as a matter of choice," he answered. "I don't think you'll impress your pater an awful lot with your spelling, if you sprinkle any K's in that word."

"That's rot," said Bunter, "I know there's one at least. Look it out in the dick, will you, Toddy?"

"Fathead!"

"Beast!"

"What about prep?" asked Peter.

"Oh, blow prep," said Bunter, irritably, "I've no time for prep, when I've got to get through this letter home. There won't be any time after prep —Squiff's going to have doughnuts in his study— I heard him tell Bob Cherry so. I think I'll put one K and chance it—I'm pretty certain that's right. And you jolly well needn't cackle, Peter Todd—you can't spell for toffee."

Peter did cackle, as he resumed prep. Billy Bunter wrinkled his fat brows over that letter home. He wanted, as he had said, to make a good impression on Mr. Bunter—a good impression might mean a remittance. And Bunter was badly in want of a remittance. Not for the first time, he had been disappointed about a postal-order he was expecting.

"I say, Toddy——."

"Don't jaw," said Toddy, without looking up. "How's a fellow to work at prep if you keep on wagging your chin?"

"Do you think there's a double-N in 'opinion,' Toddy?"

"Not quite. Now shut up."

"Well, I think it's a double-N," said Bunter, thoughtfully. "I say, Toddy, I'm going to stand a spread in the study if I get a remittance from home with this letter. I think it will be O.K. The pater's been making a lot of money lately. He's a bear, you know."

"He's a whatter?"

"A bear," said Bunter. "He was a bull last year, but he's a bear now. That's how you make money on the Stock Exchange."

"Sounds more like the Zoo to me," said Peter.

"You don't understand these things, Peter," said Bunter, loftily.

"No more than you do!" agreed Peter.

Snort from Bunter. Billy Bunter's father was a stockbroker, and at home in the holidays Bunter often heard of bulls, and bears, and stags, fearsome creatures that haunted the purlieus of Throgmorton Street. Exactly what the difference might be among "bulls," and "bears," and "stags," Bunter did not quite know—but he knew that Mr. Bunter was sometimes a bull, sometimes a bear, and at odd times a stag, changing like a chameleon according to the state of the market.

"Last hols, I heard the pater say it was going

to be a bear market, and he's a bear," went on
Bunter. "Well, when you're a bear in a bear
market, you make lots and lots of money. You see,
you sell a lot of shares you haven't got, and then
you get——."

"Run in?" asked Peter.

"No, you silly ass!" roared Bunter. "You
get the profits. Well, if the pater's making lots of
profits, there's no reason why he shouldn't stand
me a decent remittance — perhaps a fiver —
especially if he's pleased with this letter, and he
ought to be when I tell him I've succeeded in
getting Quelch's good opinion by working hard at
my lessons——."

"Ye gods!" said Peter.

"Might even be a tenner," said Bunter, hopefully. "That's why I've got to get the spelling
right—the pater's made quite nasty remarks about
my spelling—I don't know why. Now, is there a
double-N in 'opinion'? I don't mean at the end
of the word—but in the middle, before the Y——."

"The Y!" repeated Peter Todd, blankly. "Is
there a Y in 'opinion'?"

"Of course there is," said Bunter, peevishly.
"Fat lot of good asking you—you can't spell for
nuts. I wonder if Dutton knows. I say, Dutton."

Tom Dutton did not look up from prep. Dutton
had the disadvantage—or the advantage, perhaps,
as he was Bunter's study-mate—of being deaf,
and most of the conversation in No. 7 Study was
lost on him. Billy Bunter blinked at him
impatiently, as he went on with his work,
unconscious that he was being addressed.

"I say, Dutton!" roared Bunter.

Tom Dutton looked up at that.

"Eh! Did you speak!" he asked.

"How do you spell 'opinion'?"

"Pinion?" repeated Dutton. He shook his

head, glancing at his Æneid. "No, I shouldn't put it like that, Bunter. There's nothing about pinions here."

"Oh, crikey!" said Bunter, and Peter Todd chuckled.

"Sic fatus nocti se immiscuit atrae—is that where you are?" asked Dutton. "Well, I daresay Mercury had pinions, and spread them when he flew off—but Virgil doesn't say so, and you'd better not. Put it that he faded into the dark night."

"I didn't say pinion—I said opinion!" shrieked Bunter. "I'm not doing prep—I'm writing a letter."

"If you know better, what's the good of asking me?" said Dutton gruffly. "I tell you there's nothing about a pinion here—nothing at all. But if you think you know better, get on with it. Quelch will drop on you, if you hand it out in con, I can tell you that."

"I didn't say better," howled Bunter, "I said letter. Not better—letter."

"Better let her!" repeated Dutton, blankly. "Who?"

"Oh, crumbs! Know how to spell ' opinion '?" raved Bunter.

"Utter rot!" said Tom. "There's nothing about a spell here, any more than there is about a pinion. Mercury appeared to Æneas in his sleep —it was a dream, not a spell. What makes you think it was a spell?"

"I didn't say spell—I said spell——."

"Eh?"

"Is there a double-N in ' opinion '?" yelled Bunter.

"A double-ended pinion? No! I keep on telling you that there's nothing about a pinion at all. I've never heard of a double-ended pinion anyway. Have you, Toddy?"

" Ha, ha, ha!" gurgled Peter.

" You'd better not put in rot like that, Bunter. I can tell you it won't do for Quelch," said Dutton. " Now don't jaw any more—I've got to get through."

Billy Bunter did not " jaw " any more. " Jaw " was really Bunter's long suit: but he found it fatiguing with his deaf study-mate. He grunted, and went on with his letter home, while Toddy and Dutton went on with prep.

The fat Owl had finished his letter by the time his study-mates had finished prep. He read it through, and seemed satisfied.

" Look at that, Toddy," he said, " I fancy the pater will think my spelling's all right this time. What do you think?"

Peter looked at the letter. He gasped as he looked. It ran:

Deer Father,

I am riting these phew lines bekawse I think you will be pleezed to hear that I am getting on verry well in form, and that I have sukseeded in getting Mr. Quelch's good opinnyon by wurking hard at my lessons. In class this morning he komplimented me on my speling, and said that verry phew fellows in the Remove spelt like me. I thought you wood like to heer this as it shows how hard I wurk at skool. Sumtimes I am verry tired but I do not cair becawse I am keene on getting a good plaice in form, and I have no dowt that my nekst report will be a reel corker.

I am sorry to say that I am short of munny as everything is now so ekspensive. Also I am offen hungry as the phood is not reely suffishent for a fellow who is always playying strennewus games, wich gives an edge to a fellow's appytight. I should be very glad to receeve a pownd noat, and if the mater could send me a plumm kake it would be verry welkom.

> Your affectshonate Sun,
> William.

"Ha, ha, ha!" yelled Peter.

"Blessed if I see anything to cackle at," said Bunter, blinking at him. "What are you cackling at, Toddy? Think there ought to be more than one K in 'succeeded'?"

"Ha, ha! No. But——."

"I'm pretty sure about the double N in 'opinion'," said Bunter, thoughtfully. "It looks right, to me. Anything else?"

"Ha, ha, ha!" growled Peter. "If you want to impress you pater with your spelling, old fat man, you'd better write that over again, and let me give you a few tips."

"Well, that wouldn't do," said Bunter, shaking his head. "Your spelling's pretty rotten, Toddy, if you don't mind my mentioning it. Only the other day you told me that there was a 'g' in 'neigh'—and every fool knows that it's spelt N-A-Y."

"Every fool does!" agreed Peter. "But——."

"That letter's all right," said Bunter decidedly. "You needn't tell me anything about spelling, Toddy—but I'll tell you what you can do—you can lend me a stamp."

Peter, gurgling, produced a stamp: and Billy Bunter rolled out of the study with his letter— leaving Peter still gurgling.

Chapter V

OUT OF BOUNDS !

JOHNNY BULL shook his head.

"No!" he said.

"Now, look here, Johnny——!" said Bob Cherry.

"My esteemed Johnny——!" murmured Hurree Jamset Ram Singh.

"We're late!" remarked Harry Wharton.

"Jolly late," said Frank Nugent. "Don't be a goat, Johnny. We don't want to get into a row with Quelch for cutting roll."

Johnny Bull, standing stolid and solid, shook his head again. Johnny was a fellow of firm opinion. He had, indeed, the firmness of a rock: which on occasion seemed to his comrades rather the obstinacy of a mule.

The Famous Five were out of gates—and they were late. They had walked over to Highcliffe School, to tea with their friends, Courtenay and the Caterpillar. They had intended to walk back in good time for call-over at their own school. But they had talked cricket, and the time had passed somehow—and it was a long walk back across Courtfield Common—even by all the short cuts they knew. So there they were, in Oak Lane, a good mile from the school, with only a matter of minutes before the bell rang at Greyfriars for roll—and if they were going to get in before old Gosling shut the gate, it was clear that they had to find a shorter route than that by the road.

Such a route was available—but it meant going out of bounds. By the side of the lane was a high wooden fence, enclosing the grounds of the "Three Fishers," a riverside inn. A short cut across those grounds would take them to the tow-path by the Sark, and a quick and easy run to the school. But the "Three Fishers" was a place with a somewhat disreputable reputation, the haunt of racing men, and it was most strictly and severely out of bounds for all Greyfriars fellows.

There were fellows at Greyfriars, like Vernon-Smith and Skinner of the Remove, and Price of the Fifth, who sometimes paid surreptitious visits to that insalubrious resort. But such exploits were risky, and attended with painful consequences if discovered. Harry Wharton and Co. certainly never had any desire to "play the goat" like Smithy. But circumstances alter cases. It was a short cut home, or lines for cutting roll: and four members of the Co. were in favour of the short cut.

Johnny Bull was not.

"You fellows can talk till you're black in the face," said Johnny, calmly. "But we're not going out of bounds——."

"Never been out of bounds in your life, what?" asked Bob Cherry, sarcastically.

"Lots of times—but not in that kind of show," answered Johnny. "Suppose we were spotted! Any fellow spotted in that rotten show might say that he was taking a short cut. Think it would go down?"

"The spotfulness is not the terrific probability," remarked Hurree Jamset Ram Singh, "and we shall otherwisefully be preposterously late."

"Better be late, than walked in to the Head as pub-crawlers," said Johnny. "Smithy can have that sort of thing to himself."

"Put it to the vote!" said Bob Cherry.

"Good!" said Harry Wharton, laughing.

" Hands up for the short cut."

Four hands went up: Johnny Bull's remained stuck in his pockets. Johnny's view, no doubt, was the right one. Breaking bounds, in such a quarter, was a serious matter, if discovered. But the risk of discovery was, after all, remote: and lines for being late was not a risk but a certainty. The Co. did not want to have to ring up Gosling, and have their names taken: they did not want to appear as culprits in their form-master's study, under Quelch's gimlet eye. They wanted to take that short cut and chance it.

" You're out-voted, Johnny," said Frank Nugent. " This Co. goes by vote—and you're a minority of one. So shut up and come on."

" I tell you——! " grunted Johnny.

" We're wasting time! " Harry Wharton pointed out. " You've said your piece, old man— now come on."

" I tell you—— !"

" Speech is silvery, my esteemed Johnny, but silence is the cracked pitcher that goes longest to the well, as the English proverb remarks," said Hurree Jamset Ram Singh.

" Good old English proverb! " chuckled Bob. " Come on, you men! " And Bob Cherry settled the matter by making a jump at the fence, and catching the top.

" I tell you——! " hooted Johnny Bull.

" Follow your leader! " said Harry. And he clambered over the fence after Bob, and Nugent and the nabob of Bhanipur followed.

Johnny Bull gave an expressive grunt. But he took his hands out of his pockets and followed his friends. His solid commonsense seemed to be of no use to four fellows in a hurry, and he gave up the disputed point. Five active juniors dropped on the inner side of the fence, into the weedy and unkempt grounds of the riverside inn.

In the distance they could see the red-tiled old inn, with a tree-shaded path leading down to the gate on the tow-path. It was quite a short run, and the juniors did not intend to waste time in those forbidden precincts. Indeed, now that they were fairly inside, and committed to it, they were all feeling a little uneasy. Certainly, they meant no harm, and there was no harm in taking a short cut—but there was no doubt that appearances were against them, if they were seen.

" Put it on," said Bob. " Race you to the gate."

" Nice if we run into a prefect on the tow-path," remarked Johnny Bull.

" The pre's are all in hall now, fathead—think Wingate or Gwynne or Loder will be wandering along the tow-path when the bell's just going to ring for roll! If anybody sees us, it won't be a Greyfriars man."

" Quelch often walks on the tow-path——."

" Not at this time of day."

" Well, I think——."

" No, you don't," said Bob. " You exaggerate, old man. Anyhow, pack it up, and come on—we might as well have gone the long way round, if we're going to stand here while you do a chin solo."

" I jolly well think——."

" No, you don't," said Bob, and he started at a run : and Johnny gave it up once more, and raced with his friends. They had no use for words of wisdom : and really, once they were inside that prohibited fence, words of wisdom were rather superfluous—the urgent thing was to get out as fast as possible.

They sprinted for the distant gate. As they came into the path by the inn, a fat man smoking a cigar in the wooden verandah stared at them blankly. They had a moment's glimpse, as they passed, of Mr. Joe Banks, the bookmaker, with his red face, his red nose, his cigar, and his bowler hat cocked at a rakish angle on his greasy head. Then they went speeding down to the gateway as if they were on the cinder-path. Bob Cherry, in the lead, hurtled out of the open gateway rather like a thunderbolt—just as a man turned into it from the tow-path.

Crash!

It was a terrific collision. Neither saw the other till they crashed—the man turned in, just as Bob careered out, and a collision simply couldn't be avoided.

"Oh!" gasped Bob. He staggered from the shock, and sat down, and Frank Nugent tumbled over him before he could stop. The other three, panting, stopped just in time.

Bob had sat down, suddenly and hard—but the man into whom he had crashed had fared worse. He was a small, slight man, quite a light-weight: and the shock hurled him over backwards, sprawling on his back on the greasy tow-path. He sprawled there winded, gasping for breath, his hat rolling in the grass.

"Oh, my hat!" ejaculated Harry Wharton, in dismay.

"Bob's done it now!" murmured Johnny Bull. "I told you——."

"Ooooooh!" gasped Bob. "Who—what—oh, crumbs!" He staggered to his feet, "I say—oh, crikey—it's Twiss!"

"Twiss!" breathed Nugent.

"The Twissfulness is terrific!"

The Famous Five stared at the sprawling man, in dismay, almost in horror. It was little Mr. Twiss, the Head's new secretary. Not for a moment had they thought of Mr. Twiss, or

THE FAMOUS FIVE STARED AT THE SPRAWLING MAN

remembered his existence. And there he was—sprawling at their feet, knocked over and winded by Bob as he charged out of the gateway. It did not occur to them, for the moment, that it was an odd circumstance that the Head's secretary had been coming in at the gate of that disreputable inn. They were " spotted " out of bounds by someone belonging to Greyfriars: and they could hardly expect Mr. Twiss to keep silent on the subject.

Harry Wharton ran forward to give Mr. Twiss a hand to help him to rise. Hurree Jamset Ram Singh ran to retrieve his hat. Nugent and Johnny Bull lent Wharton a hand in helping Mr. Twiss up. Bob Cherry, not yet recovered from the shock, leaned on the gate-post and spluttered for breath.

Mr. Twiss was helped to his feet. He stood unsteadily, supported by the anxious juniors. They were really sorry that the little man had been knocked over, if it came to that: and there was a hope, too, that kind attentions might produce a placating effect.

" Awfully sorry, sir," gasped Bob.

" Ooooch ! " gurgled Mr. Twiss. " What—who —you rushed into me. I am breathless ! Ooooooh."

" We didn't see you, sir——," said Nugent. " We're fearfully sorry——."

" We hope you're not hurt, sir," said Harry.

" What? what? Certainly I am hurt—I have had a very painful shock," gasped Mr. Twiss. " I have been knocked over! Ugggh."

" The sorrowfulness is terrific, esteemed sahib," said Hurree Jamset Ram Singh, meekly. " Here is your estimable hat, sir."

Mr. Twiss grabbed his hat from the nabob, and jammed it on his ruffled fluffy hair. He set the pince-nez straight on his nose, and stared—or rather, glared, at the five dismayed juniors.

"Wharton! Cherry! Nugent! Bull! Hurree Singh! You have been out of bounds—that place is out of bounds! I shall report this to your form-master. Ugggh."

"We were only taking a short cut, sir——."

"What? what? Nonsense! I shall certainly report you to Mr. Quelch—I am surprised—shocked—disgusted! Pah!"

Mr. Twiss jerked himself away from supporting hands. Evidently he was in a very bad temper. The frown he bestowed on the hapless five was like unto the frightful, fearful, frantic frown of the Lord High Executioner. Still panting for breath, he turned his back on them, and walked on up the tow-path.

Harry Wharton and Co. looked at one another.

"What a go!" murmured Bob.

"I told you so!" remarked Johnny Bull. "I said——."

"Never mind what you said, so long as you don't say any more. Come on—no good being late for roll after all," said Bob.

"I told you——."

But the chums of the Remove did not stay to listen to what Johnny had told them. They raced along the tow-path towards the school, and Johnny, grunting, raced after them. There was going to be a row, that was certain, when Mr. Twiss reported them: and being late for roll would not improve matters. They arrived at the school gates with a burst of speed, just as Gosling was about to close them. And when Mr. Prout, the master of the Fifth, called the names in hall, five rather breathless voices answered "adsum" with the rest.

Chapter VI

THE SWORD OF DAMOCLES

" HERE comes Henry!" murmured Bob Cherry.

That remark was not loud enough for "Henry" to hear. Henry Samuel Quelch, master of the Greyfriars Remove, would probably not have been gratified to hear himself alluded to as "Henry."

" Now for the chopper!" sighed Nugent.

The Famous Five were not in a happy mood. They had scraped in just in time for roll, so that was all right. But as soon as Twiss came in from his walk, they expected to be called in by their form-master. It was now nearly time for prep, but the call had not yet come. Perhaps Twiss had not yet come in—or perhaps he had not yet taken the trouble to report to Quelch. It was very disconcerting. The juniors certainly did not want to face Quelch's gimlet-eye, with a tale that they had been out of bounds simply for the harmless and necessary purpose of taking a short cut. It was true, but it didn't sound true. But if they had to face that gimlet-eye, they wanted to get it over. They did not want the thing hanging over their heads, like the sword of Damocles, till after prep.

They were in the Rag, when the lean figure, and somewhat severe countenance of Mr. Quelch appeared in the doorway. The gimlet-eye roved over the crowd of juniors in the room. Obviously Quelch had not come for them—so it seemed to the breakers of bounds. They stood waiting, expecting the gimlet-eye to fix on them.

To their surprise and relief, Mr. Quelch did not look at them. The gimlet-eye fixed on a fat figure at a little distance.

"Bunter!" rapped out Mr. Quelch.

"Oh!" ejaculated Bunter. He spun round.
"Yes, sir!" Bunter blinked at his form-master in
alarm. "It wasn't me, sir."

"What! What was not you, Bunter?"

"Oh! Nothing, sir!" stammered Bunter. "I
—I mean, anything! That is, nothing! I—I mean,
if it's anything about a pie, I don't know anything
about it, sir."

"A pie!" repeated Mr. Quelch, blankly.

"Yes, sir! I mean, no, sir. I certainly haven't
had a pie to-day, sir. You can ask Skinner—he
knows! I gave him some."

There was a chuckle in the Rag. Evidently,
somebody's pie lay heavy on Billy Bunter's guilty
conscience. Mr. Quelch did not smile. He glared.

"You utterly stupid boy, Bunter——."

"Oh, really, sir——."

"Have you written your lines, Bunter?"

"Oh! Lines," gasped Bunter. It was not a
missing pie—it was lines, which was a relief to the
fat Owl. Bunter had lines—he generally had, as
he always left them till the last possible moment,
and sometimes later than that. "Oh, yes, sir!
They're in my study, sir."

"You should have brought them to me,
Bunter. Go and fetch them at once, and bring
them to my study," said Mr. Quelch, severely.

"Oh, certainly, sir."

Mr. Quelch, frowning, departed from the
doorway.

"Beast!" breathed Bunter. "I—I say, Toddy,
what had I better do?"

"Cut off and take your lines to Quelch, fathead," answered Toddy.

"But there ain't any lines," explained Bunter.

"Eh! You told Quelchy you'd written them."

" Oh! Yes! That—that was only a figure of speech, old chap. I haven't had time to write them, you know. I—I say, think it would go down if I told Quelch I left them on the study table, and they blew out of window? "

" Hardly! " chuckled Peter.

" Well, look here, old chap, you come with me, and tell Quelch you saw them blow out of window——."

" What? " yelled Peter.

" I'll do as much for you another time. Quelch would believe you—he mightn't me—you know he makes out that I'm untruthful. You come to Quelch and say——Beast! Ow! Wow! Wharrer you kicking me for? Yarooh! "

Peter Todd did not explain what he was kicking Bunter for. He just kicked. Billy Bunter yelled, and rolled out of the Rag—with the problem of those unwritten lines still unsolved.

" Not us, you fellows," murmured Bob Cherry. " Henry hasn't heard yet. Twiss must be in by this time, surely."

" Bother him! " said Harry. " We want to get it over."

" Mightn't be going to report us after all! " said Bob, hopefully. " After all, it's no business of his—the Head's secretary isn't a beak—he has nothing to do with the school—it doesn't concern him."

" That's rot! " said Johnny Bull. " He's bound to report fellows he spots pub-crawling. And that's what he thinks."

" Bound to come," said Nugent, with a nod.

" The boundfulness is terrific," said Hurree Jamset Ram Singh, dismally. " But the ridiculous suspense is preposterously infuriating."

" We shouldn't have taken that short cut," said Johnny Bull, " I told you so at the time, and——."

" Then don't tell us any more! " suggested Bob.

" Well, I did tell you so——."

" What's the row, you men? " Herbert Vernon-Smith joined the Famous Five, who were standing in a group by the window. " Did you think Quelchy was after you? You looked like it! What have you been up to? "

" Nothing really," answered Harry Wharton. " We were late and took a short cut across the 'Three Fishers' grounds, and ran into Twiss on the tow-path, and——." He broke off, as the Bounder winked.

" Did you tell Twiss you were taking a short cut? " asked Smithy.

" Yes! " growled Wharton.

" Did he believe it? "

The captain of the Remove made no reply to that.

" If you don't believe it, Smithy, say so! " said Bob Cherry, quietly. " If you think we go pub-crawling like you do, put it plain—and I'll push your nose through the back of your head."

" Thanks," said the Bounder, imperturbably. " My nose will do very well where it is. Besides, I know all about these short cuts. I was taking a short cut myself by the 'Cross Keys' last week when Wingate of the Sixth spotted me. I told him so. He gave me six of the very best——."

" Serve you jolly well right! " grunted Johnny Bull.

The Bounder laughed.

" Oh, quite! " he agreed. " It was too thin— but the best I could think out in the circumstances. You can't expect it to wash with Quelch."

" It's true! " snapped Wharton.

" Truth is stranger than fiction," said the Bounder, blandly. " Sure that Twiss saw you coming out?"

"Not much doubt about that, as Bob crashed into him in the gateway," said Nugent. "He was strewn over the tow-path."

"Oh, gum! That tears it, then. Must have been a clumsy ass to crash into him."

"How could I help it!" growled Bob. "We were putting on speed, of course, and Twiss turned in at the gate just as I was bolting out, and——."

"He turned in at the gate!" repeated Smithy, staring.

"Yes, or it wouldn't have happened."

"What on earth was Twiss doing, going into a den like the 'Three Fishers'? You're dreaming."

"Well, it's rather queer, come to think of it," said Harry, "but that's what happened—Twiss was going in as we were coming out——."

"If that's true——!"

"If!" roared Bob. He pushed back his cuffs.

"Oh, don't be a goat," said Vernon-Smith. "If that's true—if you're not making some silly mistake—you needn't worry about Twiss reporting you to Quelch."

"Why not?" asked Nugent.

"Well, look at it," said Vernon-Smith, "Twiss looks like a little tame rabbit, but, if you've got it right, there's more in him than meets the eye. Head-master's secretaries aren't supposed to drop in at pubs like the 'Three Fishers.' If Twiss really was going in, he won't want to advertise it. If you've got it right, he won't say a word to Quelch."

"Oh, rot," said Harry Wharton, uneasily.

"Bosh!" said Bob.

"Piffle!" said Nugent.

The Bounder laughed, and strolled away. A few minutes later the bell rang, and the juniors went up to their studies for prep. Harry Wharton and Co. sighted Mr. Quelch, in the distance, as they went up—but the Remove master did not glance at them, and made no sign. Evidently the sword of Damocles was to remain suspended over their heads.

"Blow the man!" growled Bob Cherry, on the Remove landing. "He must have come in—why can't he put Quelch wise and get it over."

"Blow him terrifically!" said Hurree Jamset Ram Singh.

"If we hadn't taken that short cut——!" said Johnny Bull.

"But we did!" howled Bob.

"Yes, I know we did! But if we hadn't——."

Johnny Bull's comrades glared at him. The suspense of waiting to be called in to Quelch was disturbing and disconcerting, and they were worried. Johnny Bull was right—there was no doubt about that—they oughtn't to have taken that short cut. He had told them so—that was not to be denied. But the fact that Johnny had "told them so" was not, in the circumstances, either grateful or comforting. It was exasperating.

"Now look here," said Bob, in a deep voice, "if you tell us again that you told us so——."

"Well, I did tell you so!" Johnny pointed out.

"That does it!" said Bob. "Johnny's right—he's always right, and he told us so. Now bump him for being right, and telling us so."

"Hear, hear!"

"Hold on—leggo—look here—I say—— Whoooo!" roared Johnny Bull, as his comrades suddenly grasped him, and bumped him on the landing. "I say—you mad asses—leggo—ow!"

Bump!

"Oooooh!"

"That's for being right!" said Bob. "Now

give him another for having told us so."

Bump!

"Yooo-hoop!" roared Johnny. "Look here—ow! Oh, crumbs! Wow!"

"Ha, ha, ha!"

The Co. went on to their studies, leaving Johnny Bull sitting on the landing, gasping for breath. The sword of Damocles was still suspended over their heads: but at all events Johnny was not likely to tell them any more that he had told them so!

Chapter VII

NOT A POUND NOTE !

" I SAY, you fellows! Is there one for me? "

It was morning break, and some of the Remove had gathered round the rack to look for letters. Among them was William George Bunter, blinking anxiously through his big spectacles.

" Hallo, hallo, hallo! Expecting a postal-order, old fat man? " asked Bob Cherry.

" Is the expectfulness terrific, my esteemed fat Bunter? " chuckled Hurree Jamset Ram Singh. " Hope springs eternal in the human chest, as the ridiculous poet remarks."

" Ha, ha, ha! "

" The fact is, I'm expecting a remittance from home," said Bunter. " I wrote specially to the pater a few days ago, and it's time he answered. He's making lots and lots of money on the Stock Exchange, and it might be a fiver—or a tenner, perhaps."

" The perhapsfulness is terrific."

" One for you, Bob," said Harry Wharton, glancing at the letters.

" Good! Chuck it over."

The captain of the Remove " chucked " it over, and Bob Cherry caught it. Billy Bunter blinked at the rack. It seemed to Bunter that that letter home, with its very careful spelling, ought to have pleased his honoured parent, and produced at least a pound note—while if Mr. Bunter really was making " lots and lots " of money as a " bear " on the Stock Exchange, there was no reason, so far as Bunter could see, why a fiver or a tenner should not come his way.

"Nothing for you, old fat bean," said Harry.

Grunt, from Bunter.

"Well, that's pretty rotten," he said. "Fat lot of good a fellow taking all the trouble to write home, and taking a lot of trouble with his spelling, and all that. I might as well have saved my stamp."

"Whose stamp?" asked Peter Todd.

"I say, Bob, anything in your letter?" asked Bunter, turning his spectacles on Bob Cherry, who had opened his envelope, and taken something therefrom that he had put into his pocket.

"Only a note," answered Bob.

"Only!" said Bunter. "Well, a note's a note! You can't expect to get whacking tips like I do—your people ain't rich, like mine. But if your pater has coughed up a ten-shilling note, you're in luck, old chap——."

"But it isn't a ten-shilling note," said Bob.

Billy Bunter's little round eyes gleamed behind his big round spectacles. If it was not a ten-shilling note, it could only be a pound note—and a fellow who had a pound note was a fellow in whom Billy Bunter was deeply interested.

"I say, Bob, old chap——."

"Coming out, you men?" asked Bob.

"I say, don't walk away while a chap's talking to you!" gasped Bunter, grabbing Bob's sleeve with a grubby fat paw. "I say, I've been disappointed about a postal-order, old fellow——."

"For the first time in your life?" asked Bob, sympathetically.

"Oh, really, Cherry! I say, I'll come to the tuck-shop with you and change that note, old boy——."

"I'm not taking it to the tuck-shop," said Bob, laughing.

"Well, look here, if you're not going to change it, lend it to me," said Bunter. "I'll let you have my postal-order for it to-morrow. Didn't I tell you that I was expecting a postal-order?"

"Did you?" said Bob. "I seem to have heard something of the kind. It sounds sort of familiar, somehow. Did you fellows know that Bunter was expecting a postal-order?"

"Ha, ha, ha!"

"I may get a big remittance from my pater any day, now he's rolling in it," said Bunter, eagerly. "But that postal-order's a cert, anyhow. It's from one of my titled relations, old chap, and it's absolutely certain to come to-morrow. As it happens, it will be for a pound. I say, you lend me that note, and take my postal-order when— when it comes! See?"

"The whenfulness will probably be terrific," remarked Hurree Jamset Ram Singh.

"Come on, Bob," said Harry Wharton, laughing.

"Hold on, though," said Bob. "I'm certainly not going to change this note, and if Bunter really wants it——."

"Well, you ass!" exclaimed Johnny Bull. "Have you got so many notes that you want to chuck one away?"

"You shut up, Bull!" exclaimed Bunter, warmly. "You let Bob alone! Bob can lend a pal a pound note if he likes. We're pals, ain't we, Bob?"

"Are we?" asked Bob. "First I've heard of it."

"Oh, really, Cherry!"

"Still, if you want this note——."

"Hand it over, old chap!" said Bunter, eagerly.

Bob put his hand in his pocket. A dozen

fellows stared at that proceeding. That Billy
Bunter's celebrated postal-order was likely to
arrive, nobody but Bunter believed—and perhaps
Bunter had his doubts! And even if it did
miraculously arrive, Billy Bunter was very
unlikely to use it for such a purpose as the settle-
ment of debt. And a pound was a considerable
sum in the Lower Fourth, where pocket-money
was counted in shillings.

"Look here, Bob, don't be an ass," said
Nugent.

"You shut up, Nugent!" howled Bunter. He
held out a fat hand, that almost trembled with
eagerness. "Bob, old fellow——."

"Fools and their money are soon parted!"
commented Johnny Bull, sententiously, as Bob's
hand came out of his pocket with something
crumpled in it.

"You shut up, Bull!"

"You don't often get a quid tip, Bob," said
Harry Wharton.

"You shut, up Wharton——."

"Well, no," admitted Bob, "my people ain't
rich like Bunter's, you know. I don't expect quid
tips from home."

"All the more reason to take care of that one,"
said Peter Todd.

"You shut up, Toddy!"

"Well, if you really want it, Bunter——," said
Bob, slowly.

"Yes, rather," gasped Bunter. "Never mind
what those fellows say, old chap. You can trust
me, can't you old fellow?"

"Not further than I can see you," said Bob,
shaking his head.

"Beast! I—I mean, dear old chap——."

"Ha, ha, ha!"

"Well, here you are!" said Bob. "If you

want it, old fat man, here it is. And don't worry about handing over your postal-order for it when it comes. I shan't want it—I shall be getting my old-age pension by that time."

And Bob Cherry thrust the crumpled paper into Bunter's fat paw, and walked away with his friends.

"Well, some fellows are fools!" remarked Skinner. "Hallo! What's the matter, Bunter?"

"Beast!" roared Bunter.

He rushed after the Famous Five, leaving Skinner staring. Something, evidently, was the matter. Bunter's fat face had worn, for a moment, a beatific grin—but only for a moment! Now it was red with wrath.

"I say, you fellows!" howled Bunter, as he rolled in wrathful pursuit of the Famous Five. "I say—Bob Cherry—you beast—look here! What's the good of this, you silly idiot?"

Harry Wharton and Co. turned round. Four of them looked astonished.

"Well, my hat!" said Harry Wharton. "Is that how you thank a fellow for tipping you a pound note, Bunter?"

"'Tain't a pound note!" shrieked Bunter. "Look at it!"

"Eh! What?"

"Look!" yelled Bunter.

He held it up. The chums of the Remove looked at it. It was a note. But it was not a pound note. It was nothing like a pound note. It bore not the slightest resemblance to any document issued by the British Treasury.

Dear Sir,
    The shoes are now repaired, and
may be called for when convenient.
        Yours faithfully,
            J. Snell.

It was a note! There was no doubt about that.
But a note from the shoemaker's in Friardale was
not of much use to Billy Bunter.   Certainly he
couldn't have changed that note at the school
shop!

" Ha, ha, ha! " yelled the Co. They understood
now why Bob Cherry had parted with that "note"
so cheerfully.

" What's the good of that to me? " yelled
Bunter.

" I didn't suppose it would be any good, old
fat man," answered Bob, gently. "But you seemed
to want it, and as it's no use to me——."

" Ha, ha, ha! "

" I thought it was a pound note—you said it
wasn't a ten-shilling note, so I thought——."

" Fancy Bunter thinking that a note from Snell
the shoemaker was a pound note! " said Bob.
" My dear chap, I don't get pound tips—my people
ain't rich like yours, you know."

" Ha, ha, ha! "

" Beast! " roared Bunter. " Pulling my leg all
the time——."

" The   pullfulness   was   terrific," chuckled
Hurree Jamset Ram Singh.

" Ha, ha, ha! "

Harry Wharton and Co. went out into the
quad, laughing. Billy Bunter was left with that
" note " crumpled in a fat paw, glaring after them
with a glare that almost cracked his spectacles.

Chapter VIII

ALL CLEAR !

"WHARTON!"

"Oh! Yes, sir!"

The Famous Five were chuckling over the incident of Billy Bunter and Bob Cherry's "note." But they became grave at once, as Mr. Twiss came up to them in the quad, and addressed the captain of the Remove.

Mr. Twiss was walking under the old elms, when he glanced round and saw the cheery bunch of juniors, and came across to them. They capped the Head's secretary respectfully, and a little uneasily. So far, they had heard nothing from Mr. Quelch on the subject of that unlucky short cut at the "Three Fishers." His manner had been as usual in the form-room that morning, and it was clear that he was not aware that those five members of his form had been "spotted" out of bounds in a questionable quarter. With the cheery optimism of youth, they were rather forgetting the sword of Damocles that was still suspended over their heads, till they were reminded of it by Mr. Twiss.

Now they had no doubt that the "chopper" was coming down. What Lower Fourth juniors did was not exactly any concern of the head-master's secretary: but it seemed impossible that he would fail to report what he had seen to their form-master. It was in fact his duty to do so.

The smiles faded from five faces, and they all looked very serious. Mr. Twiss blinked from face to face through his rimless pince-nez, and smiled faintly. He could see that the juniors were expecting him to walk them directly to Quelch's study.

" I have not yet spoken to your form-master, Wharton," said Mr. Twiss, in his high-pitched, squeaky voice. " I have been considering the matter. I was very much surprised, and very much shocked, to see you coming out of such a place as the ' Three Fishers,' when I was passing on the tow-path yesterday."

Harry Wharton and Co. made no reply to that.

Mr. Twiss had not been "passing on the tow-path ": he had been turning into the gateway, or the collision would never have happened. But they did not want to argue the point.

" You told me that you had been merely taking a short cut," went on Mr. Twiss, his eyes very sharp behind his pince-nez as he watched the juniors' faces.

" That was true, sir," said Harry. " We should have been late for roll if we hadn't."

" It was a very thoughtless action, Wharton. Any boy seen in such a place might make the same explanation, true or false."

" I know that, sir, of course. But it happens to be true."

" The truefulness is terrific, sir! " murmured Hurree Jamset Ram Singh.

" It was a fatheaded thing to do, and I told these fellows so at the time," said Johnny Bull. " But that was how it was."

" Well, well, I believe you," said Mr. Twiss. " I was very much startled and shocked at the time, but now that I have thought over the matter, I believe you. I do not think it necessary to trouble Mr. Quelch, in the circumstances. You acted very thoughtlessly: and you will, I am sure, realise how very foolish it was to risk placing yourselves under suspicion. I shall say nothing

about the matter—but you must let it be a
warning to you."

"Oh! Thank you, sir!" said four voices in
chorus. Johnny Bull was silent. Mr. Twiss gave
the juniors a nod, and walked away under the
elms.

He left them feeling extremely relieved.

"Good luck!" said Bob. "Not a bad little ass,
is he?"

"Well, I suppose he could see that we were
telling the truth, and there was really no need to
drag Quelch into it," said Nugent.

"Quelch would have believed us, I think," said
Harry, "but that doesn't alter the fact that we
were out of bounds. It would have meant a
detention at least."

"We're well out of it," said Bob. "All clear
now."

"The all-clearfulness is——."

"Terrific!" chuckled Bob. "Not to say preposterous. Much obliged to Twissy. You might
have thanked him too, Johnny. Or did you want
a report to Quelch and a detention or a
whopping?"

Grunt, from Johnny Bull.

"I'll keep my thanks till I've something to
thank him for," he answered. "Twiss hasn't let
us off on his own account. He's got his reasons."

"His reasons are plain enough," said Harry
Wharton, a little sharply. "He believes what
we've told him."

"He didn't believe it at the time."

"Well, he's thought it over since," said Bob,
"and he was a bit shirty at the time, too. A man's
liable to get shirty if you charge him over all of
a sudden."

"Now he's thought it over——!" said
Nugent.

"Oh, yes, he's thought it over," assented Johnny, sarcastically. "He's just said that he was passing the 'Three Fishers' when you cannoned into him. Well, was he?"

"Oh, rot," said Bob, uneasily.

"He was coming in at the gate," said Johnny. "You walloped into him face to face. Didn't you?"

"Well, yes! But——."

"And it would have come out, if he'd taken us to Quelch, and you can bet that Quelch would have wondered. Smithy said last night that he wouldn't mention it to Quelch, if we had that right —as we know we had."

"Oh, blow Smithy!"

"Blow him as hard as you like," said Johnny Bull, stolidly, "but Smithy was right, all the same."

"The 'Three Fishers' isn't out of bounds for head-master's secretaries," said Bob, with a grin. "They can trickle in there if they like."

"Only he wouldn't want the beaks to know that he liked!"

"Well, I think it's jolly good natured of him to keep mum," said Frank Nugent. "I don't want a row with Quelch, if you do."

"I don't! No more than you do," said Johnny. "But Twiss ought to have reported us to Quelch. It was his duty, and he ought to have done it. And if he hasn't it's for his own reasons, not for ours."

"Well, I'm glad he's not such a whale on duty as you think he ought to be," chuckled Bob. "I'd rather play cricket than sit in a detention class. any day. Now, then, there's just time for ginger-pop before the bell goes for class. So let's cut along to the tuck-shop—if Johnny's finished his lecture on the Whole Duty of Man."

" Ha, ha, ha ! "

" I say what I think," said Johnny Bull. " And I jolly well think——."

" I'll tell you what," said Bob, " come and have a ginger-pop—and I'll stand you a twopenny bun if you won't tell us what you think ! "

" Fathead ! "

" Same to you, with knobs on," said Bob. " Come on."

The Famous Five went to the school shop, to discuss ginger-pop and buns—much more to their taste than Mr. Twiss, and Johnny Bull's ideas on the subject of Mr. Twiss.

Billy Bunter was standing outside the little shop in the corner of the quad, his eyes and spectacles fixed on the window. Having been disappointed about a remittance that morning, Bunter was in his usual stony state. Like a podgy Peri at the gate of Paradise, the Owl of the Remove gazed longingly at good things that were beyond his reach. He blinked at the juniors as they went in, with a reproachful blink.

" Changed that note yet, Bunty? " asked Bob Cherry, affably.

" Beast ! "

Bob chuckled, and passed into the tuck-shop with his friends. They sat down round a little table, with ginger-beer and buns thereon: and a few moments later, Bunter rolled in from the quad.

" I say, you fellows ! " he exclaimed. " You're wanted. I say, the Head wants you in his study at once."

" What?" yelled the Famous Five, all together.

" He—he sent me to look for you. Better cut off, you chaps—he looked rather shirty ! I'll look after your tuck while you're gone, if you like, and —and see that nobody snaffles it."

Harry Wharton and Co. gazed at Billy Bunter. A few days ago Bunter had pulled their leg in exactly that manner, and they had fallen for it. Really, they were not likely to fall for it a second time. It was not a chicken that would fight twice! But the fat and fatuous Owl evidently hoped that it would.

" The Head wants us, does he? " gasped Bob Cherry.

" Yes, old chap, at once——."

" He seems to be cultivating quite a taste for our society," remarked Nugent.

" The tastefulness is terrific."

" I say, you fellows, I'd go at once, if I were you!" urged Bunter. " You know how stuffy the beaks get if you keep them waiting!"

" And you'll look after the tuck while we're gone? " grinned Bob.

" Yes, rather! " said Bunter, eagerly. " I'd do more than that for fellows I really like. Trust me!"

" And you'll scoff the buns, and mop up the ginger-pop, the minute we've turned our backs? "

" Yes, old chap—I—I mean No——."

" Ha, ha, ha!",   ,

" I hope you don't think I'm after your tuck, Bob Cherry——."

" Oh, my hat! " ejaculated Bob. " He hopes we don't think he's after our tuck, you men! What price that for a really hopeful nature? "

" Oh, really, Cherry! I say, you'd better get a move on," said Bunter, anxiously. " You know how waxy Quelch gets if you keep him waiting——."

" Quelch! Does Quelch want us, as well as the Head? "

" Oh! I—I mean the Head! " stammered Bunter. " Did I say Quelch? I—I mean the Head, of course. I say, he looked fierce, you know. He will be in a wax if you don't go at once. Do get a move on."

"Right!" agreed Bob. "We'll get a move on." He rose from the table, and his comrades stared at him.

"It's only Bunter's gammon, you ass," said Johnny Bull. "You're not going to the Head?"

"Oh, no! I'm going to kick Bunter all round the shop for telling whoppers."

"Oh!" gasped Bunter. "I say——."

"Good!" said Harry Wharton. "We'll all do the same."

"Hallo, hallo, hallo!" roared Bob. "Where are you going, Bunter?"

Billy Bunter did not stop to explain where he was going. He just went!

Chapter IX

TWO IN THE DARK!

"SMITHY, old chap!"

Herbert Vernon-Smith gave a jump.

Eleven strokes had boomed out from the old Greyfriars clock-tower, dully through the night. At that hour, all Greyfriars School was dark and silent. Some of the beaks might be still up, in their studies: but all the forms, from the Sixth to the Second, were in bed and asleep—or should have been. On this particular night, however, there was at least one exception—the Bounder of Greyfriars was wide awake. And as the last stroke of eleven died away, he slipped quietly from his bed, and began to get his clothes on, in the glimmer of moonlight from the high windows.

There was a faint sound of regular breathing in the long dusky dormitory: and an intermittent rumble of Billy Bunter's snore. But the Bounder did not expect to hear anything else: and a low whispering voice from the next bed startled him.

"Reddy, you ass!" he breathed.

Tom Redwing sat up in bed.

"You're up, Smithy," he muttered. "Look here, old chap——."

"Quiet! Don't wake the dorm."

"You're breaking out?"

"Oh! No!" said the Bounder, sarcastically. "I've got up and dressed myself to take a stroll in the corridor." He laughed softly. "Don't be a goat, Reddy! I've got to see a man about a horse. Go to sleep."

Tom Redwing peered at him in the gloom. He

was anxious—but almost as angry as anxious. Remove fellows wondered sometimes at the friendship between the quiet, steady Redwing, and the wild and reckless Bounder, in whose restless nature there seemed to be an ineradicable kink of blackguardism. But that ill-assorted friendship was very deep and real: and it was the reason why Tom was awake that night when his chum was about to creep softly from the sleeping dormitory.

"Look here, Smithy," he muttered, "I suppose it's no good asking you to chuck this because it's a rotten thing to do——."

"How well you know me!" agreed Smithy.

"But if you can't be decent, you might have a little sense," snapped Redwing. "Quelch has had his eye on you all this term——."

"Dear old Quelch!" murmured the Bounder. "Fast asleep now, Reddy—and not dreamin' of me. If the dear man's dreamin', it's more likely to be of pius Æneas or the Seven Against Thebes." And Smithy chuckled again.

"You know you're under suspicion, Smithy. I saw Wingate's eye on you when you went out after class to-day."

"So did I! That's why I didn't drop in at the 'Cross Keys.' I thought it would be safer later."

"For goodness' sake, Smithy, don't be a fool! It's too risky," urged Redwing, earnestly. "You know what it means, breaking out at night—you'd be sacked like a shot if they spot you——."

"Speech may be taken as read!" yawned the Bounder.

"I suppose it's no use talking to you——."

"Not in the least! You're losin' your beauty sleep for nothin'."

"Hallo, hallo, hallo!" came a drowsy voice. "Is that somebody up?" Bob Cherry lifted his head from the pillow, and stared round, "Is that you, Smithy?"

"Find out," snapped the Bounder.

"Look here, Smithy——!" urged Redwing.

"Oh, wake the whole dorm!" snarled Vernon-Smith. "I'll leave you to it!" And he slipped away to the door.

"That goat Smithy!" said Bob. "He'll run into a beak or a pre, one of these times, and serve him jolly well right."

"The rightfulness will be terrific," came another voice. Evidently the nabob of Bhanipur had awakened also.

"Who's that jawing?" Bolsover major was awake, too. "Can't you fellows keep quiet and let a fellow sleep?"

"Quiet, you fellows, for goodness' sake," muttered Redwing, anxiously. "It's risky enough for Smithy anyway——."

"Smithy out on the tiles!" There was a chuckle from Skinner. "Good old Smithy! He will do it once too often, some time."

"I guess that guy surely does ask for it!" came a nasal yawn from Fisher T. Fish. "I'll tell a man he does."

"Silly ass!" said Frank Nugent.

"Silly rotter, you mean!" grunted Johnny Bull.

More and more fellows were awakening at the sound of voices. Vernon-Smith did not hear them: the door had opened, and closed, without a sound, and the Bounder was gone.

Smithy was not insensible, perhaps, to the anxiety—not unmingled with angry disgust—of his chum Redwing. But if that feeling influenced him, it did not influence him to the extent of restraining him from his reckless escapades. Smithy had his good qualities: there was more good than bad in him: but he had

a love of excitement, of the thrill of danger for its
own sake, that seemed to make it impossible for
him to toe the line as other fellows did.

He was well aware of what he was risking: he
knew that "breaking out" at night had only one
penalty: the "sack," short and sharp. That risk
gave an added zest to his adventure.

He had boundless confidence in himself, in his
cunning and resource. His luck had always been
good—and he banked on his luck. It was "pie"
to the Bounder to carry on in his own arrogant
way, regardless of authority, a law unto himself,
to delude the "beaks" and beat watchful prefects.
He was quite cool as he crept away silently down
the dark corridor, and crossed the wide landing to
the staircase.

After all, it was easy, for a fellow with plenty
of nerve—and Smithy had never lacked nerve.
The whole House was buried in silence and
slumber. There was a door on the junior lobby
which he could leave unlocked for his return. He
would be back in an hour or so, and nobody the
wiser. He had done it before, and it was easy to
do again. He stepped stealthily down the stairs,
without a sound. There was no glimmer of light
—all was black darkness. He descended the stairs
with his right hand following the banister as a
guide. And he went swiftly. There was always a
possibility, if a remote one, of a "beak on the
prowl," and he was keen to get out as soon as
possible.

Stealthily, silently, but swiftly, he went down,
step after step, his hand gliding down the polished
oak banister. And then, suddenly, it happened.

That anyone could be ahead of him on the
staircase would have seemed impossible, to
Smithy, had he even thought of it, in the darkness. A master would of course have turned on

the staircase light. Nobody—unless a fellow breaking out like Smithy—could be supposed to be creeping down the staircase in the dark—as silently as Smithy, for he heard no sound.

He gave a gasp of utter amazement and alarm, as he suddenly bumped into an unseen figure in the darkness.

Someone, unseen, unsuspected, was in front of him, going down the staircase silently in the dark, close to the banister. Smithy, moving more swiftly, had overtaken him, and, inevitably, bumped into him!

"Oh!" gasped the Bounder.

His gasp was echoed by a startled exclamation.

"Oh! Who—what——."

A hand in the darkness swept round, grasping at the junior.

Smithy did not recognise the husky, startled voice, but he knew that it was a man's voice, not a boy's. It was no breaker of bounds that he had run into so unexpectedly—it was a man—it must be a master—and he had fairly walked into that master's hands. He gave a desperate wrench as he was grasped, with a wild hope of yet escaping unrecognized, lost his footing, and slipped on the stairs. The unseen man, evidently as wildly startled as Smithy himself, stumbled over him, and they sprawled on the stairs together.

And, as they sprawled, and rolled, and bumped, and panted, a light suddenly flashed on, above: and Mr. Quelch, his lean figure encased in a dressing-gown, stared down blankly from the landing at the two sprawling figures.

Chapter X

ONCE TOO OFTEN !

" VERNON-SMITH ! "

" Oh ! " breathed the Bounder.

He had rolled down two or three stairs, he was bumped and bruised and breathless, hardly knowing whether he was on his head or his heels. But he dragged himself loose from the unseen man who sprawled with him, and scrambled up—just as the landing light flashed on. That light gleamed full on his face as he stared up at the lean figure on the landing, and he met the gimlet-eyes of his form-master.

" Vernon-Smith ! " repeated Mr. Quelch, with compressed lips.

Quelch had been disturbed by the sudden outbreak of uproar in the middle of the night : he had hurriedly donned his dressing-gown and come out on the landing to investigate. He could hardly have expected to see a member of his form up at that hour. Still, he did not seem greatly surprised. He had had a doubtful and distrustful eye on that particular member of his form for a long time.

His face was very grim, as he stared down at the Bounder. A single glance took in every detail, noting that the junior was fully dressed, even to his collar and tie : Quelch did not need telling that Smithy had been going out of the House. The Bounder's long run of luck had failed him at last : he was fairly caught " breaking out " at night !

He realised it, as he looked up at Mr. Quelch, and his heart sank. Only a few minutes ago, Tom Redwing had been urging him to give up that reckless escapade: but the scapegrace of Grey-friars had had no use for good advice. He rather wished now that he had found a use for it.

For a long moment, Mr. Quelch stared at the Bounder, his face so grim that it might have been that of the fabled Gorgon. Then his glance shifted to the figure that was still sprawling breathlessly, panting and gasping and gurgling, on the stairs.

" Is that Mr. Twiss? " exclaimed the Remove master.

" Twiss! " muttered Smithy, and he stared round at the man with whom he had collided in the dark—revealed now in the light. He gritted his teeth. It was Twiss—what had that little ass been doing, stealing about like a ghost in the dark?

Mr. Twiss sat up dizzily. He was winded, startled almost out of his wits, spluttering for breath. The Bounder had had a shock: but Twiss, plainly, had had a greater one.

He blinked up at Mr. Quelch, like an owl in the sudden light. His rimless pince-nez slanted on his nose: his fluffy hair was wildly ruffled, standing almost on end, and his usually pallid face was crimson.

" Urrrggh! " gurgled Mr. Twiss. He made an effort to rise, and dragged himself up, with the aid of the banisters. " Urrgh! Mr. Quelch—urrggh! "

" What has happened, Mr. Twiss? " asked the Remove master. " Did you find this junior going out? "

" I—I hardly know," gasped Mr. Twiss. " I—I was descending the stairs—I—I could not sleep, and I—I was going down for a book I left in Common-Room, and—and all of a sudden I felt somebody behind me—— Oh, goodness gracious! I—I—I was so startled—oooogh! "

FOR A LONG MOMENT, MR. QUELCH STARED
AT THE BOUNDER

Mr. Quelch eyed the fluffy little man, crimson and breathless and confused, hanging weakly on to the banister: and his lip curled ever so little. No doubt it had been startling enough for Mr. Twiss to discover somebody behind him suddenly in the dark: but it was pretty evident that Twiss had not only been startled, but frightened.

"I—I—I——," burbled Mr. Twiss. "This is a boy of your form, I think, Mr. Quelch." Holding to the banisters with one hand, Twiss set his glasses straight with the other, and peered at Vernon-Smith. "I—I was—was quite startled—I —I may say alarmed. Surely this boy should not be out of his dormitory at this hour of the night, Mr. Quelch."

"Most assuredly he should not, sir," answered Mr. Quelch. "I am sorry that you have had such a shock, Mr. Twiss, and that it was due to a boy in my form. I trust, sir, that you are not hurt."

"I—I think I—I am a little bruised——I—I think I stumbled over the boy——I—I fell down several stairs," mumbled Mr. Twiss. "I—I do not feel quite myself. I—I think I—I will return to my room."

Mr. Twiss came up the stairs unsteadily, his hand on the banister. Vernon-Smith followed him up, his face set.

The Bounder had recovered from the shock now, though he was still feeling shaken. But little Mr. Twiss seemed to be nothing but a bundle of nerves. Smithy wondered savagely whether the little ass had supposed that it was a burglar behind him in the dark.

The Bounder was "for it," he knew that. But he had the courage of his delinquencies, and he was cool and collected now, ready to face what was coming to him. He felt only a savage scorn for the frightened, confused, stammering little secretary.

Mr. Twiss reached the landing, still gasping, when a deep voice boomed out.

"What is all this? What is this disturbance? Quelch! What has happened?" It was the fruity voice of Mr. Prout, the master of the Fifth Form.

Prout, too, had been disturbed by the noise, and had turned out, and the sound of opening doors told that others had been roused also.

Mr. Quelch compressed his lips bitterly. It was bad enough to find a boy of his form breaking bounds at night: worse, for other masters to arrive on the scene. Prout, his portly figure draped in a voluminous dressing gown of many colours, rolled up, staring from Quelch to Twiss, and from Twiss to Vernon-Smith, and back to Quelch again.

"What has happened, Quelch? What is this alarm? Is it a fire—or——?" boomed Mr. Prout.

"Nothing of the kind, Prout," snapped Mr. Quelch, " it is merely——."

"Is anything the matter?" came Mr. Capper's voice, and the master of the Fourth came into the light on the landing.

"I heard a noise—it sounded like someone falling downstairs." It was the acid voice of Mr. Hacker, the master of the Shell. " Has there been an accident?"

Mr. Quelch breathed hard and deep.

The Bounder's cheeks burned. All the masters were staring at him, evidently surprised to see a junior standing there fully dressed. Smithy hardly dared look at Mr. Quelch. He could guess what his form-master was feeling like.

"There is no occasion for alarm." Mr. Quelch's voice seemed to grind like a saw. " A boy of my form was out of his dormitory, that is all. And——."

"All?" said Mr. Hacker, very expressively.

And he gave an audible snort as he whisked away.

"Really," said Mr. Capper, "it is very annoying to be disturbed in this way, at such an hour——."

"I should say so!" boomed Prout. "I should most certainly say so. I should say that it was not merely annoying—I should say that it was scandalous! We have all been disturbed—we have been brought out of our beds——."

"There is nothing to keep you out of bed, Mr. Prout," Quelch almost yapped!

"What? What? Really, Mr. Quelch! A boy of your form causes all this uproar and disturbance at midnight——. I repeat, sir, that it is scandalous! Scandalous!" boomed Prout. "Unprecedented—I may say, unparalleled!" Prout snorted, and whirled away, with a sweep of a vast dressing-gown. "Scandalous!" he repeated, over a plump shoulder, as he went. "Come, Capper! There is nothing the matter—nothing but a boy of Quelch's form disturbing the House at midnight—a mere trifle, no doubt!"

"Hem!" said Mr. Capper.

Mr. Twiss, still gasping, was going to his room, which opened on the landing. The door closed on him and his gasps.

Left alone with that delinquent of his form, Mr. Quelch fixed his gimlet-eyes on the Bounder, gleaming like cold steel.

"Vernon-Smith!" His voice was low but deep.

"Yes, sir," muttered the Bounder.

"Have you been out of the House?"

"No, sir."

"You were going out?"

Vernon-Smith made no reply to that. The Bounder was far from particular about the truth when he was dealing with "beaks" or prefects. But it was obviously futile to deny what was perfectly clear.

"Very well," said Mr. Quelch, his voice more like a saw than ever, "I shall take you back to your dormitory now, Vernon-Smith. You will be taken before your head-master in the morning, and Dr. Locke will deal with you."

The Bounder, with all his nerve, paled a little. He had risked it a dozen times or more—now he had risked it once too often. Now that it had happened, he had the nerve to face it. But his heart was like lead at the thought of that interview with his head-master in the morning.

"I hadn't been out of the House, sir," he muttered. "It's not ten minutes since I left my dormitory, and——."

"You need say nothing, Vernon-Smith. Whatever you have to say, you may say to Dr. Locke when you come before him," said Mr. Quelch, coldly. "Now follow me."

The Bounder, in miserable silence, followed him to the door of the Remove dormitory.

Chapter XI

UP BEFORE THE BEAK !

" I SAY, you fellows! "

Billy Bunter rolled up to the Famous Five, in the quad, with a cheery excitement in his fat face. There were a good many serious faces in the Greyfriars Remove that morning. Even fellows who did not like Smithy were rather concerned about him. Bunter, apparently, saw no occasion to be concerned. Bunter rather liked a spot of excitement—and there was quite a large spot in the Remove that sunny morning after prayers.

Harry Wharton and Co. were unusually grave. They did not pal with the Bounder, but they were on more or less friendly terms with him, and in any case they would have felt sympathy for a fellow up before the Head. Tom Redwing was with the Co., his face dark with a distress he could not conceal. Billy Bunter blinked at the troubled group of juniors quite cheerily.

" I say——! "

" Oh, blow away, Bunter," said Bob Cherry, curtly.

" Oh, really, Cherry! I say, Smithy's for it," said Bunter. " I say, Quelch took him to the Head when we came out after prayers."

" We know that, fathead."

" I expect it's the sack," said Bunter. " I say, 'taint often that a fellow gets bunked, is it? I say, think Smithy will be bunked, Redwing? "

Redwing winced, but made no reply.

" Oh, shut up, you fat ass," said Bob, " Smithy won't be bunked—he wasn't out of the House when they nailed him."

"Oh, that wouldn't make much difference," said Bunter, shaking his head. "They jolly well know he was going out on the razzle-dazzle. It's the sack all right, you can take my word for that."

"Now run away and play," said Frank Nugent.

"Oh, really, Nugent! What I mean is, do you fellows think it will be an expulsion in Hall, with all the school lined up, and the whole bag of tricks?" asked Bunter. "If it's that, I expect we shall cut a class. If we get out of maths with Lascelles——."

"Dry up!" grunted Johnny Bull.

"Oh, really, Bull! It would be corking to get out of maths, wouldn't it? Or do you think the Head will just whiz him out quietly?" Bunter blinked inquiringly at the juniors through his big spectacles. "What do you think, Wharton?"

"I think you're a fat ass!" answered the captain of the Remove.

"Oh, really, Wharton! What do you think, Bob?"

"I think you're a burbling bandersnatch."

"Beast! Of course, I'm sorry for Smithy," said Bunter. "He's asked for it, of course, and it serves him jolly well right: still, I'm sorry for him. You fellows may not be, but I've got a sympathetic nature, I hope. He's rather a beast, and he's got a rotten temper, and he's mean with his money—only yesterday he refused to cash a postal-order for me, just because it hadn't come—still, now he's up for the sack——."

"Turn round, Bunter," said Bob.

"Eh! What do you want me to turn round for?"

"I'm going to kick you."

"The kickfulness is the proper caper," agreed Hurree Jamset Ram Singh. "Turn roundfully, my esteemed idiotic Bunter."

"Beast!"

Billy Bunter turned round—but he did not wait to be kicked. He departed, to bestow the delights of his conversation on more appreciative fellows.

Harry Wharton and Co. were left to their rather glum meditations. They had had plenty of trouble with the Bounder, at one time and another, and nobody could have been more thoroughly " down " on his wild and reckless ways—but now that he was so badly up against it, everything was washed out but concern for the luckless fellow.

" Brace up, Reddy," murmured Bob Cherry uncomfortably, " 'taint the long jump for Smithy this time. He never went out——."

" They know he was going out!" grunted Johnny Bull.

" You can't bunk a man for what he was going to do—if he never did it," said Bob. " Bank on that, Reddy."

Redwing nodded without speaking.

The Remove fellows were waiting for news. Vernon-Smith was with the Head—up for judgment. Many eyes turned on the head-master's study window. The juniors would have given a good deal to know what was going on in that rather dreaded apartment. Nobody envied Herbert Vernon-Smith, standing before his head-master, to answer a charge of attempted " breaking-out " at night. The minutes seemed very long.

" Hallo, hallo, hallo!" ejaculated Bob, suddenly. " Here's Smithy."

All eyes were turned on the Bounder, as he came out of the House. He came with his hands in his pockets, his face cool and unconcerned. There was always a touch of swagger about the scapegrace of Greyfriars, and it was more pro-

nounced now, as he strolled into the sunny quad.
Whatever Smithy's feelings were, there was no
sign of them in his face. The Bounder was not a
fellow to wear his heart upon his sleeve.

"What's the verdict, Smithy?" called out
Skinner. "Sacked?"

Smithy glanced round at him, but did not
trouble to reply. Billy Bunter grabbed his arm
with a fat grubby paw, eager for news.

"I say, Smithy, sorry you're bunked, old chap.
Is it going to be in Hall? Did the Head say——
ow! wow! ow! wow! Beast!" Bunter jerked
away that fat paw, as the Bounder gave it a sharp
rap.

"Smithy, old man." Tom Redwing came up
breathlessly. "For goodness' sake—tell me——."

The Bounder's hard face softened a little.

"O.K.," he answered, "you're not losin' me
this time, Reddy!"

"Not sacked?" asked Johnny Bull.

"Sorry to disappoint you—no."

"Oh, don't be an ass!" said Johnny. "I'm
glad you've got off, and if you've got any sense at
all, you'll let it be a warning to you. After
this——."

"Speech may be taken as read," said Smithy.
"I'll come along to No. 13 Study when I want a
sermon. Pack it up till then."

Johnny Bull breathed hard.

"We're all glad, Smithy," said Harry
Wharton, quietly.

"Glad I'm up for a Beak's flogging?" asked
Smithy. "Thanks."

"If that's all, you're in luck."

"A flogging!" repeated Redwing. His face
fell. "Well, you couldn't expect much less,
Smithy! Thank goodness it's no worse, old
fellow."

" Oh, I'm feeling jolly about it, of course," said the Bounder, sarcastically. " Sort of thing a fellow would look forward to."

" You might have been turfed out," said Bob. " You would have been, if you'd been caught outside the House instead of inside."

" Exactly what the Old Man said," drawled Vernon-Smith. " As it is, I'm let off with a flogging." He set his lips. " I wouldn't care—I can stand a whopping—if the old bean had got on with it. But it's going to be a public execution—the whole school in hall—sort of example to all the fellows—Gosling comin' in to take me up—— You fellows can expect an entertainment after third school—almost as good as going to the pictures."

His eyes were smouldering as he spoke. With all his assumption of cool indifference, it was clear that Smithy was feeling this deeply—not so much the flogging itself, for he was hard as nails : but the disgrace of the infliction in the crowded hall, under the staring eyes of all Greyfriars : his own form, and all the other forms, lined up to witness the " execution."

But it was only for a moment that his feelings were revealed. The next, he laughed lightly.

" What rotten luck," he drawled. " I've done the same thing a dozen times or more—lucky they don't know that !—and then I get dished because a silly little ass goes mooning down in the middle of the night for a silly book. I'd like to punch that man Twiss's silly rabbit face."

" Well, you can hardly blame Twiss," said Nugent. " He couldn't help you walking into him in the dark."

" Why couldn't he be fast asleep in his burrow, like any other rabbit ? " snarled Smithy, " and if he wanted to go down mooning for a book, why couldn't he switch on the light, like a sensible man? I should have given him a jolly wide berth if he had."

"Queer that he didn't," remarked Bob.

"Oh, he's a queer little beast," said Vernon-Smith, contemptuously. "I wish now I'd tipped him down the staircase, blow him."

"Well, that's rot," said Johnny Bull. "No good blaming Twiss because he happened to be in the way when you were kicking over the traces. That's not sense. If you hadn't gone out of the dorm——."

"Tell your pals the rest," interrupted the Bounder. "They may like sermons—I don't!"

And he walked away with Redwing, leaving Johnny Bull staring. Apparently Smithy was disposed to lay some of the blame for his disaster on little Mr. Twiss, and he had no use for solid common-sense from Johnny.

Johnny Bull breathed very hard.

"I suppose I can't punch a fellow's head when he's up for a flogging," he said. "But I've a good mind—a jolly good mind——."

Johnny left it at that.

Chapter XII

THE "EXECUTION"

IT was over!

The last sounding swish of the birch had died away through the silent Hall. From Herbert Vernon-Smith, not a sound had come.

Hall was packed. Every fellow of every form was there, from Sixth-Form seniors down to fags of the Second Form—the prefects in their places, with their canes under their arms: the masters, with grave faces: the hapless culprit, quiet and subdued, but with a hint of defiance in his glinting eyes. A public flogging was a rare occasion at Greyfriars, in latter days—the hard old days were long gone when that ancient hall had often echoed to the swishing of the birch in the hands of grim old head-masters and to the painful howls of the victims. Greyfriars men were "whopped" when they required the same, but "six on the bags" in a study was the usual limit. Only on very rare occasions—very rare indeed—was there a public "execution": with the school assembled in the Hall, masters and boys all present, and the culprit "hoisted" in the old-fashioned way—and no doubt it was all the more impressive for that reason. The Head had felt it his duty to make a public example of Vernon-Smith—and there were few who did not think that, tough as it was, the Bounder was getting off cheaply. Smithy prided himself on carrying on in reckless defiance of authority, on being a law unto himself: and now he had come up against the inevitable result, and come up against it hard.

It was a severe infliction. There was nothing
of the grim old Busby type about the head-master
of Greyfriars: but he had his duty to do, and he
did it. And kind old gentleman as the Head
seemed at happier moments, there was no doubt
that he could whop! Skinner whispered to Snoop
that he wondered where the old boy packed the
muscle, and Snoop grinned, and Billy Bunter
giggled. But most of the fellows were grave and
quiet. Smithy had asked for it—and more—but it
was tough, and they sympathised.

But it was over at last. Gosling set Smithy
down, and he stood, a little unsteadily, his face
pale. Not a sound had escaped him—the Bounder
was tough all through, hard as hickory, and he
would have disdained to allow a single cry to leave
his lips. But very few fellows could have gone
through that castigation in silence.

It was over—and the school dismissed. In
silence, they crowded out of Hall. Tom Redwing
slipped his arm through Smithy's and led him
away. Some fellows would have spoken to him—
but the look on Smithy's face did not encourage
them. It was pale, set, with eyes smouldering like
live coals. Redwing led him away in silence, and
the door of No. 4 Study in the Remove closed on
them.

"Poor old Smithy!" said Bob Cherry, in the
quad. "It's rough luck."

"The roughfulness of the luck is terrific," said
Hurree Jamset Ram Singh, dismally.

"Fellow shouldn't ask for what he doesn't
want!" grunted Johnny Bull.

"I know that, ass! But it's tough all the
same," said Bob. "Smithy likes to fancy himself
a fellow who doesn't give a boiled bean for beaks
and pre's—and he will feel this."

" He, he, he ! " contributed Billy Bunter. " Bet you he will ! The Head seemed to think he was beating carpet ! I say you fellows, I think I'll go and ask Smithy how he feels."

" Better leave him alone, you fat ass ! " said Harry Wharton, " Smithy won't be wanting to see anybody just now."

" That's just like you, Wharton. You're not sympathetic," said Bunter, reprovingly. " You haven't got my kind heart."

" I haven't got your fat head, thank goodness. Leave Smithy alone."

" Yah ! " retorted Bunter. And he rolled away, to inquire how Smithy was feeling—perhaps from kind-heartedness, but more probably from an inquisitive desire to see how Smithy was taking it.

In No. 4 Study Smithy was not looking as if he wanted kind inquiries from a kind-hearted Owl. He was leaning on the study table, breathing in gasps. He had succeeded in keeping up an aspect of iron endurance and indifference while many eyes were upon him. But it had fallen from him now like a cloak.

Tom Redwing stood silent, in miserable distress. Every mutter of pain from his chum went to his heart: and he was uneasy, too, and a little alarmed, at the evil gleam in the Bounder's eyes. Only too plainly he could read the fierce and savage resentment that ran riot in the breast of the scapegrace.

The Bounder stirred at last, lifting a pale bitter face, and looking at him across the table.

" You think I asked for this ? " he muttered, savagely.

" Well, old chap——! " said Tom. He paused. All Greyfriars knew that Vernon-Smith had asked for what he had received, and more: that he had deserved it, and that it might have been worse for him. But it was not a tactful moment for saying so.

"Well, if I asked for it, I've had it!" said Vernon-Smith, between his teeth, "and others may get what they've asked for, too." His eyes burned.

"Smithy, old man——."

"Don't 'Smithy old man' me! That little beast Twiss——."

"Twiss couldn't help——."

"I don't care whether he could help it or not. He's got me this! And the Head, too——."

Redwing started, in real alarm.

"Smithy! Are you mad? What do you mean?"

"Never mind what I mean," sneered the Bounder. "You'd better not know. There are ways of hitting back—even at the Great Panjandrum! No good askin' you to join up in a rag on the Big Beak."

"I should jolly well say not!" exclaimed Redwing, aghast. "For goodness' sake, Smithy, don't be mad. Do you want to be sacked after all?"

"Oh, I shall be jolly careful," jeered Smithy. "That moon-faced rabbit Twiss won't be wandering about in the dark next time. They won't get anything on me—after it's happened."

"For goodness' sake, Smithy——."

"Oh, don't jaw," said the Bounder savagely. "Do you think I want pi-jaw now? Leave a fellow alone."

"But—old chap——."

"Oh, leave a fellow alone!" snarled Vernon-Smith.

He moved restlessly about the study, his brow black, his eyes burning. Tom Redwing stood looking at him in silence for a few moments, and then quietly left the study. The Bounder was in

no mood for the company of even his best friend
—his only friend at Greyfriars. In his present
temper he was as likely to quarrel with friend as
with foe. Redwing's face was troubled, as he went
down the Remove passage: but he hoped, and
believed, that when the effects of the flogging had
worn off, Smithy would forget his wild words.

The study door opened again, a few minutes
later, and Skinner looked in. He was about to
enter: but as he caught the Bounder's look, he
stopped in the doorway.

"Feeling a bit better, old scout?" he asked.

"Find out! And get out."

Harold Skinner shrugged his shoulders and
walked away. The Bounder kicked the door
savagely shut after him.

But after a few minutes more it re-opened.
This time it was the fat face and big spectacles of
Billy Bunter that looked in. The fat Owl blinked
curiously at the dark scowling face that was
turned on him.

"How are you feeling now, Smithy?" he
asked, genially. "I thought I'd give you a look-in
——. Don't feel like sitting down for a bit, what?
He, he, he."

"Get out!"

"Oh, really, Smithy! You might be civil when
a fellow asks you a civil question. I wouldn't make
a lot of fuss about it, if I were you," said Bunter,
encouragingly. "After all, what's a licking?"

"What?"

"A fellow ought to be able to take a licking
without doing a song and dance about it, old chap!
I wouldn't! Grin and bear it, you know," said
Bunter.

"You fat fool!"

"Well, that's my advice," said Bunter. "I
wouldn't make a fuss over a whopping. I can take

it, I hope. I'm not soft! Brace up, old chap, and
——. What are you going to do with that stump,
Smithy?   I say—leggo my collar—wharrer you
think you're up to——. Keep that stump away—
oh, crikey! Whooop!"

Billy Bunter roared.

Bunter had stated that he wouldn't make a fuss
over a whopping. But he seemed to change his
fat mind as the Bounder grabbed his collar with
one hand and laid on the stump with the other.
He did make a fuss—quite a tremendous fuss—
he roared, and yelled, and howled, and spluttered:
and he was still roaring, and yelling, and howling,
and spluttering, when the Bounder pitched him
into the passage and slammed the study door on
him. The Remove passage echoed to sounds of
woe as the fat Owl tottered away, wishing from
the bottom of his fat heart that he hadn't paid
that kind-hearted visit to No. 4 Study.

Chapter XIII

UPSIDE DOWN !

" CHERRY ! "

" Yes, sir."

" Kindly refrain from shuffling your feet."

"Oh! Yes, sir! I mean, no, sir!" stammered Bob.

Henry Samuel Quelch was not in his bonniest mood in class that afternoon. There was a frown upon his brow, and a glint in his gimlet-eyes. The Remove knew the signs: and most of them made up their minds to walk warily. Even Billy Bunter made some slight effort to give attention to Quelch's words of wisdom in that class. Even Lord Mauleverer sat up and took notice. Seventeenth-century history did not exactly thrill the Lower Fourth, but they took what interest they could in Charles, and James, and the Revolution of 1688. Bob Cherry, indeed, was keeping his eyes fixed on Quelch, as if he simply yearned to know about 1688 and all that! But it was almost impossible for Bob to keep still.

However, Quelch having rapped out to him, Bob endeavoured so to do. He knew, of course, what was the matter with Quelch, as all the fellows did.

There had been a Head's flogging in the Remove. Quelch, certainly, had endorsed the Head's sentence with the fullest approval: if anything, he was disposed to think that the Head had not laid it on hard enough. But it was very irritating and annoying to Quelch, all the same. Other masters, in Common-Room, commented on it—

Hacker raised his eyebrows, Prout boomed, Capper and Twigg made remarks, Wiggins shook his head: it was, in fact, a topic in Common-Room: and when Common-Room had a topic, they worried it like a dog with a bone. Quelch, like all form-masters, disliked criticism of his form: and if other beaks suddenly stopped talking when he appeared in the offing, he knew why. It was all very annoying.

To Quelch's credit, he did not "take it out" of the Bounder. Smithy was in form, with a sullen brow and a glinting eye, in a mood to answer his form-master with impertinence if picked upon. Quelch was not, as a rule, patient with sullen looks, but he could be considerate to a fellow who had been through it so severely: and he took no notice of Vernon-Smith, not only ignoring his scowling face, but passing him over in the lesson. Which all the juniors thought was very decent of Quelchy. But if Quelch did not take it out of Smithy, he was exceedingly tart with the rest of the form.

"Mauleverer!"

"Oh! Yaas, sir," gasped Mauly, in alarm.

"Do you consider it decorous to yawn in class, while your form-master is speaking?"

"Oh! No, sir! Certainly not, sir."

"If you do so again, Mauleverer, I shall cane you."

A history class, in Mauly's opinion, was enough to make a stone image yawn. After that, however, he manfully suppressed his feelings.

"I guess Quelch is sure fierce this afternoon," Fisher T. Fish whispered to Tom Brown, and the New Zealand junior nodded.

"Fish!" It had been the faintest of whispers, but Quelch seemed to have uncommon keenness of hearing that afternoon. "Did you speak to

Brown, Fish?"

"Oh, gum! I mean, yep!" gasped Fisher T. Fish.

"Take fifty lines, Fish."

Fisher Tarleton Fish did not whisper again.

"Bunter!"

"Oh, crikey!" ejaculated the alarmed Owl, as the gimlet-eye fixed on him.

"You are not paying attention, Bunter."

"Oh, yes, sir! I heard everything you were saying, sir," gasped Bunter. "I—I haven't missed a word, sir. I—I'm awfully keen on history, sir."

Quelch gave him an expressive look. However, he seemed satisfied with that, and the gimlet-eye turned from Bunter, much to the fat Owl's relief.

Billy Bunter, in point of fact, was on the alert, like the rest of the form. But Billy Bunter had other matters on his mind. It was not only that he was lazy—he was always that. It was not only that he had an instinctive repugnance to learning anything: that was nothing new. It was not only that he regarded a lesson as a bothering infliction that a fellow had to get through somehow, and forget as soon afterwards as he could: that was his fixed and permanent view on the subject of education. But Bunter was feeling many lingering and painful twinges from the stumping in No. 4 Study. The Bounder had laid on that stump not wisely but too well. Every now and then Bunter gave a painful wriggle: and only terror of Quelch made him suppress an occasional yell. In such circumstances, how was a fellow to fix his attention on a dreary drone? Quelch, fortunately, did not know that Bunter regarded his instructive voice as a dreary drone.

It was not a happy lesson. Quelch, of course, did not realise that he was being unduly tart. He was simply keeping an inattentive form up to the

mark.   But many eyes turned longingly on the
form-room clock, of which the hands seemed to
crawl.

When Quelch began to ask questions on the
lesson most of the fellows concentrated.   Billy
Bunter was rubbing a plump spot where he had a
pain, when the gimlet-eye turned on him.

" Bunter ! "

" Oh ! Yes, sir," groaned Bunter.

" The year of the English Revolution ? "

That really was an easy one. They had gone
over it in the lesson, and even Lord Mauleverer
could have answered promptly.   Perhaps even
Bunter could have done so but for those troublesome twinges which had monopolised his attention. As it was, he couldn't. He blinked at his
form-master.

" Answer my question, Bunter."

" Oh, certainly, sir ! " Bunter wrinkled his fat
brows in an effort of thought. Bunter was never
good at dates—he loathed all dates, except the
edible variety. He had a vague idea that there
was a double number in it, and that was all.

" Bunter ! I——."

It flashed on Bunter.

" 1066, sir," he gasped. One date was much the
same as another to Billy Bunter, and there was a
double figure in that. He hoped it would do.

Quelch's look did not seem to indicate that it
would do.

" Bunter ! Did you say 1066, Bunter ? Are you
not aware, Bunter, that 1066 was the year of the
Norman Conquest ? " rumbled Mr. Quelch.

" Oh, yes, sir," said Bunter, cheerfully.   Even
Bunter knew that.

" Bless my soul ! Do you suppose that the
English Revolution occurred in the same year as
the Norman Conquest ? " hooted Mr. Quelch.

" Didn't it, sir? " asked Bunter. " I—I mean
——." He gathered from Mr. Quelch's look that
it didn't! " I—I mean, of—of course it didn't, sir.
I—I wonder what made me say 1066, sir! I—I
didn't mean 1066, sir, of—of course. I—I meant
——."

" Well, what did you mean, Bunter? "

" I—I—I mean——I—I know the date, of
course, sir—I—I never forget dates——I—I shall
have it in a minute, sir——."

" If you do not answer my question, Bunter, I
shall give you the date to write out five hundred
times after class."

" Oh, crikey! I—I—if—if you'll give me a
minute, sir——," groaned Bunter.

" I will give you one minute, Bunter. If you
open your book, I shall cane you. One minute! "
rumbled Mr. Quelch, and he turned his attention
to other happy members of his form, leaving
Bunter perspiring.

The fat Owl gave a start, as he felt something
slipped into his fat hand, under cover of the desk.
He blinked down at a slip of paper on which a date
was written. Tom Brown had hastily scribbled the
required date, and passed it along under the desks,
from hand to hand, to the hapless Owl.

Bunter's fat face brightened. He was all right
now, when the gimlet-eye turned on him again.
He was prepared to answer Quelch's question—
the good-natured New Zealand junior had got him
out of his fix. It was too dangerous for any fellow
to whisper. But Browney had found a way.

" Well, Bunter? " The gimlet-eyes transfixed
the fat Owl again. " Are you prepared to give me
the year of the English Revolution? "

" Oh, yes, sir," answered Bunter, full of cheery
confidence now. " 8891, sir."

Bunter had not noticed that he was holding that

slip of paper upside down!

Mr. Quelch almost jumped.

"WHAT!" he roared. He seemed hardly able to believe his ears. "Did—did—did you say 8891, Bunter?"

"Ain't that right, sir?" stammered Bunter, in dismay. "I—I think it was 8891, sir."

"Ha, ha, ha!" came a howl from the Remove. The Lower Fourth were not exactly in a hilarious mood that afternoon. But Bunter on dates was too much for them. They yelled.

"Silence!" rapped Mr. Quelch. "Bunter! Is this stupidity or impertinence? Are you not aware, Bunter, that the present year is in the twentieth century?"

"Oh, yes, sir," said Bunter, blinking at him. "Of course, sir."

"Then what do you mean by 8891?"

"Ain't—ain't that right, sir?"

"A date six thousand years in advance of the present date?" almost shrieked Mr. Quelch. "What do you mean, Bunter?"

"Oh!" gasped Bunter.

He blinked down at the paper in his fat hand. There was the date, written plainly enough in pencil: 8891, the way Bunter was holding it.

Dates were much of a muchness to Billy Bunter: merely bothering things that had to be handed out when a beak asked for them. But it dawned even on Bunter's fat brain that there was a mistake somewhere, and that he had considerably post-dated the English Revolution.

"Bunter! The date is 1688——."

"Oh!" stuttered Bunter. He realised now what had happened. "I—I meant to say 1688, sir, only I had it upside down—I—I mean——."

"Ha, ha, ha!"

"Silence in the class! Bunter, is that a paper

in your hand!"

"Oh! No, sir! Yes, sir! I—I—I mean, no, sir," babbled Bunter. "I—I haven't got anything in my hand, sir, and—and there's nothing written on it, and I wasn't holding it upside down, and——."

"That will do, Bunter! You will write out the date 1688 five hundred times after class! After which," added Mr. Quelch, with almost ferocious sarcasm, "you will perhaps remember at least one date in English history, Bunter."

The prospect of remembering at least one date in English history did not seem to console Billy Bunter very much. His fat face was lugubrious, as the clock-hand crawled slowly round, until at last the welcome hour of dismissal came.

Chapter XIV

BUNTER KNOWS HOW!

" LEND me——."

" Stony! " said Peter Todd, shaking his head sadly.

" Oh, really, Toddy! Lend me——."

" Hasn't that whacking remittance come? " asked Peter, sympathetically. " Wasn't your pater pleased with your spelling, after all? Too bad, when he's rolling in money because he's a wolf— did you say a wolf——? "

" A bear, you silly chump! " snorted Bunter. " You're a bear on a falling market, and a bull on a rising market, see? So the pater's a bear——."

" I see," agreed Peter. " That accounts for your manners, of course, if your pater's a bear! "

" Oh, don't be a funny ass! " howled Bunter. " Look here, lend me——."

" Nothing doing! "

" A pen——."

" A whatter? " ejaculated Peter Todd. He stared across No. 7 Study at Bunter. When Billy Bunter began with " Lend me," Toddy naturally supposed that it was a coin of the realm that Bunter wanted. Apparently he had, for once, mis-judged his fat study-mate. All Bunter wanted was a pen—though that was rather mysterious, as three pens lay on a study table—Toddy's, Dutton's, and Bunter's own.

" A pen," repeated Bunter, " I've got those rotten dates to write for Quelch. 1688 five hundred times. I—I don't think I'll keep Quelch waiting, Toddy—he ain't in a good temper to day. Have you got a pen in your desk? "

" You want some new specs, old fat man, if you can't see three pens lying right under your silly nose," said Peter.

" Three ain't enough," explained Bunter, " I want four."

" You want four? " repeated Toddy, blankly. " Are you going to use four pens all at once, you frabjous owl? "

" That's it," said Bunter, " I got the tip from Fry, in the Fourth Form. You see, you fasten four pens together, one over the other, with a string, and write with them all at once. Fry's done lines for his beak that way, and it worked."

" It might work with Capper," chuckled Peter Todd. " But if Quelch saw an impot with the same line written over four times——."

" Yes, but this ain't lines," argued Bunter, " Quelch is too downy for that, I know. But writing a date is different, see? I've got to write the same date over and over again. Well, with four pens tied together, I write four at once, and being the same date Quelch won't suspect a thing. I do it in a quarter the time, Peter, and my time's of value," added Bunter, with dignity.

" It must be, as you've been frowsting about doing nothing ever since class," agreed Peter. " If you take my advice, old lazybones, you won't try to pull Quelch's leg like that."

" I'm not asking you to give me advice, Peter— I'm asking you to lend me a pen. Look here, have you got another pen in your desk? " demanded Bunter, impatiently. " You needn't worry about advising a chap who's got twice your brains."

" Oh, my hat! " said Peter. " Well, here's a pen, old brainy barrel. You can have that old exercise-book too, if you like."

" Eh! I don't want your old exercise-book!

What use is an old exercise-book?"

"To pack in your bags when you take your impot in to Quelch," explained Peter.

"Yah!" was Bunter's reply to that.

Peter Todd chuckled, and left the study. Billy Bunter sniffed, and proceeded to carry out the big idea. It seemed a good thing to Bunter.

Fastening several pens together, to write more than one line at a time, was not exactly a new idea. Its use depended largely on the beak with whom it was worked. Capper, the master of the Fourth, was a mild, somewhat inattentive, and very unsuspicious gentleman: and a Fourth-Form man could palm off on him an imposition in which lines were repeated. But even Bunter realised that if a downy bird like Quelch saw an impot beginning

    Conticuere omnes intentique ora tenebant
    Conticuere omnes intentique ora tenebant
    Conticuere omnes intentique ora tenebant
    Conticuere omnes intentique ora tenebant

there would be thunder in the air.

But with dates it was different. Bunter's dates had to be repeated, so that was all right.

The fat junior jammed the four pens together, and secured them with a knotted string. Then he dipped the four nibs into the ink, and started. It did not come easy at first. Still, what a chap like Fry could do, a really brainy fellow like Bunter evidently could do. He had no doubt about that.

"Blow!"

The four pens, somehow, came apart. Perhaps Bunter hadn't knotted the string very securely. The fat Owl blinked in great exasperation at a sea of blots.

He breathed hard through his little fat nose. Then he laboured to secure the pens more securely. Bunter, as a rule, was neither industrious nor persistent in any task. But he could be both persistent and industrious in dodging work. Indeed, Bunter would take more time and trouble in eluding a task than would have been required to get it done.

He re-started after the interval.

Slowly, but surely, he got on with it. " 1688 " gradually covered the page with endless repetitions. Bunter was quite sick of that date before he had repeated it five hundred times.

Still, with that dodge he had picked up from Fry of the Fourth, he had only to write it one hundred and twenty-five times. to make up the total of five hundred. That dodge was a time-saver.

It was finished at last. Bunter blinked over it with satisfaction. Quelch, of course, expected him to write that date five hundred times, not merely one hundred and twenty-five times. Quelch could expect what he liked! There was " 1688 " five hundred times repeated, and Quelch would never dream of that time-saving device. How could he?

Glad to be done with it, Billy Bunter took his paper, and rolled down the Remove passage. A few minutes later he was tapping at his form-master's study door.

" Come in ! "

Bunter rolled in.

Mr. Quelch glanced up from a pile of Latin proses, raising his eyebrows a little.   For once, Bunter was prompt with the delivery of an impot. Quelch's expression became quite kindly.   He hoped that this was a sign of amendment in the laziest and most dilatory member of his form.

" Ah ! Bunter ! " said Mr. Quelch, quite genially. " You may hand me your paper, my boy."

Bunter handed him the paper.

Mr. Quelch glanced at it. His eyebrows lifted again, higher than before. He seemed puzzled for a moment. Bunter, with inward trepidation, saw the genial expression disappear from his face, as if wiped away with a duster. Was it possible that the beast suspected something?

Alas! It was!

" I—I hope it's all right, sir," stammered the fat Owl, " I—I've written it five hundred times, sir. I—I counted."

Mr. Quelch did not reply for a moment. He was scanning that paper with an eye as keen as any gimlet. If he was counting, he had to admit that the total was correct—Bunter was sure of that. Yet he did not seem satisfied, somehow.

Bunter had been careful with his total. But he had not been quite so careful with his spacing. He hadn't thought about that. A fellow couldn't think of everything—at all events, Bunter couldn't. Bunter's paper looked like this:

1688	1688	1688	1688
1688	1688	1688	1688
1688	1688	1688	1688
1688	1688	1688	1688
1688	1688	1688	1688
1688	1688	1688	1688
1688	1688	1688	1688
1688	1688	1688	1688

And so on.

Those blocks of four puzzled Mr. Quelch for a moment. But only for a moment. He laid down the paper, and looked at Bunter.

His hand strayed to his cane. But he withdrew it. His crusty face relaxed into a grim smile.

" Bunter! "

" Oh! Yes, sir! " mumbled Bunter.

" Forty years ago," said Mr. Quelch, " I was a schoolboy."

" Oh! W-w-w-were you, sir? " stammered Bunter. He realised that Mr. Quelch must have been a boy, in his time, though no one would have supposed so, to look at him! Still, he did not see why Quelch should tell him so.

"I was," said Mr. Quelch, "and when I was in a junior form, I was acquainted with a trick of fastening pens together——."

"Eh!"

"By which device," said Mr. Quelch, "more than one line could be written at a time."

"Oh!" gasped Bunter.

"This trick," said Mr. Quelch, "could sometimes be played with success upon an inattentive or absent-minded master. I did not approve of it, even as a schoolboy, Bunter. I approve of it still less as a school-master."

"Oh!"

"And I recommend you," added Mr. Quelch, "to use only one pen! You may go, Bunter."

Billy Bunter went—with feelings too deep for words.

Chapter XV

SMITHY'S SCHEME !

"IT'S mad, Smithy!" muttered Tom Redwing.

"Is it?" jeered the Bounder.

"You can't do it!"

"Can't I?"

They were in No. 4 Study, after prep. Most ot the Remove had gone down to the Rag: but Smithy was not disposed to meet the crowd in the day-room, and Tom Redwing stayed up in the study with his chum. Smithy was moving restlessly about the room, his hands in his pockets, his brow moody, his eyes glinting. Tom's eyes were on him in deep anxiety. He knew that mood of the Bounder—a mood in which he was utterly reckless of consequences. He had dreaded what Smithy might do, in his savage resentment: and now that he knew, he was alarmed.

Vernon-Smith came to a halt, and stood staring at his chum, with a sneer on his hard face.

"It's not so risky as you fancy," he said. "Not that I care!"

"They'll think of you first thing," urged Redwing. "It's no good telling you that what you're thinking of is rotten—you know that! But the risk—I tell you they'll think of you first of all —you were flogged this morning, and something happens in the Head's study the next night— they've only got to put two and two together."

"I'm not so sure of that. A chap who's just had a flogging wouldn't be expected to risk another just afterwards. But what's the odds—if they can't prove anythin'? Even if they guess, they've got to

have proof. If they ask me whether I did it, do
you think I shall answer, 'Oh, yes—I cannot tell a
lie: I did it with my little hatchet'?" The Bounder
laughed scoffingly. "Let them suspect what they
like! I stick to it that I never left the dorm after
lights out, if I'm questioned. Who's to prove anythin' else?"

"You were caught last night——."

"Think that little bunny-faced blighter Twiss
will be goin' down for a book again in the middle
of the night?" jeered Smithy.

"No! But anything might happen—a master
might be up——."

"I'm leaving it late to make sure. It was only
eleven last night when that fool Twiss was mooning about. I shall make it midnight. Anybody
likely to be up at midnight?"

Redwing was silent.

"It's as safe as houses, and you know it,"
sneered Smithy. "You want to stop me, because
you don't like the idea. Think I can't see through
you?"

"I know I'm wasting my breath, Smithy.
But——."

"Don't waste any more, then."

"It's rotten, Smithy! When you're cooler,
you'll see that as plainly as I do. The Head's a
good man and a just man. You had it hard, I
know. But if you will kick over the traces, what
do you expect?"

"Is this a lecture or a sermon?"

Tom Redwing bit his lip.

"It's a rotten game to rag the Head's study—
rotten, and disrespectful, and caddish," he broke
out, hotly, "and it's rottener still to rely on telling
lies to see you through if you're suspected."

"Can it!"

"You wouldn't tell lies among the fellows——."

"That's different. Beaks are fair game," said Vernon-Smith. "They can whop a man if they bowl him out—they can't expect him to give himself away."

"I know that's how you look at it, Smithy. But you're wrong-headed about it. Other fellows don't have to lie themselves out of scrapes—Wharton, or old Bob, or Mauly——."

"Is that sixthly or seventhly?"

Redwing breathed hard. He knew that it was useless to argue with the scapegrace of Greyfriars, when his wilful mind was made up. It evoked only mockery from the Bounder.

"You don't feel like turning out to-night, to keep cave in the passage while I'm in the Beak's study?" grinned Smithy.

"You know that I couldn't have a hand in anything of the kind."

"Of course not! Aren't you a jolly old model—like Wharton, or old Bob, or Mauly?" mimicked the Bounder. "I'd ask Skinner or Snoop, but they haven't the pluck. Well, I don't want any help."

"It's mad," said Tom, "I tell you——."

"It's safe as houses, and you know it," said the Bounder, coolly. "I've got it all cut and dried. The Head never locks his study door. That's easy. I go down with my pyjamas tucked into my trousers—if I'm spotted, they can't make out that I was going out of bounds like that." He chuckled. "But I shan't be spotted, Reddy—there won't be anybody up to spot a fellow at the jolly old witchin' time of night. I shan't be more than ten minutes in the Beak's study—but you can bet your Sunday hat that it will be a sight for gods and men and little fishes when I'm through with it."

"Smithy, old man——."

"Keep mum, that's all," said Smithy, "and if you hear me stirring to-night, don't jaw, and wake the fellows, as you did last night. Nobody's going to know who shipped the Head's study, if I can help it."

Redwing sat silent, looking at him. Studies had been "shipped" before, at Greyfriars—it was not unknown for even a master's study to be "shipped." But the idea of shipping the Head's study was certainly not likely to occur to any mind less wildly reckless than the Bounder's, and as Redwing had said, even the Bounder would never have thought of it had he been cooler. But Smithy was not cool now—he was seething with angry and passionate resentment, and not to be reasoned with.

"You don't like the idea?" jeered Smithy.

"You know I don't."

"Lump it, then!" said Vernon-Smith. "Keep mum about what I've told you, that's all."

"You know that I shall do that. But——."

"That's enough! Give us a rest. And——." The Bounder broke off, as the study door was suddenly opened from without. A fat figure rolled in—and stopped.

"Oh!" ejaculated Billy Bunter. "Haven't you fellows gone down? I—I thought you'd be down in the Rag——I—I—I mean, I—I looked in to speak to you, Smithy——."

"You fat idiot! What do you want?"

"Oh! Nothing! I say, you fellows, ain't you going down?" asked Bunter. "I say, Wibley's going to do some of his impersonations in the Rag, I hear—awfully funny when he does old Prout, you know—you fellows shouldn't miss it. That's what I came to tell you, Smithy——I—I didn't think you'd gone down, and I wasn't after anything——."

"Oh, get out!" growled Vernon-Smith.

"Oh, really, Smithy! If you think I was after

your chocolates——."

" What?"

" I never knew you had chocs in the study cupboard! How could I?" demanded Bunter, warmly.
" I came up to tell you that Wharton wants to
speak to you—it's about the cricket, you know
——."

" Hand me that stump, Reddy!"

" Beast!"

Billy Bunter did not wait for the stump. He
had had more than enough of that stump for one
day. He faded promptly out of No. 4 Study, and
the door slammed behind him.

Chapter XVI

STRUCK DOWN !

HERBERT VERNON-SMITH made no sound as he slipped from his bed in the dark.

The last of twelve strokes had died away in the night. It was midnight: and at that hour, the last light was out, the most belated beak had gone to bed: all Greyfriars slept.

Whether Tom Redwing was awake in the next bed, Smithy did not know—and he did not care. In his better moments, Redwing had much influence over him: but in his present mood, opposition only made him more stubbornly obstinate. His face was set and bitter, as he scrambled into his trousers. He did not intend to dress—if, by ill chance, he was " spotted " on his way down, he wanted it to be clear that he had not intended to leave the House: some tale of intending a " rag " on another dormitory would see him through. But such a mischance was very unlikely: what had happened the previous night could scarcely happen a second time.

There was a faint stirring—and then he knew that Redwing was awake. But Tom did not speak —he would not risk drawing attention to Smithy's mad escapade. If Smithy carried out his scheme of " shipping " the head-master's study, it could not be kept too secret, even in the Remove.

The Bounder guessed that his chum's eyes were on him, in the gloom. He did not heed. Silently, in his socks, he crept away to the door— and even the wakeful Redwing, listening, did not hear a sound as the door opened and closed again.

Smithy was very cautious—caution itself, though he had no doubt that the coast was clear. He was taking no chances. All was dark—but he knew every inch of the way. Silently he crept down the passage, across the landing—doubly cautiously he crept down the stairs, taking his time, listening intently. He made no sound—and no sound came to his hears in the silent House.

Some fellows might have hesitated to traverse dark passages and stairs at such an hour. Billy Bunter's fat imagination would have peopled the shadows with lurking burglars. But the Bounder was not troubled with nerves. The darkness and the silence were nothing to him.

He stood, at length, in the corridor on which the head-master's study opened. His heart beat a little faster as he stopped at the door.

The thought came into his mind of the tremendous " row " on the morrow, when it was discovered that the Head's study had been " shipped." He knew that Redwing was right— they would think of him at once: the scapegrace who had been flogged only that day. What did it matter, if they could prove nothing? Anyhow, he was not turning back.

His hand was steady as he groped for the door-handle in the blackness. To his surprise, the door moved under his hand—it was ajar.

He had expected to find it unlocked: he had not expected to find it unlatched. But there it was, and he pushed it open, without a sound.

He stepped in, his feet noiseless on the soft carpet.

The next moment, he stood transfixed, his heart giving a great bound. A startled gasp escaped him involuntarily, unconsciously.

The study was dark: the blinds drawn, shutting out the glimmer of the stars. But across the wide room, on the further side of the Head's writing-table, was a twinkle of light.

It was the gleam of a torch!

Only for a split second was it visible. It was shut off instantly. Whoever held that light had heard him.

He heard a panting breath in the darkness. He was wildly startled: but the other, unseen, was as startled as he.

Vernon-Smith's heart thumped.

He was not alone in the room.

Who was there—who could be there, in the dark, at midnight, with only the glimmer of a tiny torch to light him?

The thought of burglars had never entered the Bounder's mind at all as he threaded his way by dark staircases and passages in a silent House at midnight. But it rushed into his mind now. For what else could it mean?

There was a panting breath—a hurried rustle —the rustle of papers. Vernon-Smith could see nothing but the gleam of the light instantly extinguished. But he could hear—he heard the panting breath, the rustling paper, the scrape of a chair as someone, moving hurriedly, knocked against it in the dark . Someone was at the Head's desk—a panting, startled man: and he knew what that man was, what he could only be—a thief in the night!

For the moment, the Bounder was as if paralysed: his bulging eyes staring into the gloom, his heart leaping and thumping. But as he heard the unseen man moving, he realised his peril, and backed swiftly to the doorway.

Almost at the same moment an unseen figure, rushing across the room to the door, crashed into him, knocking him backwards.

He staggered, throwing out his hands, catching as he fell at the invisible figure that had crashed into him, hardly knowing what he did. His right hand closed on an arm—and held. But it held only for a moment. A clenched fist lashed from the darkness, crashing into his face with stunning force, and he spun over with a cry and thudded to the floor.

He heard, as his senses swam, the patter of running feet in the dark corridor. The man who had struck him down was running. But he heard, and knew, no more. There was a low moan, and silence: and the Bounder of Greyfriars, crumpled, inert, lay in the darkness just within the doorway, stunned and senseless.

Chapter XVII

WHAT HAPPENED TO SMITHY ?

HARRY WHARTON awoke. His eyes opened, in the glimmer of light from the high windows. Something had awakened him—he hardly knew what: but he knew that somebody was moving in the dormitory. He lifted his head from the pillow and looked round him. Faintly, from the night, came the sound of a chime. It was half-past twelve.

The moon was high in a clear sky. Its light glimmered in the long dormitory: he could see the many beds, each with its black shadow on the floor. From the silence came the intermittent rumble of Billy Bunter's deep snore. But there was some other sound—someone was stirring.

He stared towards the door. A cold draught in the air told him that it was open: and in the glimmering moonlight he saw that it was wide open, and that a shadowy figure was standing there.

His lip curled as he looked. The thought of Smithy came into his mind at once—that it was the scapegrace of the Remove who was returning at that late hour from some reckless excursion. It was like the Bounder to carry on with his wild ways, in spite of the flogging—or even because of it.

But was it Smithy? He made out a figure in pyjamas, standing with his back to the room, looking out into the passage. Dimly as he made it out, he saw, after a moment or two, that it was not Smithy's. He sat up in bed, staring at the shadowy form. It was not Smithy: but it was a Remove man, watching the dark passage outside and listening — why, the captain of the Remove could not imagine.

"Who's that?" he called out, softly. "What's up?"

The half-seen junior at the door gave a sudden start, and spun round towards him. Then Wharton saw his face in the moon-glimmer, and recognized Tom Redwing.

"Quiet!" came a breathless whisper.

"Redwing——!"

"Quiet! Don't wake anyone. Quiet."

Harry Wharton sat silent, staring at him. He could read the trouble and anxiety in Redwing's face, and he did not need telling that it was something to do with Smithy. Redwing would not have been out of bed at that hour on his own account. He turned his glance towards Vernon-Smith's bed, and now that he looked at it he could see that it was unoccupied.

Quietly, he slipped from his own bed, and joined Redwing at the doorway. If Smithy was out of bounds again, so soon after the offence for which he had been flogged in Hall, he could understand Redwing's anxiety. The reckless scapegrace was hardly worth being concerned about: but Tom was concerned about him, all the same.

"What's up, Reddy?" he asked, in a low whisper, "Smithy breaking out again?"

"No! No! It's not that! It's a rag——."

"A rag?" repeated Harry.

"Keep it dark! Smithy was wild—you know him!" muttered Redwing. "He was going to ship the Head's study——."

"The mad ass!" breathed Wharton.

"I know! But—but—he said he would be ten minutes. That was enough—but—but why doesn't he come back? He's been gone half an hour. I've been listening all the time—there hasn't been a sound—he can't have been nailed. But—but why hasn't he come back?"

Redwing put his head out of the doorway again, staring into the blackness of the passage. All was silent—still. He hardly knew what he feared—but he knew that something must have delayed the Bounder—something must have happened: he could not begin to guess what. Why did not Smithy return?

"I can't understand it," he muttered. "Smithy's not the fellow to tumble downstairs in the dark, or anything like that——."

"Hardly."

"But why——? I can't make it out. He can't be all this time in the Head's study—but what ——?"

"Sure that was his game?" asked Harry.

"Yes, yes, he said so."

"Um! Yes! But——," Harry Wharton paused.

"He can't have gone out, if that's what you're thinking. He couldn't go out of the House in his trousers and socks."

"No! But—if he's only gone down to a study ——."

"That's what I can't understand. They've not got him—there hasn't been a sound—but something—something——," muttered Redwing. "He's a reckless ass, but he would get through as quickly as he could—and get safe back. Why doesn't he come?"

Wharton shook his head. He was as perplexed as the Bounder's chum. Every minute that Vernon-Smith was out of his dormitory added to the danger of discovery. Ten minutes would have been ample—a quarter of an hour more than ample. And he had been gone half an hour: and there was still no sound or sign of his return.

"Something must have happened to him," muttered Redwing.

"What could have happened?"

"I don't know. But—I'm going down to look for him! I can't make it out—but something's wrong. Some accident—something—he wouldn't be staying all this time, if he could help it."

Harry Wharton nodded.

"I can't make it out any more than you can, Reddy. But it's jolly queer. I'll come down with you, if you're going."

"It will mean a row for you, if—if——."

"You're not going alone," said Harry.

They had been speaking in low voices at the door: no one else in the Remove dormitory had awakened. And they were careful to wake no one as they slipped on trousers and socks, and then stepped out quietly into the passage. In a minute more, they were crossing the landing to the staircase—stepping lightly and softly, for Mr. Quelch's room was near at hand. As quietly as the Bounder half an hour before them, they crept down the stairs to the study landing below.

All was dark and silent there, and the lower staircase was a black well. In the silence they could hear each other's suppressed breathing. They groped down to the ground floor, and there they stopped, to listen, at the foot of the staircase. But there was no sound from the gloom—the Bounder was not coming.

"He must be still in the Head's study," whispered Wharton.

"But why——?"

"Goodness knows! We shall soon see."

A minute more, and they were in the corridor outside the door of the head-master's study. There was no sound from the study—if the Bounder was there, he was silent. Redwing groped for the door. and his hand met open space.

"The door's open," he breathed.

"Then he must be here."

"Smithy!" whispered Redwing. He peered into the dark interior of the room. He could see nothing. "Smithy!"

"Smithy, you ass!" muttered Wharton, "answer if you're there."

There was no answer from the blackness. Then, as they listened with anxious intentness, a strange sound came—low and faint: a low, barely audible moan. Harry Wharton started, the blood rushing to his heart. He caught Redwing's arm.

"Did you hear——?" His voice came in a gasp.

"Smithy!" panted Redwing.

He ran into the study, stumbled over something that lay in the darkness, and almost fell. A startled cry broke from him.

"Good heavens! Smithy——."

"What is it?" gasped Harry Wharton.

"Get a light—quick! It's Smithy—it must be Smithy—lying here—switch on the light, quick!"

Redwing was groping at the unseen form over which he had stumbled. Wharton found the switch inside the doorway and flashed on the light.

He stared, with starting eyes, at the scene in the study—Redwing, on his knees beside the still form stretched on the carpet: the Bounder, his face upturned, colourless, with a great black bruise on the forehead.

"He's hurt," groaned Redwing. "Smithy, old man!"

Wharton could only stare, stupefied. The Bounder lay unconscious under the eyes of the two horrified juniors. But he was coming to—the

moan they had heard was the first sign of returning consciousness. And as Redwing lifted the
sagging head, and rested it against his knee,
Vernon-Smith's eyes opened, and another faint
moan escaped him. His dizzy eyes flickered in the
light.

"Reddy!" he muttered.

"I'm here, Smithy, old fellow. You're hurt
——."

"I had a knock."

There was silence again, for a long minute.
The Bounder lay with his aching head resting on
Redwing's knee, without stirring. But he was
recovering a little—a faint flush of colour came
back into his white face. His voice came again,
faint, but stronger than before.

"He's gone?"

"He—who?"

"The man who knocked me out."

"The man who knocked you out!" repeated
Harry Wharton. "There's nobody here, Smithy."

"I know! I thought I heard him running, as I
went down. Stick to me, Reddy—you go and call
Quelch, Wharton."

"Call Quelch——," Wharton stared. "Smithy
—here—at this time of night——."

"This can't be kept dark now—the Head's
been robbed——."

"Smithy!"

"Can't you understand? The thief was here—
he knocked me out and ran—he was at the Head's
desk—do you think I'm wandering in my mind,
you fool?" snarled the Bounder. "Look at the
Head's desk—I expect you'll see signs of him."

Harry Wharton gave the Bounder a long, hard
look. Then, in silence, he crossed the study to the
head-master's writing-table, and looked round it.
The table had a column of drawers on either side

—and Wharton started, and caught his breath, as he saw that one of them was pulled open—a rough gash in the wood showing that the lock had been forced.

" Well? " came an impatient mutter from the Bounder.

" I'll call Quelch," said Harry, quietly.

He hurried from the study. A couple of minutes later Mr. Quelch, roused from sleep, was listening with a startled face to what he had to tell.

Chapter XVIII

SOMETHING UP !

" I SAY, you fellows."

" Hallo, hallo, hallo ! "

" Something's up ! " said Billy Bunter.

" Not really ? " asked Bob Cherry.

" Yes, rather." Billy Bunter nodded his fat head sagely, " I can jolly well tell you fellows that something's up ! "

At which the Famous Five smiled.

Almost every fellow at Greyfriars School knew, or suspected, that something was " up " that sunny morning. Apparently it had now dawned upon the powerful intellect of William George Bunter.

The Famous Five, as a matter of fact, knew more about it than most fellows. Harry Wharton had told his chums of the strange happening in the night. They had been discussing it when Billy Bunter rolled up to them in the quad after breakfast. The fat Owl blinked at them seriously through his big spectacles.

" You fellows wouldn't know," he remarked. " You fellows never hear anything. But it's pretty plain that something's up. You can take my word for that."

" That settles it ! " said Harry Wharton, gravely. " And what is it that's up, old fat man ? "

" It's something to do with Smithy, I fancy," said Bunter, wisely. " He's been fighting."

" Smithy been scrapping ? " asked Frank Nugent.

" Well, haven't you seen him this morning ? "

asked Bunter. "He's got a lump over his eye as if a mule had kicked him——. Think he was out of bounds last night, and got into a scrap with some of his precious pals at the 'Cross Keys'? That might be it."

"Oh, my hat!" gasped Harry Wharton. "No, I'm sure Smithy hasn't been out of bounds, Bunter. You can wash that out."

"Think it was Redwing?" asked Bunter.

"Eh!"

"I mean to say, he's got a rotten temper, and I've often wondered why Redwing doesn't punch his head. They were having a row in their study after prep last night——."

"Rot!" said Johnny Bull.

"Well, perhaps not exactly a row," said Bunter, "but they were jolly well arguing over something, and Smithy was ratty. I thought they'd gone down when I went to No. 4 to look for the chocolates—I mean, when I dropped in for a chat with Smithy——."

"Ha, ha, ha!"

"Well, you can cackle, but I can tell you that Smithy was in a beastly temper as usual—he was simply insulting," said Bunter. "Anyhow, Smithy's got a jolt from somewhere. Quelch must have noticed it——."

"Think so?" asked Bob.

"Well, it stands to reason—he's seen him at prayers, and at brekker, so he must have noticed it," argued Bunter. "Think Smithy's up for another flogging, Wharton?"

Harry Wharton laughed.

"I hardly think so," he answered. "I don't fancy that Smithy's in a row at all, Bunter. Try again."

"Well, something's up, and if it isn't Smithy, what is it?" asked Bunter. "I wonder if it's

Loder of the Sixth——."

"Loder!" repeated the Famous Five, blankly.

"Well, suppose the beaks have spotted him?" suggested Bunter. "We all know the sort of man Loder is. If the Head knew, he would sack him like a shot. Think Loder's up for the sack, you fellows?"

"Better ask Loder—he would know," suggested Bob Cherry.

"Ha, ha, ha!"

"Oh, really, Cherry!" Bunter sniffed. "If you fellows can't see that something's up, it only shows what duffers you are. Didn't you see Quelch's face—he always looks like a grim old gargoyle, I know, but this morning he looks like—like—like a Gorger."

"Like a whatter?" gasped Bob Cherry. "Oh! Do you mean Gorgon?"

"I don't care whether it's a gorger or a gorgon, but that's what Quelch looks like. And the other beaks, too," said Bunter. "I heard Prout say to Capper that it was unpara—unpara—I mean, what's that long word he uses? Oh, I know—unparallelogrammed——."

"Ha, ha, ha!" yelled the Famous Five.

"Blessed if I can see anything to cackle at. That's what Prout said to Capper," declared Bunter. "I heard him. And I heard Hacker speaking to Twiss, too—he said he'd heard nothing during the night, and Twiss said he hadn't, and that jolly well shows that something happened, see?" said Bunter, triumphantly. "I expect I should have heard the next minute what it was, only Hacker saw me, and I had to move on. You know the Acid Drop! He'd make out that a fellow was listening to what he was saying."

"And the listenfulness was not terrific?" grinned Hurree Jamset Ram Singh. "The esteemed Bunter hears these things without listening."

" Well, I keep my eyes open," said Bunter, " You fellows would know more about what goes on, if you did the same. I say, seen Skinner? Skinner may know something about it. You fellows never know a thing."

And the fat inquisitive Owl rolled away in search of Skinner and possible information on the interesting subject of what might be " up " at Greyfriars that morning.

" I suppose it will be all over the school soon," remarked Bob Cherry. " It can't be kept dark about burgling the Head's study. It's a matter for the police."

" I believe Quelch phoned to Inspector Grimes at Courtfield after he sent us back to the dorm last night," said Harry. " The police must have been here. May be here now for all we know—or Bunter knows."

" They won't do much good here. I expect the johnny who knocked Smithy out is far enough away by this time, with what he snaffled from the Head's desk."

" Some cracksman from London, most likely," said Nugent.

Harry Wharton shook his head.

" I shouldn't think so, from what I saw," he said, slowly. " That drawer in the Head's desk had been forced open—a chisel or something—a cracksman could have picked the lock easily enough, and he wouldn't risk making a noise breaking it open. It was broken open in the clumsiest way."

" Not professional work, what? " grinned Bob. " Local talent, perhaps! Some jolly old tramp— I wonder how he got in."

" Grimey will find that out."

" Hallo, hallo, hallo! Here's Smithy! By gum, that sportsman last night must have given him a whale of a jolt," said Bob.

Many eyes that morning had turned on the Bounder's disfigured face. The heavy black-and-bluish bruise on his forehead leaped to every eye. Only too plainly, he had received a terrific jolt from the unknown man in the Head's study. Apart from that ugly bruise, however, the Bounder showed few if any signs of what he had been through. He was hard as nails. His expression was far from pleasant as he came up to the Famous Five, and his eyes glinted as the juniors involuntarily glanced at his disfigured forehead.

" Looks pretty, doesn't it? " he sneered.

" It must have been a bit of a shock," said Bob.

" Yes, it was a bit of a knock," said Vernon-Smith, between his teeth. " I'd like to meet the man who handed it out—I'd give him something back. Not much chance of that, I suppose—he had lots of time to get clear before I was found. I came to tell you that you're wanted, Wharton—you and I and Redwing—Grimey wants to hear anything we can tell him."

" Is Grimes here, then? " asked Nugent.

" Yes, in the Head's study. I believe he's been making investigations." The Bounder sneered again. " Fat lot of good. We can't tell him anything of any use, but I suppose he wants to take notes. That's about as far as he'll get, I expect. Come on, Wharton."

The captain of the Remove went into the House with Smithy. They joined Tom Redwing, and the three of them followed Mr. Quelch to the Head's study. The Co. remained in the quad, where they were once more favoured with the attention of Billy Bunter. Bunter rolled up with an excited fat face.

"I say, you fellows! What do you think?" exclaimed the fat Owl.

"I told you yesterday," answered Bob, "I think you're a burbling bandersnatch, old fat man."

"Oh, really, Cherry! I say, there jolly well is something up, as I told you!" exclaimed Bunter. "I say, what about Grimes being here?"

"Grimes!" repeated Bob.

"Yes, rather! Inspector Grimes from Court-field police-station!" trilled Bunter, "I've found it all out. Mind, it's true about Grimes—two or three fellows have seen him—and he's jolly well in the Head's study now. I say, he can't have come here to run Smithy in, can he?"

"Oh, suffering cats! Hardly!" gasped Bob.

"Well, you can take my word for it that something's up. My belief is that something must have happened last night," said Bunter. "I shouldn't wonder if that's why Grimey has come over from Courtfield. You can jolly well cackle as much as you jolly well like, but you'll jolly well find that I'm right—there's something up!" declared Bunter. "Mark my words, you fellows—before you're much older you'll hear that there's something up."

And Billy Bunter rolled off again in search of further thrilling items of news, leaving the Co. chuckling.

Chapter XIX

INSPECTOR GRIMES INVESTIGATES

" HERE are the boys, sir!" said Mr. Quelch.

Dr. Locke was seated at his writing-table. His glance turned on the three juniors as they followed the Remove master into the study, and he frowned a little as he looked at the Bounder. The Head's kind old face was clouded, and there was a wrinkle in his brow. The present state of affairs was very disturbing to him. A robbery had taken place—an unheard-of occurrence in Dr. Locke's placid existence. No doubt, in the scholastic calm of Greyfriars, Dr. Locke knew that there were head-hunters in Borneo, and cannibals in Central Africa. But he had never anticipated rubbing shoulders, as it were, with the underworld. What had happened was a great shock to him. He had greeted Inspector Grimes, of Courtfield, with his usual urbane courtesy: but he would almost as soon have seen a grisly spectre in his study.

The three juniors stood quietly before their head-master. The Bounder did not look, or feel, uneasy.

It had had to come out about his surreptitious nocturnal visit to his head-master's study. But his reckless scheme of "shipping" the study had not been carried out, after all: for which he was now duly thankful. He had no doubt of coming through easily, especially after the injury he had received.

There was a stocky figure standing by the study window—Inspector Grimes, of Courtfield, plump and red-faced. Plump and red as his face was, almost sleepy, his eyes were very keen: and they scanned the three juniors with a very penetrating look. Mr. Grimes did not stir or speak, and the juniors hardly noticed that he was there.

"You know why I have sent for you, my boys," said the Head. "Your form-master has told me all the circumstances: but I desire to hear what you have to say, and Mr. Grimes may have some questions to put to you. It appears that you, Wharton, and Redwing, came down in the night to look for Vernon-Smith."

"Yes, sir," said Harry.

"I understand: but I do not understand, Vernon-Smith, why you came down to this study, in the first place. You left your dormitory, at midnight, and came to this study—why?" The head-master's voice grew sterner as he put that question.

"I'm sorry, sir," said the Bounder, meekly. Smithy could be meek, when he liked. "It was a lark, sir—I can see now how silly it was—but ——."

"A lark!" repeated the Head. "What do you mean by a ' lark,' Vernon-Smith?"

"I—I was going to put some gum in your ink-pot, sir."

"What! Bless my soul!" exclaimed the Head, blankly.

Tom Redwing compressed his lips a little. He knew, only too well, what the Bounder's intentions had been. But for the unexpected encounter with the midnight pilferer, the study would have been "shipped," and found in the morning in a state of the wildest disorder.

Mr. Quelch fixed gimlet-eyes very sharply on Smithy. He did not know what Redwing knew: but he had no doubt—not the slightest doubt—

that the scapegrace of Greyfriars had planned
something much more serious and damaging than
a fag trick of putting gum into an inkpot. But the
Remove master did not speak.

" Bless my soul! " repeated the Head. " It was
your intention, Vernon-Smith, to play a foolish,
unthinking prank in your head-master's study—a
prank of which a small boy in the Second Form
might be ashamed."

" I'm very sorry, sir." Smithy was meakness
itself, " I know it was silly, sir—I see that quite
plainly now. And I never did it, sir, as it happened
—I was knocked out as soon as I got into the
room." Smithy passed a hand over the black
bruise on his forehead, just to remind the Head
that he had been injured. He thought it worth
while to keep that in Dr. Locke's mind.

There was a pause.

" Vernon-Smith! " said the Head, at last, " but
for the consequences of your act I should request
your form-master to administer a severe punish-
ment for such a foolish, unreflecting, disrespectful
prank. In view of the injury you received, I shall
not do so."

" Thank you, sir," murmured the Bounder.

" No doubt what has occurred will be a warning to you," said Dr. Locke. " Your reckless
action placed you in actual danger, as it transpired.
Let this be a lesson to you, Vernon-Smith."

" Oh, yes, sir."

Dr. Locke glanced across at Mr. Grimes.

" If you desire to question the boys, sir——."

" Certainly, sir." Mr. Grimes stepped from the
window. " I should like to hear from you, Master
Vernon-Smith, exactly what occurred. At what
time precisely did you leave your dormitory?"

" Midnight had just struck, sir."

" You came down in the dark?"

" Yes, sir. I had no idea that anyone was here, of course, till I saw the light of a torch as I came into the room."

" You did not see the man who held the torch? "

" No: it was put out instantly."

" You saw nothing at all of him? "

" Nothing whatever, sir."

" What happened then? "

" I realised that it must be a burglar, and backed to the door. He must have rushed for the door at the same time, for he rushed into me, and I caught at him as I was knocked over. Then he gave me—this." The Bounder touched the bruise on his forehead.

" You were stunned? "

" I must have been. I don't know anything afterwards till Wharton and Redwing found me here. But I heard him running, as I fell—I am sure of that. He ran down the corridor."

" As frightened as you were, apparently," said Mr. Grimes.

The Bounder gave him a look.

" I was not frightened," he answered, disdainfully. " I was startled, of course. If I'd had a chance, he wouldn't have knocked me out like that."

Mr. Grimes smiled.

" Now, Master Redwing, it appears that you came down to look for your friend, as he did not return to the dormitory. You too came down in the dark, I suppose? "

" Yes, sir," answered Tom.

" At what time was this? "

" Some minutes after half-past twelve."

" Then Master Vernon-Smith must have lain here unconscious for at least half an hour. Did you see, or hear, anything unusual as you came down? "

" Nothing at all, sir."

" Or you, Master Wharton? "

" Nothing, sir."

" No sound of anyone stirring? "

" No, sir."

"You found Master Vernon-Smith unconscious here? "

" I stumbled over him, sir," said Redwing. " I called to Wharton to switch on the light, and then we saw him. He was just beginning to come to."

" You saw no sign of a burglar? "

" Not till Smithy told us to call Mr. Quelch," said Harry. " Then I looked at Dr. Locke's desk, and saw that a drawer had been broken open."

" Thank you, Master Wharton. That is all— at present."

The Head made a sign, and the three juniors left the study. Inspector Grimes stood with a deeply thoughtful expression on his face. Dr. Locke and Mr. Quelch regarded him in silence. Whether the Courtfield inspector was cogitating deeply, or whether he was utterly at a loss, they did not know. Mr. Grimes spoke at last, as a bell began to ring.

" I will take up no more of your time now, sir. I have some investigations to make which will be better carried out while the boys are in class. I may have something to tell you later—I certainly hope so."

And Dr. Locke proceeded to the Sixth-Form room, and Mr. Quelch to the Remove: and Mr. Grimes was left to his meditation and investigations, whatever they were.

Chapter XX

BUNTER WANTS TO KNOW !

" IT'S bub-bub-bub—— "

" What? "

" Bub-bub—bub——." Billy Bunter stuttered, in his excitement. " It's bub-bub-bub—burglars." He got it out at last.

Harry Wharton had rejoined his friends in the quad. It was only a few minutes now to class, and they were waiting for the bell when Bunter rolled up, spluttering with excitement, his little round eyes almost popping through his big round spectacles. Evidently the Owl of the Remove had news—startling and thrilling news.

" Bub-bub-burglars! " gasped Bunter. " What do you fellows think of that? "

" Bub-bub-burglars," was it? " asked Bob. " What sort of burglar is a bub-bub-burglar? "

" Oh, really, Cherry! I've found it all out! " gasped Bunter. " I've got it from Wingate of the Sixth—he knows."

" And he's told you all about it? " grinned Bob.

" Well, he didn't exactly tell me—I heard him talking with Gwynne," explained Bunter. " They were up last night. Quelch was up. All the prefects were up. Some of the beaks, too—Quelch called them up. There's been a burglary in the Head's study."

" You don't say so! "

" I jolly well do! " asserted Bunter. " Thousands of pounds gone. Thousands! "

" That all? " asked Frank Nugent. " Not millions? "

"No—thousands," said Bunter. "Of course, the Head wouldn't be likely to have millions of pounds in his study, Nugent."

"About as likely as thousands, I should think," said Harry Wharton, laughing.

"Well, that's all you know!" retorted Bunter. "Rolls of banknotes—stacks of them—heaps! A regular pile of banknotes. And I say, Smithy's mixed up in it."

"Mixed up in the pile of banknotes?" asked Bob.

"Ha, ha, ha!"

"No, you fathead—not in the banknotes, in the burglary. That's where he got that cosh on his cocoanut," said Bunter, breathlessly. "I say, some fellows went down in the middle of the night and found Smithy lying in the Head's study, covered with blood——."

"As bad as that?" gasped Wharton.

"Yes—I expect the burglar knocked him out with his jemmy," explained Bunter. "Burglars use jemmies, you know—they're a sort of what-do-you-call-it that they use for busting open thingummybobs——."

"Oh, scissors!"

"Smithy got it on the nut," said Bunter. "Wingate mentioned his name. So you can take it from me that Smithy got that cosh in the Beak's study last night, and he got it from the burglar. He seems to have walked right into the burglar— silly ass! That's how it happened—I've got it straight from Wingate—he was talking to Gwynne in the Prefects' Room, and the window was open and I happened to hear him, being just under the window. Some fellows came down and found him——."

"Found Wingate?"

"No, you ass—found Smithy, weltering in his gore——."

"Smithy's a tough nut," said Bob. "He looks pretty fit this morning for a chap who's been weltering in his gore over-night."

"Ha, ha, ha!"

"The welterfulness was probably not terrific," chuckled Hurree Jamset Ram Singh.

"Well, I know, and you don't," said Bunter. "You fellows go about with your eyes shut, and never find out anything."

"Not by listening under open windows, any-way," said Nugent.

"I wasn't listening, you beast—I couldn't help hearing what they said, when I'd stopped to tie my shoe-lace, could I? I say, I wonder who those fellows were who came down and found Smithy?"

"I wonder!" said Harry, gravely.

"Ha, ha, ha!"

"You can cackle, but I tell you, it's straight. I'd like to know who the fellows were. Quelch came down——."

"And caught the burglar?" asked Johnny Bull.

"No—as far as I can make out, the burglar bolted after knocking out Smithy with the butt of his automatic——."

"As well as with his jemmy?" asked Bob.

"Eh? I—I meant the butt of his jemmy—I mean, the jemmy of his automatic—I mean——," Bunter was getting a little mixed. "I mean, he coshed Smithy on the cocoanut with his jemmy, and then he must have bolted with the banknotes, and that's jolly well why old Grimey is here this morning! I told you fellows that something must have happened last night! Didn't I?"

"You did!" agreed Bob. "Bunter's the man for the news, you fellows. He told us there was something up! And there is."

" Ha, ha, ha! "

" Quelch called up the prefects, and they searched the House," went on Bunter. "They found a window open—the window of the Sixth-Form lobby—that's how the burglar went, of course. I expect that's how he got in, too. I say, ain't it exciting, you fellows? "

" Thrilling," said Bob. "You seem to have heard quite a lot while you were tying up your shoe-lace, Bunty."

" I should have heard the rest, I expect, if Gwynne hadn't shut the window," said Bunter. " I say, I'd like to know who those fellows were who came down and found Smithy. I say, where's Smithy? I'm going to ask him. He looks in a beastly temper this morning, but I'm jolly well going to ask him. Seen Smithy? I heard somebody say that he was let off classes this morning because of that cosh. Know where he is? "

" He's gone up to his study," said Harry, laughing. " Better not bother Smithy—he's not in the best of tempers. Besides, I can tell you, if you want to know."

" You! " said Bunter. "Rot! You never know anything. You wouldn't have known there was something up at all, if I hadn't told you. Mean to say you know who the fellows were who came down and found Smithy in the Head's study last night? "

" Sort of."

" Gammon! " said Bunter. "Who were they? "

" Redwing and I."

" Oh! " gasped Bunter. "Why, you beast, you know all about it, then! You jolly well knew there was something up all the time. Why, you beast——."

" Ha, ha, ha! "

" Hallo, hallo, hallo, there's the bell! " exclaimed Bob Cherry. " Let's have the next instalment of the thriller in break, Bunty."

" I say, you fellows——."

" Come on," said Bob. " Henry doesn't like to be kept waiting—even on the morning after the night before."

" But I say, you fellows, there's old Grimes." Billy Bunter's eyes, and spectacles, fixed on a stocky figure emerging from the House. " I say, Grimey's here because of the burglary, you know. Think he's going to look for clues? " Billy Bunter eyed the plump inspector inquisitively, curiously, almost hungrily. " I say, it's pretty rotten to have to go in to class with all this going on, ain't it? I say, think a fellow might risk cutting a class? "

" I wouldn't risk it with Quelch! " chuckled Bob.

" Still, a fellow might be late! " argued Bunter. " Suppose a fellow never heard the bell, or forgot the time——."

" Come on, you fat duffer," said Harry Wharton. And the Famous Five headed for the Remove form-room.

But Billy Bunter did not follow them. Inquisitiveness was Bunter's besetting sin: he always wanted to know. And on this unusually thrilling occasion, more than ever did Bunter want to know.

Instead of following the other fellows in, Billy Bunter rolled off in quite another direction. Quelch was strict on punctuality: still, there was a sporting chance that he might believe that a fellow hadn't heard the bell, or had forgotten the time, or both. Billy Bunter was going to risk it: and when Mr. Quelch gathered his flock in the form-room, the fattest member of his form was conspicuous by his absence.

Chapter XXI

NO LUCK FOR BUNTER !

INSPECTOR GRIMES was busy. He seemed unaware that he was under observation.

But he was! From a little distance a pair of little round eyes, and a pair of big round spectacles, were fastened on the plump gentleman from Courtfield.

Billy Bunter watched him breathlessly.

Mr. Grimes was rooting about at the window of the Sixth-Form lobby. Bunter knew why. He knew that that window had been found open in the night, when Quelch had called up the prefects to search the House. Bunter did not need telling that that was where the burglar had made his exit after knocking Smithy out in the Head's study. Obviously, the inspector was looking for clues. Bunter was breathlessly interested.

Billy Bunter had read a good many detective novels. He knew all about clues, and the interpretation thereof. He was well aware that an amateur detective, if not an official one, could deduce, from a spot of cigarette-ash, not only who had committed the crime, but the size of his feet, the colour of his hair, and his style in neckties. Of course, an official detective-officer, with the disadvantage of practical training and experience, couldn't be expected to do wonderful things like that. Still, Grimey might find out something— and Billy Bunter fairly burned with curiosity to know what.

Mr. Grimes was making a most meticulous examination of the stone sill under that window.

He had something in his hand—Bunter wondered whether it was a magnifying glass. Mr. Grimes spent quite a long time at the sill. Then, bent double, his plump figure rather suggesting a barrage-balloon, he proceeded to scan the earth under the window, occasionally stirring the grass with a plump finger, concentrated on his search.

Bunter, at first, watched from a respectful distance. But objects were rather dim to the Owl of the Remove at a distance, and gradually he edged nearer. He heard Mr. Grimes give a grunt, which seemed, to Bunter, to have a note of satisfaction in it. What had he discovered?

Nearer and nearer the inquisitive fat Owl edged, till he was only a few yards behind the inspector's plump back. Mr. Grimes seemed oblivious to him, and of everything but his task. But suddenly he resumed the perpendicular, glanced round, and stared at Bunter.

"Oh!" gasped Bunter. He was taken quite by surprise: he hadn't expected that sudden move. He goggled at Mr. Grimes.

To his relief, Mr. Grimes did not look angry. Indeed, a faint smile came over his stolid red face. It dawned on Bunter that Mr. Grimes had not, after all, been unconscious of the fat junior blinking at him: he had known that Bunter was there all the time.

"Oh!" repeated Bunter. "I—I say——."

"Master Bunter, I think," said Mr. Grimes. He had had the pleasure, or otherwise, of making Billy Bunter's acquaintance long ago. Evidently he remembered him. Circumferentially, at least, Bunter was a fellow not easily forgotten.

"Oh! Yes!" gasped Bunter. "G-g-good morning, Mr. Grimes."

"Good morning," said Mr. Grimes, politely.

"N-n-nice morning, ain't it?" said Bunter.

"Very!" agreed Mr. Grimes.

"I expect you've found the footsteps—I mean the footprints?" ventured Bunter.

"Do you?" said Mr. Grimes.

"Well, that's the window where the burglar got out last night," said Bunter. "They found it open when they searched the House, you know."

"Ah!" said Mr. Grimes.

"Must have left some sign when he jumped out," said Bunter. "It's rather high from the ground, isn't it? I expect you've spotted it."

"Indeed!" said Mr. Grimes.

"If you haven't, I daresay I could help!" said Bunter.

"Eh?"

"I'm a Greyfriars Scout, you know," explained Bunter. "I'm considered pretty good at picking up signs. I don't miss much."

"Oh!"

"I'd be jolly glad to help!" said Bunter.

"It's very kind of you, Master Bunter, to offer to expend your valuable time in assisting the police in their duties," said Mr. Grimes, with a deep, deep sarcasm that was a sheer waste on Billy Bunter. Bunter was blind and deaf to sarcasm.

"Oh, not at all, Mr. Grimes," said the fatuous fat Owl. "Anything I can do, I'll be jolly glad. Trust me! I fancy I could pick up any sign you've missed."

Mr. Grimes gazed at William George Bunter. He looked very thoughtful. It did not occur to Bunter that he was considering whether to box Bunter's fat ears for his cheek or not.

But Mr. Grimes was an amiable and good-tempered plump gentleman, and he decided not. Having gazed at Bunter, he turned away, and went into the House by the lobby door.

Bunter blinked after him. He was surprised

by this sudden departure of Mr. Grimes, when they had been getting on so nicely with their chat.

"I say, Mr. Grimes!" he squeaked.

Mr. Grimes did not reply. He disappeared into the lobby, and shut the door after him. Bunter was left blinking.

It really looked as if Mr. Grimes had no use for Bunter's kind assistance in the execution of his official duties. However, being on the spot, Bunter proceeded to look for "signs" under the lobby window. But if the Courtfield inspector had made any discovery there, Bunter made none. Even with the aid of his big spectacles, added to his knowledge of scoutcraft, the fat junior was unable to spot a single trace of anyone having jumped from that window. He concluded that the fleeing burglar must have climbed out very carefully instead of jumping out, and wondered whether Mr. Grimes had been able to deduce as much.

The chime of the quarter caused the fat Owl to blink up at the clock-tower. He was fifteen minutes late for class. A quarter of an hour late was rather a good allowance in dealing with a master like Mr. Quelch. But Bunter did not turn his steps immediately in the direction of the form-room.

He rolled into the House, but not to the Remove room. From the corner of the corridor he blinked cautiously in the direction of the Head's study. While masters and boys were in form, and the Head with the Sixth, it was a chance for Bunter to view the scene of the burglary, and blink at the burgled desk, which he was intensely curious to do.

The coast was clear: and the fat Owl rolled up the corridor to the Head's door, turned the door-handle, and rolled in.

"Well?"

That monosyllable came like a shot.

Bunter jumped.

He had taken it for granted that the Head's study would be vacant, with the head-master in the Sixth-Form room. But it was not vacant. Mr. Grimes was there.

The inspector was leaning over the Head's writing-table, perhaps making some examination of the burgled drawer in which Billy Bunter was so keenly interested. But he jerked upright as Bunter rolled in, and stared—or rather glared—at him.

"Oh!" stuttered Bunter. "I—I thought—I—I mean—I—I didn't—I—I wasn't—I—I mean to say—oh, lor'!"

"What are you doing here?" snapped Mr. Grimes.

"Oh! Nothing! I—I mean——."

"You had better go," said Mr. Grimes.

Bunter thought so, too: and he went.

"Beast!" he breathed, as he rolled down the corridor.

After which, Bunter decided that he had better turn up for class. Really, it was high time. He rolled off to the form-room, where all the Remove stared at him as he rolled in, and Mr. Quelch fixed him with a grim gimlet-eye.

"Bunter!" rumbled Mr. Quelch. "You are twenty minutes late for class."

"Oh! Yes, sir! I never heard the time, and I forgot the bell——."

"What?"

"I—I mean, I never heard the bell, and I forgot the time," gasped Bunter. "Not knowing the bell, sir—I mean the time—I—I——."

Billy Bunter's voice trailed away. He had hoped that this would be good enough for Quelch. But Quelch was always rather a doubting Thomas, where Billy Bunter was concerned. His speaking countenance indicated only too plainly that it was not good enough. He picked up the cane from his desk.

"You will take fifty lines for unpunctuality, Bunter."

"Oh! Yes, sir."

"And," added Mr. Quelch, grimly, "I shall cane you for untruthfulness, which is a much more serious matter. Bend over that chair, Bunter."

"Oh, lor'!"

Whop!

"Wow! ow-ow-wow! Wow!"

"You may go to your place, Bunter."

Billy Bunter went to his place—wriggling.

Chapter XXII

CORNERED !

"I SAY, you fellows!"

Billy Bunter blinked into the changing-room, where Harry Wharton and Co. and a good many other fellows had gathered. It was a half-holiday that afternoon, and the heroes of the Remove were booked for cricket with Hobson and Co. of the Shell. When cricket was the order of the day, minor matters like burglaries naturally took a very secondary place: and the Co. had, in fact, forgotten all about the exciting incident of the night, for the time. Billy Bunter reminded them of it.

"Seen Grimey?" he asked.

"Grimey?" repeated Bob Cherry, looking round. "He's gone, long ago."

"Oh, good!" said Bunter. "He won't be in the Head's study then, blow him. He was there when I looked in this morning——."

"You looked in at the Head's study!" exclaimed Harry Wharton.

"Well, a fellow wants to see what's happened," said Bunter. "I was going to give that desk the once-over—where the burglar burgled it, you know. I shouldn't wonder if I found a clue."

"Something that Grimey has missed, what?" asked Johnny Bull, sarcastically.

"That's it," assented Bunter. "Grimey's rather an old donkey, you know. He was rooting about under the lobby window this morning, but of course, he never spotted anything. I offered to help——."

"What?" yelled Bob.

"I mean, with my knowledge of scoutcraft, you know, I might be jolly useful in picking up sign——."

"Your which of whatter?" gasped Bob. "Why, you fat chump, you couldn't pick up a sign if it stuck out a mile. You couldn't trail anything but a jam-tart or a dough-nut."

"I'm used to jealousy," said Bunter, with a sniff. "I'm a pretty good Scout, I fancy, Bob Cherry."

"The fancifulness is terrific," chuckled Hurree Jamset Ram Singh.

"Didn't Grimey jump at your offer, Bunter?" asked Squiff, with a grin.

"Well, he was civil," said Bunter. "He said it was kind of me to offer to assist the police in their duties——."

"Ha, ha, ha!" yelled the juniors. They could guess, if Bunter couldn't, that Mr. Grimes had been indulging in sarcasm.

"Blessed if I see anything to cackle at. Then he walked off—I don't know why," said Bunter. "I didn't know he had gone to the Beak's study —but there he was, when I went in, and he glared at me like a Gorger—I mean a Gorgonzola——."

"Ha, ha, ha!"

"But if he's cleared off, all right," said Bunter. "I'm jolly well going to see where the burglar boggled—I mean burgled——."

"You'd better not let the Head spot you prying in his study, you fat chump," said Peter Todd.

Billy Bunter winked, a fat wink.

"I'm wide," he said. "That's all right, Toddy. I've had an eye open for the Head—he's in his garden now, jawing to Twiss. I saw him. The Head won't spot me. I'm wide, I can tell you."

"You are!" agreed Toddy. "Never saw a

wider chap."

" The widefulness is terrific."

" Double-width, at least," said Bob Cherry, with a nod.

" You silly ass, I don't mean wide," snapped Bunter. " Too jolly wide to be spotted by a beak, I fancy. I say, where's Smithy?" Bunter blinked over the crowd of faces in the changing-room. " Ain't Smithy going to play cricket?"

" Not with a lump like a duck's egg on his frontispiece," said Bob. " Smithy's taking a rest."

" Bit soppy, to make such a fuss about a cosh on the conk," said Bunter. " I wouldn't! I hope he ain't sticking in his study this afternoon—I—I mean, is he sticking in his study, Redwing?"

" Smithy's in his study, if you want him!" said Tom Redwing, curtly.

" Well, I don't want him, of course—but he shouldn't be slacking in his study," grunted Bunter. " Soppy, I call it! A fellow may have a bit of a headache, but I don't believe in slacking and frowsting about."

" Bunter doesn't believe in slacking and frowsting about!" said Bob Cherry.

" Ha, ha, ha!"

" Besides, if he's got a headache, it would be much better for him to lie down," said Bunter. " Quelch would give him leave to go up to dorm, if he asked. Why not cut up to the study and tell him, Redwing?"

" Fathead!"

" Is there anything to eat in Smithy's study?" asked Bob Cherry, staring at the fat Owl suspiciously.

" Oh, really, Cherry! If you think I know anything about that box of chocs in Smithy's study——"

" Ha, ha, ha!"

" What I think is, that a fellow shouldn't be soppy, and make a song and a dance about a bit of a tap on the crumpet. I've a jolly good mind to go up and say to Smithy——Whoooop! Keep that bat away, Redwing, you beast! Wharrer you shoving that bat at me for? " yelled Bunter.

Without explaining why he was shoving his bat at Bunter, Tom Redwing shoved again: and the fat Owl faded out of the doorway of the changing-room.

" Beast! " floated back, as Bunter departed.

Leaving the fellows in the changing-room laughing, Billy Bunter rolled away in the direction of the Head's study.

There were two important matters on Billy Bunter's fat mind that afternoon. One was the box of chocolates in Smithy's study—the other was his curiosity to pry at the burgled desk. With Smithy taking a rest in No. 4 in the Remove, the former was evidently out of reach of his fat fingers —so the fat Owl gave his attention to the latter.

The coast was clear this time: with Inspector Grimes gone from Greyfriars, and the Head and his secretary both in the Head's garden. Billy Bunter arrived at his head-master's study, opened the door and blinked in, and then rolled in. It was rather a risky game to pay a surreptitious visit to that awesome apartment: but Billy Bunter had taken his precautions, and he had great faith in his own "wideness." It seemed to Bunter safe as houses, and when there was no danger, Bunter was bold as a lion. He rolled in and shut the door after him.

Then he proceeded to give the Head's writing-table the " once-over." It was easy enough to spot the drawer that had been "burgled." All the other drawers were shut and locked—but the burgled drawer was partly open, and empty. The lock, and the wood surrounding it, had been crudely and roughly broken by the instrument that had forced open the drawer, and it could not be wholly shut again till it was repaired.

Billy Bunter blinked at it wisely through his big spectacles. He blinked at it from very angle. Bunter had no high opinion of Inspector Grimes and his abilities—but considerable faith in his own. Besides, he knew a lot about detective work from the detective-novels he had read. Bunter would have been very bucked to pick up a clue: and if there was a clue to be spotted, he had little doubt that he would spot it.

But after ten minutes of industrious blinking, Bunter had to admit that if a clue was there, he couldn't locate it.

The burglar did not seem to have played up, as it were, as burglars do in detective novels. He seemed to have left no sign whatever to be picked up by eagle eyes: even eagle eyes assisted by a big pair of spectacles. There was absolutely nothing to be seen but an oaken drawer that had been roughly wrenched open with a chisel.

Bunter grunted.

Still, he had gratified his inquisitive curiosity, and seen what was to be seen, little as it was: and that was something. He rolled towards the door.

He stopped suddenly.

His fat ears pricked up like those of a startled rabbit. His fat hand was almost on the door handle, when a sound came from the corridor without—a sound of footsteps.

"Oh, crikey!" breathed Bunter.

He stood transfixed, in sheer terror. Was it the Head coming in? If he were caught in that study——!

His fat heart palpitated as he listened. The footsteps were approaching the study door—foot-

steps of more than one person. They were coming
—and there was Bunter, palpitating with terror,
to meet their eyes the moment the door was
opened! The Owl of the Remove was fairly
cornered!

He gave a wild blink round the study. There
was no escape, and his only thought was to get
out of sight—escape might come later if they
didn't spot him there. The footsteps were almost
at the door, when Bunter crammed himself
desperately behind a massive, high-backed armchair that stood in a corner. He was hardly out of
sight when the door opened.

"Pray step in, Mr. Grimes."

It was the Head's voice.

Bunter's fat head almost swam. That beast
Grimes had come back, and the Head had brought
him to the study. That meant that they were
going to "jaw." They had come to stay! And if
they found Bunter there——!

Billy Bunter could only hope that they
wouldn't.

Chapter XXIII

"AN INSIDE JOB!"

"AN inside job, sir!"

Dr. Locke looked inquiringly at Inspector Grimes. The Head's learning was great—his erudition wide and deep. He knew many languages and many other things. But he did not know what an "inside job" was.

"An inside job," repeated the inspector. "A job done from the inside, sir—not a case of burglary from outside. Not a case of house-breaking, sir. Nobody entered this building last night."

Dr. Locke blinked at him.

"I don't quite understand, Mr. Grimes. Surely some extraneous person must have entered the House, or the robbery could not have taken place." Then he gave a little start, "You do not mean to imply that some person resident in the House could have——."

He broke off, blankly.

"Exactly, sir," said Mr. Grimes, with a nod, "I am afraid it may be a shock to you, sir. But there is no doubt about it in my mind. Some person belonging to this establishment was pilfering here, when the boy Vernon-Smith unexpectedly interrupted him."

"Bless my soul!" said the Head, faintly.

"I am sorry, sir. But I must apprise you of the facts. The pilferer is to be looked for in this school."

"Impossible!" said the Head.

Inspector Grimes let that pass. He sat stolid,

waiting for the schoolmaster to assimilate what he had told him.

"I have every confidence in every servant employed at this school, sir," said the Head, a little warmly.

"No doubt, sir. At the present moment, the perpetrator is absolutely unknown. There is no more reason to suspect a servant than to suspect any other person here."

Dr. Locke gazed at him, quite aghast.

"At the moment, sir, no one can be excluded. It is, as I have said, an inside job—and the wanted man is here—here under this roof."

"Bless my soul!" repeated Dr. Locke. "Mr. Grimes! I cannot, of course, doubt your professional skill and efficiency. But this—this is beyond credence. You have, of course, some reason for supposing——."

"I am not supposing, sir, but stating facts," said Mr. Grimes, "and I can make the matter clear to you in a few words. The person who robbed your desk desired, no doubt, to give the impression that a burglary had occurred. A window was left open for that purpose."

"But I have supposed, sir—everyone has supposed—that the burglar escaped by that open window——."

"Precisely what he intended you to suppose, sir, and no doubt hoped that the police would suppose."

"Oh!" murmured Dr. Locke.

"I have made the most careful and meticulous examination, sir, of the window, the sill outside, and the grass below the sill. The result is the assurance that no one either entered or left the House by that window last night."

"Then it was a—a trick?"

"A simple trick, sir—or rather, a childish one:

DR. LOCKE BLINKED AT HIM

but all that he could do to give the hoped-for
impression that the pilferer had come from outside."

" But——," murmured the Head.

" Even before examining the window for
traces, sir, I was aware that it was an inside job.
Inside information is an indication of an inside job,
sir. The person—man or boy or whatever he was
—knew where to look for the money."

" He knew——? "

" Obviously, sir. There are dozens of drawers
in your desk here. In one of them, money is kept.
That may be known to many persons in this building, but it could not be known to any extraneous
person. But it was the money-drawer that was
broken open, sir."

" Oh! "

" We can hardly suppose, sir, that a stranger,
in strange surroundings, happened on the right
drawer by sheer chance, or even knew that there
was money in any of the drawers at all."

" I—I had not thought of that——."

" This is not your line of country, sir," said the
inspector, with a faint smile. " It is everyday
work to me."

" Oh! Quite! But——."

" In that drawer, sir, from what you have told
me, there was a considerable sum in cash—ten
five-pound notes, five ten-pound notes, and fifty
pound notes—one hundred and fifty pounds in all.
The whole sum is missing. Whoever broke open
that drawer knew that it was there—knew, at all
events, that money was there. Are many persons
in this House, sir, aware that cash was habitually
kept in that particular drawer? "

" I—I hardly know. Certainly it was no
secret," said the Head. " Cash for various require-
ments is kept there, and has always been kept

there. I have frequently had occasion to take cash from the drawer in the presence of others."

" Then a good many persons may have known ——."

" Certainly: though I had not, of course, supposed that anyone would be interested in the matter."

" Some person in need of money might be extremely interested, sir, in knowing where to lay his hands on it," said the inspector, drily. " In short, sir, this is not, as it appeared at the first glance, a case of burglary—but a case of pilfering. The thief is still here, and I have no doubt whatever that the money is still here."

" Here?" repeated the Head.

" I mean, at hand—somewhere in the school. It is very easy, sir, to reconstruct the affair, in so simple a matter as this. Some unscrupulous person, in need of cash, knew where to find it. He crept down in the night, opened a ground-floor window to give an impression of an intruder from outside, stole into this study, broke open the money-drawer, and helped himself to all that was there."

" Oh! " breathed Dr. Locke.

" Quite possibly," said Mr. Grimes, " he may have intended, after securing his plunder, to break open other drawers, to add colour to the pretence of a burglary. But he was interrupted suddenly by a foolish boy coming into the room to play a thoughtless prank."

Mr. Grimes paused. The Head, with a deeply clouded brow, was silent.

" We know from Master Vernon-Smith what happened next. The pilferer shut off his light instantly—his chief concern, I imagine, was to avoid being seen—and identified. In the dark, he rushed for the door, knocked out the boy who was in his way, and ran. His first thought, naturally, was merely to escape—to escape unrecognized. In that he succeeded. But the person, sir, is obviously still here—and the money also: and a search——."

"A search?" repeated Dr. Locke. He gazed at Mr. Grimes almost in horror. "A search, sir—impossible."

"Quite unnecessary, sir," said Mr. Grimes, cheerfully, "I was about to say that a search would reveal the pilfered money in the pilferer's room, if he kept it there—which he would not do, if he had his wits about him—or any wits at all."

"Oh!" said the Head.

"It is clear, sir, that the—the person hoped that the theft would be attributed to an outside burglar. But he could not feel sure of that, especially as Vernon-Smith's interruption prevented him from adding plausible details as he may have intended. He would not dare to keep the plunder in his own quarters in case of a search."

"But what——?"

"It was easy, sir, as there was no immediate alarm, the boy Vernon-Smith having been knocked unconscious. Finding that there was no alarm, I imagine that the pilferer crept out of his room again, and concealed the bundle of notes in some hidden recess, where, if it was found, it could throw no suspicion upon himself."

"Oh!"

"I am aware, sir, that a general search would be extremely repugnant to you. But it would be useless also: for I have no doubt whatever that, wherever the money may be, it is not in the quarters of the person who purloined it."

Dr. Locke nodded, slowly.

"I shall, with your concurrence, take certain

measures," said Mr. Grimes. " In the meantime I suggest that nothing of what I have told you shall be mentioned outside this study. The pilferer cannot fail to guess that I suspect an inside job, but the less he is put upon his guard the better."

" Nothing shall be said, Mr. Grimes."

"Very good, sir! I need take up no more of your time at present." Mr. Grimes rose, " I shall hope soon, sir, to have further information for you."

Dr. Locke sat with a troubled face after the plump inspector had left him. He had had a shock. A burglary would have been bad enough—quite an undesirable spot of excitement in the school, from the head-master's point of view. But an " inside job "—some untrustworthy person in his very household—that was much more discomfiting and distressing.

For long, long minutes, the Head sat in silence, thinking it over. At last, he rose and left the study. The door closed behind him.

Then—and not till then—did a fat head and a fat face rise from behind the back of the armchair in the corner.

Between excitement and terror, Billy Bunter's little round eyes were almost popping through his big round spectacles.

" Oh, crikey!" breathed Bunter.

It was Bunter's chance to escape, at last. He lost no time—anxious to get clear before some other beast came into the study. He crept round from behind the armchair, and tiptoed to the door. He opened the door a few inches, and blinked into the corridor. All was clear: and Bunter rolled out of the study, and rolled away, and like Iser in the poem, he rolled rapidly.

Chapter XXIV

CHOCS FOR BUNTER !

" TODDY, old chap——."

" Can it," said Peter Todd.

" Bob, old fellow——."

" Bow-wow ! "

" I say, Inky——."

" Brr-r-r-r ! "

" But I say, I've found it all out ! " gasped Bunter.

Even that startling statement did not draw attention to Billy Bunter. Whatever the fat Owl might or might not have found out, nobody wanted to know. Cricket was going on, on Little Side. Harry Wharton and Tom Brown were at the wickets, and Hobson of the Shell was putting in some really good bowling that made the captain of the Remove, so to speak, sit up and take notice : and the Remove batsmen waiting at the pavilion were interested in the batting and in the bowling, but not in the least in William George Bunter.

Billy Bunter gave an angry snort.

He was full of news—packed with news—he was the fellow who knew ! Nobody else knew— except the Head and Mr. Grimes—what Bunter knew ! He was fairly bursting with news and excitement.

Bunter liked to be the fellow with the news ! He liked to know the latest happening, the newest item of gossip, and to relate the same to fellows who hadn't heard. Now he had a really thrilling and tremendous spot of news—quite a whale of a tale ! It was annoying and exasperating when nobody wanted to hear it.

After getting out of the Head's study Bunter had found the House almost deserted: most of the fellows were on the cricket ground. So thither rolled Bunter to impart his thrilling news. He found plenty of fellows there to whom to tell his startling tale—but they all turned deaf ears. They watched Harry Wharton dealing with Hobby's bowling, and did not even look at Bunter.

"I say, you fellows——!" hooted Bunter.

"Dry up, old fat man," said Squiff.

"Oh, really, Field! I say, I've found it all out, and I'll jolly well tell you——."

"Go and tell somebody else, for goodness' sake," said the Australian junior. "Give us a rest."

"Beast! I say, Inky, old chap——."

"The talkfulness is too terrific, my esteemed Bunter."

"But I say——."

"A still tongue is a stitch in the side that saves ninepence, as the English proverb remarks."

"You silly ass! I say, Hazel——."

"Roll away, barrel," said Hazeldene.

"I say, Nugent——."

"Well hit!" roared Bob Cherry. "Good man! Bet you that's three."

The batsmen were running. It was, as Bob predicted, three: and brought Tom Brown to the batting end. All eyes were on the New Zealand junior, as he faced Hobson of the Shell for the last ball of the over.

"I say, Bull——."

"Hobby's a good man with the leather," remarked Johnny Bull, ruthlessly regardless of Bunter. "But Browney will put paid to him, you see."

"I say, Ogilvy——."

"Don't bother."

" I say, Wibley——."

" Is that fat bluebottle still buzzing!" exclaimed Bob Cherry, looking round. " Buzz off, Bunter, and buzz somewhere else."

" I say, Redwing——."

" Hallo, here comes Smithy!" exclaimed Tom Redwing. " Jolly good innings, Smithy—squat down here, old chap. Head better?"

The Bounder grunted in reply to that inquiry. He was not looking amiable, and the dark bruise on his forehead showed up to great advantage in the bright sunshine. He had a lingering headache, and he looked, as he felt, disgruntled. But evidently he had tired of his own company, and come down from the House to see how the cricket was going on.

" I say, Smithy!" bleated Bunter. The Bounder, as the man who had encountered the pilferer in the Head's study, was sure to be interested in Bunter's startling tale. " I say——."

" Oh get out!" grunted Smithy.

" But I say——."

" Good old Browney!" roared Bob Cherry. " That's a boundary."

It was a boundary and the Remove crowd gave Tom Brown a cheer. Billy Bunter was not interested in boundaries. He grabbed Vernon-Smith's sleeve.

" I say, Smithy, old chap——."

" Leave me alone, will you?" snapped Smithy, jerking his sleeve away.

" But I say," gasped Bunter, " I've found it all out. I heard old Grimey talking to the Head——."

" Don't tell me what you've heard at a keyhole, you fat prying owl!" growled Vernon-Smith.

" It wasn't at a keyhole." Bunter grabbed Smithy's sleeve again, " I say, do listen to a chap. I heard old Grimey say to the Head——Beast!

You jolly well kick me, and I'll jolly well——
yaroop!"

Billy Bunter retired from the scene. The
Bounder, evidently, was not in a good temper: and
nobody seemed to have any use for Bunter's news,
whatever it was. And now that Vernon-Smith
was on the cricket ground, Billy Bunter's thoughts
turned to that box of chocolates in No. 4 Study—
inaccessible so long as Smithy was there,
accessible now that Smithy wasn't there. This was
Bunter's chance. If Smithy had not yet scoffed
those chocolates——!"

Bunter was anxious to thrill anyone who would
listen, with his startling tale. But he was still more
anxious to scoff those chocs, if they were still
available. Smithy might go back to the House
any minute—the tale could wait, but the chocs
couldn't. The fat Owl rolled away to the House.

All was clear in the Remove passage. Now that
Smithy had gone out, not a fellow remained in the
studies that sunny half-holiday. Billy Bunter
rolled into No. 4 Study—and the first object that
met his eyes, and his spectacles, was that box of
chocolates on the study table.

It had been opened. Smithy, apparently, had
been sampling the contents. But the box was still
nearly full, when Bunter grabbed off the lid. He
gazed ecstatically at the stack of chocolates.
Smithy often had nice things like that—rare in
other studies, rarest of all in Bunter's.

The Owl of the Remove did not linger in No.
4—Smithy might come back. Staying only to cram
a couple of fat chocolates into a capacious mouth,
to go on with, Bunter grabbed the box, and rolled
out of the study.

Neither did he linger in the Remove passage.
If Smithy came back to his study, it was certain
that he would miss the box at once, and look for

it—and very probably for Bunter! The fat Owl hurried up the passage to the little stair at the end that led up to the Remove box-room.

A minute more, and he was safe in the box-room. There was a bolt on the door, which Bunter promptly secured, in case of pursuit. Then he sat down on a big trunk that belonged to Lord Mauleverer, and started on the chocolates.

A few minutes later, Bunter was glad that he had taken the precaution of shooting the bolt. He gave a jump, and almost choked over a chocolate half-way on the downward path, as he heard a light step on the box-room stair.

The door-handle turned. Billy Bunter's eyes, and spectacles, fixed in alarm on the door. He had no doubt it was Smithy, after him and the chocs —who else could it be?

Whoever it was, he seemed surprised to find that the door did not budge. The wood creaked under a strong and heavy pressure from without. Bunter's fat heart palpitated. Smithy—if it was Smithy—seemed to suppose that the door had jammed somehow, not that it was bolted inside.

Creak! creak!

" Oh, crikey!" gasped Bunter, in terror that the bolt might give. " I say, you can't get in, you beast—it's no use shoving, so yah!"

To his surprise and relief, the pressure on the door ceased instantly. There was a sound of a quick light footstep that died away down the box-room stair.

" Beast!" breathed Bunter.

Smith—if it was Smithy—was gone: but Bunter had little doubt that the beast would be waiting for him below, to catch him as he came down.

But the fat Owl knew a trick worth two of that. The box-room window overlooked flat leads, from

which it was easy, even for Bunter, to scramble
down to the ground with the aid of a massive old
rain-pipe. Billy Bunter chuckled, a fat chuckle.
He had a safe line of retreat—and that beast,
Smithy, could wait for him at the box-room stair
as long as he jolly well liked! It did not occur to
him for one moment that the hand that had tried
the door was not Smithy's—whose else could it
have been?

The alarm over, Billy Bunter's attention
returned to the chocolates, and he resumed enjoying life. There were many chocolates in the box:
but there could not be too many for Bunter. He
had bolted the door—now he sat on Lord
Mauleverer's trunk and bolted the chocolates—
and then he opened the box-room window and
bolted himself!

Chapter XXV

BUNTER SPREADS THE NEWS !

" I JOLLY well shan't tell you now."

"Thanks!" said Harry Wharton, politely.

"Ha, ha, ha!"

There was a cheery crowd in the Rag. Having beaten the Shell, the heroes of the Remove were feeling pleased with themselves and things generally. Billy Bunter, rolling into the Rag, found them talking cricket—playing the Form match over again, as it were, and still absolutely without interest in Bunter and the tale he had to tell.

Bunter had found some listeners, however. He had told his minor, Sammy of the Second. He had told Tubb of the Third. Temple, Dabney and Co. of the Fourth Form had condescended to listen: and then he told Skinner, and Snoop, and Stott, of the Remove. Coker of the Fifth came along with Potter and Greene while he was telling Skinner and Co. and paused to hear—and then Coker told Bunter that he was a grubby little eavesdropping tick, and ought to have his head smacked—and, on further consideration, smacked it. Bunter was rubbing a fat ear as he rolled into the Rag: and snorted as "cricket jaw" fell on both his fat ears from all sides.

" I mean, I've a good mind not to tell you !" amended Bunter.

"You've got a good mind?" asked Bob Cherry.

"Yes, I jolly well have."

"First I've heard of it. I didn't know you had one at all, let alone a good one. Why don't you use it sometimes?"

"Yah! I say, you fellows, if you knew what
I know, you'd jolly well sit up and take notice. A
hundred and fifty pounds spotted about the school
——."

"Eh!"

"What?"

"A hundred and fifty pounds!" said Bunter.
"Fivers, tenners, pound notes, spotted about
Greyfriars somewhere. That's what I was going
to tell you, though I've a jolly good mind not to,
now."

A dozen fellows stared at Bunter. He had
attention at last.

"Wandering in your mind—if you've got one
to wander in?" asked Bob.

"Been dropping your loose change about?"
asked the Bounder, sarcastically.

"Ha, ha, ha!"

Bunter gave Herbert Vernon-Smith a rather
uneasy blink. He had rather expected to hear
something from Smithy on the subject of
chocolates when he saw him again. But Smithy
did not seem to be thinking about chocolates,
much to the fat Owl's relief.

"Has your postal-order come, Bunty?" asked
Frank Nugent, laughing. "Cashed it and dropped
the money?"

"Ha, ha, ha!" yelled the juniors.

"Oh, really, Nugent! It's the Head's cash,"
explained Bunter. "The tin that was snooped
from his desk last night. It wasn't a burglary
after all—it was an inside job. See?"

"A whatter?" ejaculated Bob.

"An inside job," said Bunter, with an air of
superior wisdom. "It's called an inside job when
it's done inside, see? That's what Grimey called
it, and I suppose he knows."

"And Grimey told you?" asked Johnny Bull with a snort.

"He jolly well told the Head, and I jolly well heard him!" retorted Bunter. "And I jolly well know all about it, and you jolly well don't. Precious little goes on that I don't get wind of, I can tell you."

"Bunter's in the know," said Bob. "Bunter always will be in the know, so long as they make keyholes to doors. What about kicking him?"

"The kickfulness is the proper caper," said Hurree Jamset Ram Singh. "Turn roundfully, my esteemed prying Bunter."

"How could I help hearing, when I was in the room?" demanded Bunter. "Think I'd listen syrupstitiously? I was parked behind the Head's armchair in the corner—think I was going to let him catch me in his study? I couldn't help hearing what they said, could I? You might listen syrupstitiously, Bob——."

"What?"

"Or you, Inky! Not me," said Bunter. "As it happened, I heard the lot. I say, you fellows, I wonder who snooped the dough? Grimey said it was somebody in the school, and he's still here, of course."

"What utter rot!" exclaimed Harry Wharton.

"The rotfulness is terrific."

"Chuck it, Bunter!"

"Kick him!"

"I tell you, that's what Grimey said!" roared Bunter. "He said it was an inside job, and the snooper is somebody in the school, and he's still here, and he's hidden the loot about Greyfriars somewhere—not in his own room in case there was a search, and there's fivers and tenners and pound notes spotted about somewhere, and nobody knows where, and——."

"It's impossible!" exclaimed Harry.

"Well, that's what Grimey said," declared Bunter. "Think you know better than Grimey? I say, you fellows, he wasn't looking for footsteps —I mean footprints—under the lobby window this morning—he knew there weren't any—that's why he was looking for them—I mean why he wasn't ——."

There was a buzz in the Rag now. Bunter had got away with it at last. The burglary—as a mere burglary—was already fading as a topic. But the idea of a hundred and fifty pounds hidden somewhere about the school caused a sensation.

"Grimey said that a burglar wouldn't know which was the money-drawer," went on Bunter. "He said the snooper knew. See?"

"By gum!" exclaimed Vernon-Smith. He passed his hand over the bruise on his forehead, and his eyes glinted. "Grimey was right, if Bunter heard him say that. How the dooce would a burglar know the Head kept money in that drawer, or in his desk at all? By gum!"

"You can't believe that the man's at Greyfriars, Smithy!" exclaimed Bob.

"Isn't it as plain as your face—which is saying a lot?" retorted the Bounder. "I wonder I never thought of it. Grimey was bound to spot it—he's come across inside jobs before this."

"Smithy, old man——!" said Redwing.

"Oh, don't be an ass, Reddy! The man who knocked me out last night wasn't an outsider— he was an insider—of course he was." The Bounder evidently had no doubt on that point.

"But who——?" exclaimed Squiff.

"Echo answers that the who-fulness is terrific," said Hurree Jamset Ram Singh, shaking his dusky head.

"Look here, it's all rot," exclaimed Bob

Cherry. " Why, if the snooper's here, he might be anybody! You didn't see him, Smithy——."

" No—he took jolly good care of that, and I know why, now," said the Bounder, his eyes gleaming. " But now I know he's here——."

" You don't," said Bob. " That fat ass has got it all wrong, if he really heard anything at all——."

" Oh, really, Cherry! I jolly well word every heard—I mean I jolly well heard every word——."

" You ought to be jolly well kicked, anyhow," growled Johnny Bull.

" Beast! "

" I guess this is the cat's whiskers," said Fisher T. Fish. "A hundred and fifty pounds—why. that's over four hundred dollars in real money. I'll say it's worth nosing around a few to locate it."

" Might be hidden anywhere," said Peter Todd.

" Anywhere but near the snooper's own quarters," remarked Frank Nugent. " But it wouldn't stay hidden long, I should imagine. As soon as the snooper thinks it safe he will get it out of the place, surely."

" I say, you fellows, I'm going to look for it! If a fellow found it, they'd have to stand him something out of it—at least a fiver! " said Bunter, eagerly. " Perhaps a tenner! What? "

" Grimey may find it," said the Bounder, sardonically. " But if Bunter finds it, Grimey won't! "

" Why, you beast, think I'd touch it! " roared Bunter, in great indignation. " Think I'd touch what wasn't mine, you swob? "

" Oh, chuck it, Smithy," said Bob. " You know Bunter wouldn't——."

" I know he snoops every fellow's tuck that he can lay his fat paws on," sneered the Bounder. " If we see Bunter blowing cash at the tuck-shop, I shan't believe, for one, that his postal-order's come!"

"Why, you — you — you ——!" stuttered Bunter, in spluttering wrath. "I say, you fellows, you jolly well know——."

"Chuck it, Smithy," said Harry Wharton, sharply. "Don't be a rotter."

The Bounder shrugged his shoulders.

The day-room was in a buzz now. The mere idea of a "hidden treasure" somewhere about Greyfriars was exciting. Mr. Grimes, when he advised the Head that nothing should be said outside the study, had been happily unaware of a fat Owl drinking in every word behind the armchair in the corner. Before prep that evening, there was hardly a man at Greyfriars who had not heard the startling story, and did not know that a bundle of tenners and fivers and pound notes was "spotted" somewhere about the school.

Chapter XXVI

A SPOT OF EXCITEMENT

MR. QUELCH glanced over his form in class the following morning with a sharp suspicious eye.

He could see that something was " on " in the Remove.

There were many signs of suppressed excitement. Fellows whispered to one another. Many glances turned on the form-room clock. That was by no means uncommon—but now quite an unusual number of the Lower Fourth seemed interested in the time, which could only mean that they were unusually anxious to get out. The fattest member of the form seemed hardly able to keep still. Twice, and thrice, Mr. Quelch had rapped out at Bunter for whispering in class. It booted not—there was Bunter whispering again.

Something of great interest, it was plain, stirred the Greyfriars Remove. The lesson was geography: Mr. Quelch, with the aid of a large map spread on the blackboard, was putting his form wise about the latest fashions in European frontiers. But only too clearly it was not geography that was exciting his form. Attention in the form-room ought to have been wholly concentrated on the acquirements of geographical knowledge. But things were not as they ought to have been.

Mr. Quelch frowned. He could not begin to guess what all this excitement was about. But it was out of place in the form-room.

" Bunter ! " rapped out Mr. Quelch.

"Oh! Yes, sir," gasped Bunter. "I—I wasn't speaking to Toddy, sir."

"You were whispering to Todd, Bunter."

"Oh! No, sir! You can ask Todd, sir. He heard me."

"Bunter! Repeat to me at once what you were saying to Todd!" rapped Mr. Quelch. Quelch was going to get to the bottom of this.

Billy Bunter blinked at him in dismay. Nearly every fellow in the Remove was eager for break, in order to begin a "treasure-hunt." Billy Bunter was the most eager of all. But he did not want to confide that to Quelch. Bunter loved to be the fellow with the news, and he had enjoyed spreading the startling tale of a bundle of cash hidden in some secret nook about the school. He was willing, indeed eager, to tell the tale to any Greyfriars man. But he didn't want to tell it to a beak —very much indeed he didn't.

"Do you hear me, Bunter?" inquired Mr. Quelch, in a deep rumbling voice.

"I—I never spoke to Toddy, sir. I—I only said——."

"Tell me at once what you said, Bunter."

"I—I—I said——."

"Well," rapped Mr. Quelch.

"I—I said it was a—a fine morning, sir," gasped Bunter.

"Oh, my only summer hat!" murmured Bob Cherry. "If Bunter thinks that that will do for Quelchy——."

Mr. Quelch gazed at the fat ornament of his form. He gazed at him like the fabled basilisk. Then he picked up the cane from his desk.

"Bunter! If you do not immediately give me a truthful answer, I shall cane you. What did you say to Todd?"

"Oh, lor'! I—I only said I—I was going to

look in the Cloisters in break, sir!" gasped Bunter. "We—we're allowed in the Cloisters, sir."

"Is that what Bunter said to you, Todd?"

"Yes, sir," answered Peter.

Mr. Quelch stared at them both, puzzled. That the Remove were all excited about something, and Bunter most excited of all, was clear. But there was nothing particularly exciting about taking a walk in the old Cloisters, so far as Mr. Quelch could see.

"You will take fifty lines for talking in class, Bunter," he said, at last.

"Oh! Yes, sir."

Geography resumed the tenor of its way. For some minutes even Bunter gave Mr. Quelch a little attention. But it was only too clear that the Remove weren't interested in geography.

"Fish!" rapped out Mr. Quelch, suddenly. Fisher T. Fish gave quite a jump, as his name was shot at him like a bullet.

"Aw! Yep, sir!" he gasped.

"What were you saying to Skinner, Fish?"

"I—I—I guess——."

"Answer me at once, Fish!"

"I—I was jest remarking, sir, that on the Noo Yark exchange an English fiver would be worth about fifteen dollars in genooine spondulics," stammered Fisher T. Fish.

There were grinning faces in the Remove. Fish, evidently, had been calculating the value in American money of the fivers in the hidden bundle. But Mr. Quelch, of course, could not guess that one.

Every fellow in the Remove and almost every fellow in every other form at Greyfriars, knew all about Inspector Grimes's belief that the purloined notes were hidden in the school. But the Head, as requested by Mr. Grimes, had said nothing on the subject, so the beaks were still in the dark.

"Upon my word!" said Mr. Quelch, more puzzled than ever. Fishy's reply let in no light on the mysterious excitement in his form. "Fish! You should not discuss such matters in class. Take fifty lines."

Geography re-started after the interval. Once more there was a respite from whispering. But thoughts were straying, that was plain. Mr. Quelch's eyes were beginning to look like glittering gimlet-points.

"Hazeldene!"

"Oh! Yes, sir," stammered Hazel.

"You are not paying attention, Hazeldene. I have pointed out the city of Prague. Where is the city of Prague situated, Hazeldene?"

"I—I—I think——."

"I have asked you, Hazeldene, where the city of Prague is situated. Upon my word—Bunter, are you whispering to Snoop?"

"Oh, crikey!"

"Bunter! Tell me this instant what you said to Snoop!" thundered Mr. Quelch.

"I—I only said I wondered whether it was in Gosling's wood-shed, sir," gasped Bunter.

"Bunter! Have you taken leave of your senses! You wondered whether the city of Prague was in Gosling's wood-shed! What do you mean, Bunter?"

"I—I didn't mean—I—I mean I never—I—I —I——."

"Is this an impertinent jest, Bunter?"

"Oh! No, sir! Yes, sir! Oh, lor'! Wow!" roared Bunter, as Mr. Quelch's pointer, hitherto used on the map, was now used on his fat knuckles. "Wow-ow!"

"Silence, Bunter!"

"Yes, sir! Yow-ow-ow-ow! Wow!"

"If you continue to make those ridiculous noises, Bunter, I shall cane you."

Billy Bunter made a great effort to suppress the ridiculous noises. He sucked his fat knuckles in silent anguish.

It seemed to the Remove that the form-room clock never would indicate 10.45. But, at long last, it did, and the juniors got out in break: to their great relief, and perhaps to their form-master's also.

They fairly scampered out into the quad when freedom came. Mr. Quelch stood looking after them with a puzzled frowning brow. What was "on" in his form that morning? Clearly something was. Coker, of the Fifth, passed him, going out of the House with his pals Potter and Greene, and Mr. Quelch heard from Coker:

"Bit exciting, ain't it? Sort of treasure-hunt."

"All the fags are after it," said Potter. "Might have a shot at it ourselves."

They passed on, leaving Mr. Quelch gazing at their backs. Temple, Dabney and Co., of the Fourth, came out with a rush.

"We're on this, you men," Cecil Reginald Temple was saying.

"Oh, rather," said Dabney.

"Bless my soul!" said Mr. Quelch. It dawned on him that the excitement that morning was not confined to the Remove. It was shared in other forms—even the Fifth, a senior form.

Mr. Quelch walked out, and stopped to speak to Wingate, of the Sixth, who was discussing something with Gwynne and Sykes of that form. All three seemed deeply interested in their topic, whatever it was: but the Greyfriars captain turned politely as Mr. Quelch stopped to speak.

"Wingate! There seems to be some excitement among the boys," said the Remove master,

" I do not understand it. Have you any idea of its cause? "

" Oh! I—I think so, sir," said Wingate. " There's a story going round the school that the banknotes taken from the Head's desk on Tuesday night are hidden about the place somewhere."

" Bless my soul! Who could have set such a rumour in circulation! "

" I have no idea, sir, but everybody seems to have heard it—it's all over the school," answered Wingate, with a smile. " The fags are all going treasure-hunting, I believe."

" Dear me! " said Mr. Quelch.

He went back into the House, to see the Head about it.

Chapter XXVII

THE TREASURE-HUNTERS !

" WHAT about our box-room? " asked the Bounder.

Harry Wharton laughed.

" As likely as any other spot, I imagine! " he answered.

" Just about," grinned Bob Cherry. " Plenty of places to choose from—about a million or so."

" The jolly old bundle must be somewhere," remarked Frank Nugent.

" Only, where? " said Johnny Bull. " Like looking for a needle in a haystack. Any special reason for looking in our box-room, Smithy? "

" Yes! " said Vernon-Smith.

The chums of the Remove gave him attention at once. So far as they could see, there was absolutely no clue, no hint of a clue, to the hide-out of the bundle of notes. It might have been hidden almost anywhere: and in a rambling, ancient pile like Greyfriars School, there were innumerable nooks and crannies where a small packet could lie concealed. Almost everybody was keen on the " treasure-hunt ": eager fags of the Second and Third swarmed in the most unexpected places: Shell and Fourth and Remove were all agog—even a good many Fifth Form men, and even some of the high and mighty Sixth, were rooting about in odd corners. " Hidden treasure," even though it would not appertain to the finder, was a magnetic attraction. But it had to be admitted that the chances of success were slight.

" Cough it up, Smithy," said the captain of the

Remove. " I suppose it might be in a box-room
as likely as anywhere else. But why our box-
room specially?"

"Because the door's fastened," said Vernon-
Smith. " Skinner went up after prep last night—
I daresay you know he parks his cigarettes in the
box-room—and he couldn't get in and get his
fags."

" And so the poor dog had none!" sighed Bob
Cherry.

" But that's odd," said Harry. " Why should
anybody fasten the door of our box-room?"

"That's what I wondered," said Smithy. " It
can't be locked—the key's been missing for ages
—but there's a bolt on it. I cut up before class to
see if Skinner was right, and the door wouldn't
open—it's been bolted inside. Whoever did it
must have got out by the window. Well, why?"

" The whyfulness is terrific."

" By gum," said Bob. " Looks as if somebody
or other wants to keep fellows from wandering
into that box-room."

" Exactly!"

" We'll draw that box-room for a start, then,"
said Harry Wharton. " We can get in by the
window—if there's no beaks about."

" Good egg!" said Bob. " No end of a catch
if we bag the giddy treasure—one up for the
Remove! Come on."

And the bunch of juniors walked away, to circle
round the school buildings—with an eye open for
" beaks " and " pre's." Clambering up to high
windows was very much against all rules: and had
the eye of authority fallen upon them in the act,
that enterprise would have been nipped in the bud.

They stopped by the massive old rain-pipe that
gave access to the flat leads under the box-room
window. Descent was an easy matter, as Billy

Bunter had found—ascent was more difficult. But little difficulties were not likely to stop schoolboys on the track of treasure!

Herbert Vernon-Smith grasped the rain-pipe and began to clamber up. The Famous Five stood watching him, ready to climb in their turn. They were all in an eager mood now.

"It's a jolly old sporting chance, anyhow," remarked Bob Cherry. "And it won't take us ten minutes to root through the box-room—half-a-dozen of us."

"Many hands make the cracked pitcher go longest to a bird in the bush," agreed Hurree Jamset Ram Singh.

"Inky, old man, that jolly old moonshee who taught you English at Bhanipur must have been a real whale on proverbs," chuckled Bob.

"Ha, ha, ha!"

"My esteemed Bob——."

"Dear me!" said a high-pitched voice behind the juniors. "Whatever does this mean? What are you boys doing here?"

The Famous Five spun round, as if touched by the same spring. They stared at little Mr. Twiss. Vernon-Smith, half-way up the rain-pipe, twisted to look down, and glared at him. For a moment he had feared that it was a "beak"—which would have meant lines or a gating.

"It's all right, Mr. Twiss," said Bob. "We're getting up to our box-room. Some sportsman has bolted the door on the inside."

"Dear me! Surely it would be better to speak to your form-master," said Mr. Twiss. "No doubt Gosling could enter by his ladder and unfasten the door."

"Well, we're rather pushed for time, sir," said Bob. "Break doesn't last long—and we're after the treasure."

"The—the what?" ejaculated Mr. Twiss, staring at him.

"Haven't you heard about the Head's bank-notes, sir?" asked Bob. "It's all over the school that they're hidden somewhere about Greyfriars."

"Nonsense!" snapped Mr. Twiss.

"Hem! We—we thought of looking in the box-room, sir——."

"Vernon-Smith! Come down at once! You are risking life and limb," said Mr. Twiss, sharply.

The Famous Five exchanged glances. Twiss, in their opinion, was a nervous little rabbit of a man, and very likely the Bounder, clinging to the rain-pipe, looked to him in a perilous position. He was not a master, and really had no right to interfere: but evidently he was going to do so.

"Smithy's all right, sir," said Harry.

"I cannot allow this, Wharton! You are well aware that Mr. Quelch would not allow anything of the kind. Vernon-Smith, come down at once."

The Bounder, clinging to the rain-pipe, gave Mr. Twiss a dogged look. It irked the rebel of the Remove to obey masters and prefects: and he was not going to obey little Twiss if he could help it. Who the dickens was Twiss?

"Do you hear me, Vernon-Smith?"

"Aren't you our head-master's secretary, sir?" asked Vernon-Smith.

"Eh! What? Yes. What do you mean, Vernon-Smith?"

"They haven't made you master of the Remove by any chance?" said the Bounder, with cool impertinence.

"Smithy, old man——!" murmured Bob.

"Better chuck it, Smithy," said Harry Wharton. All the party were irritated by Mr. Twiss's interference: but it was evidently injudicious to carry on. Only the Bounder thought of doing so, regardless of Twiss.

"Vernon-Smith! You are impertinent!" exclaimed Mr. Twiss. "I shall report your impertinence to your form-master. Now come down at once."

"You've no right to give me orders, Mr. Twiss."

"What? What? I tell you to come down."

"Smithy, old chap——!" said Nugent.

"Rats!" said Smithy. And with cool disregard of Twiss, he resumed clambering up the rain-pipe.

Harry Wharton and Co. stood in dismay. This meant a report to Quelch, and a row. The Bounder was the man for rows! Twiss, evidently, was angry: and they expected him to walk away in quest of Mr. Quelch at once.

But Mr. Twiss did not walk away. He made a stride towards the rain-pipe, reached up, and grasped Vernon-Smith's ankle.

"Come down at once!" he snapped.

The Bounder set his teeth. All his obstinacy was roused now. He hung on to the rain-pipe.

"Will you come down, Vernon-Smith?"

"No!" snapped the Bounder.

"Smithy——!" exclaimed Harry Wharton.

"Smithy, you ass——."

"My esteemed Smithy——."

"Look out!" roared Bob, in alarm. "Oh, my hat! Oh, suffering cats and crocodiles!"

Mr. Twiss was jerking angrily at the Bounder's ankle, and Smithy's hold was too precarious for that. He came suddenly slithering down the rain-pipe, and landed with a heavy bump, sprawling, on the earth.

"Oh!" he roared, as he landed.

"Dear me!" gasped Mr. Twiss.

Harry Wharton and Co. ran to help the

"COME DOWN AT ONCE!" HE SNAPPED

Bounder up. Vernon-Smith's face was furious. Mr. Twiss blinked at him through his rimless pince-nez.

"You foolish boy! I hope you are not hurt! It was wholly your own fault! Such recklessness ——."

Vernon-Smith's reply, if he had made one, would certainly not have poured oil on the troubled waters. But the Famous Five gave him no opportunity of cheeking Mr. Twiss any further. They surrounded him and hustled him away. Mr. Twiss stood blinking after them as they went.

"Leave go, you fatheads! Look here, I'm goin' up that pipe!" snarled the Bounder. "Who's that dashed little ass to butt in?"

"Kim on!" said Bob Cherry.

"I tell you——."

"Oh, don't be a goat, Smithy," growled Johnny Bull. "You're up for six already, if Twiss goes to Quelch. Do you want another Head's flogging?"

"Why couldn't the meddling little beast mind his own business?" hissed the Bounder. "I've got a bushel of aches and pains from that bump. He's always shovin' in where he's not wanted."

"Let him rip," said Bob, soothingly. "You can't row with Twiss. We'll have another shot after third school. There's not much left of break now, anyhow."

The Bounder grunted angrily, but he suffered the chums of the Remove to lead him away: perhaps realising that he couldn't row with Twiss. He was still rubbing sore spots, with a scowling brow, when the bell rang for third school, and the Remove trooped back to their form-room.

Chapter XXVIII

BUNTER IS AMUSED

" HE, he, he! "

Thus William George Bunter.

Bunter seemed amused.

After third school, Harry Wharton and Co. were in the quad. They intended to have another " shot " at the Remove box-room, but they were waiting for Smithy, who had been kept back by Mr. Quelch when the Remove came out. They could guess that Twiss had spoken to Quelch, and that Quelch had something to say to Smithy on the subject.

Billy Bunter gave a fat ear to the talk among the Famous Five as they waited for Vernon-Smith. Bunter's fat face was irradiated by a wide grin—a grin so wide that it seemed almost to extend from one fat ear to the other. And he chuckled explosively. Bob Cherry looked round.

" Shut off that alarm-clock, Bunter," he said.

" Eh! I haven't got an alarm-clock! Wharrer you mean? "

" Well, whatever it is, shut it off! " said Bob.

" You silly ass! " hooted Bunter, realising that it was his fat cachinnation to which Bob alluded. " I say, you fellows are enough to make a cat laugh. Mean to say you've been clambering up to the box-room window because the door was bolted, and you fancied—he, he, he! " Bunter chortled. " Think the snooper parked the bank-notes in the box-room, and bolted the door? He, he, he."

" What is that fat chump cackling at? " asked

Johnny Bull. "It looks like it, doesn't it, you burbling bloater?"

"He, he, he!" Bunter almost wept with mirth, "You see, I jolly well know who bolted that box-room door."

"You do!" exclaimed Harry Wharton, staring.

"He, he, he!"

"Who did it then?" demanded Frank Nugent.

"He, he, he! I did!"

"You!" roared all the Famous Five together.

"He, he, he!" Bunter gurgled. The idea of the Famous Five fancying that the "treasure" might be hidden in the box-room because the door was bolted was enough to make Bunter gurgle—when he had bolted that door himself! "Oh, crikey! You've been clambering up to the window after the banknotes—he, he, he—because the door was bolted—he, he, he—and I bolted it yesterday afternoon—he, he, he! Oh, crumbs! He, he, he."

Bunter spluttered with merriment.

"You fat, foozling, frumptious, footling frump!" said Bob Cherry. "What the thump did you bolt that door for, if you did bolt it?"

"Because that beast Smithy was after me," giggled Bunter. "See? Not that I had the chocs from his study, of course——."

"You had Smithy's chocs——?"

"No!" roared Bunter. "Nothing of the kind. Don't you get telling Smithy I had his chocs. He never had any chocs, so far as I know, and they weren't in a box, and the box wasn't on his study table when he went down to Little Side—and if it had been, how should I know, as I never went to the study?"

"Oh, my hat!"

"I never touched that box," said Bunter,

warmly. "It wasn't there when I went in. Besides, I left it without even touching it. Not that I went there, you know. I was down in the Rag when I went to Smithy's study—I mean when I didn't went—I mean——."

"I know what you mean," said Bob. "You bagged Smithy's chocs, and took them up to the box-room to scoff. Is that it, you fat brigand?"

"Oh, really, Cherry! I've told you I never touched Smithy's chocs—as if I'd touch his chocs!" said Bunter, disdainfully. "I'm a bit too particular for that, I hope. And there weren't very many, either, they didn't last me ten minutes——."

"Ha, ha, ha!"

"But you know Smithy!" said Bunter. "Suspicious beast! It would be like him to think of me when he missed his chocs. Fellows do, as you jolly well know! So I thought I'd bolt the box-room door in case he came up, and when he came up after me, he couldn't get in, see?"

"Smithy came up after you!" said Harry Wharton, blankly.

"Yes, and I got away by the window," grinned Bunter. "That's how the door was left bolted, see? He, he, he!"

The Famous Five stared at Bunter.

"I don't make this out," said Bob. "If Smithy got after Bunter, and couldn't get into the box-room, he must have known the door was bolted. But it was Smithy who thought the bolted door might be a clue——."

"Rot!" said Bunter. "Smithy jolly well knew. I tell you he came up after me, and pushed at the door, and I jolly well told him it was no good shoving, too. I jolly well knew he'd be waiting for me, that's why I cleared by the window."

It was quite mystifying to the Famous Five.

"And you fellows thought——!" chuckled Bunter.

"Hallo, hallo, hallo! Here's Smithy."

Herbert Vernon-Smith came out of the House, with a sullen brow. Billy Bunter sidled behind the Famous Five as he came up. Smithy had not mentioned the subject of chocolates, so far: but the fat Owl could not feel quite easy in his fat mind.

"No need to climb in at the window," grunted the Bounder. "That rabbit Twiss has told Quelch, and Gosling got in with his ladder while we were in class, and the door's unbolted now. We can walk in if we like. Quelch has given me a detention for cheeking Twiss."

"Might have given you six!" said Johnny Bull.

"Oh, rats! Coming up to the box-room?" snapped the Bounder. "It's open now, but it was bolted, and you know what that looked like."

"He, he, he!"

"Bunter says that he bolted that door yesterday," said Harry.

"What?" yelled Smithy.

"You didn't know?" asked Bob.

"You footling ass, should I have fancied that the snooper did it, if I'd known Bunter did it? Talk sense."

"Well, this is a bit mixed," said Bob.

"The mixfulness is terrific."

"What was Bunter doing in the box-room, then?" snapped Vernon-Smith. "He doesn't go there to smoke, like Skinner. What were you there for, you blithering fat ass?"

"Oh! Nothing!" said Bunter, hastily. "Nothing to do with chocs——."

"Chocs!" repeated Vernon - Smith, unpleasantly. "Oh! I see! That's where my box of chocolates went, is it?"

"No, it ain't!" roared Bunter. "I wasn't eating chocs when you shoved at the door, and I never hid the box behind Mauly's trunk, and it ain't there now."

Vernon-Smith stared at the fat Owl.

"I never shoved at the door, you fathead! I never went up to the box-room at all yesterday. What do you mean?"

"Oh!" ejaculated Bunter, "wasn't it you? I—I wondered why you didn't say anything—a fellow would expect you to blow off steam. I thought it was you, and I jolly well cleared by the window, because I thought you'd be waiting outside! Not that I had the chocs, you know! Nothing of the kind."

"Somebody else, and Bunter thought Smithy was after him!" said Bob. "Well, let's go and draw the jolly old box-room, now it's open."

"Hold on a minute!" said Vernon-Smith. There was a glint in his eyes. "Let's have this clear. You were in the box-room scoffing my chocs, Bunter——."

"No! Nothing of the kind. I—I—I haven't tasted chocs for weeks. I—I went there to look for a—a—a book——."

"You howling ass, never mind the chocs! I want to know what happened."

"Oh! If you ain't going to make a fuss about the chocs, Smithy—not that I had them, of course ——."

"No, you ass! No, you fathead! No, you prize porker! Now tell me what happened while you were in the box-room."

"Oh, all right," said Bunter. "You came up after me, and shoved at the door, and I jolly well told you you couldn't shove it open, too. I mean,

I thought it was you. It was somebody."

" Didn't he speak? "

" Not a word! Just sneaked down the box-room stairs as soon as I spoke," said Bunter. " Of course, I thought it was you, waiting syrup-stitiously for a chap to come out——."

" Might have been Skinner after his smokes," said Bob.

" Oh, don't be an ass! Skinner would have slanged the fat chump for bolting him out—so would I—so would any Remove man," snapped Vernon-Smith.

" Well, nobody but a Remove man would go up to our box-room," said Nugent. " Nobody else ever goes there."

" What a brain! " said the Bounder, with a sneer.

" Well, what the dickens do you mean? " exclaimed Nugent. " You know as well as I do that nobody outside the form ever goes up to our box-room."

" Oh, quite! " jeered the Bounder. " Nobody at all—unless it was somebody who had a special reason—somebody who might have hidden a packet there, and wanted to help himself from the packet—and sneaked off quietly when he found that somebody was in the box-room——."

" WHAT! " gasped the Famous Five, all together.

For a moment, they stared at the Bounder. The next moment, six juniors tore into the House: leaving Billy Bunter blinking after them blankly through his big spectacles.

Chapter XXIX

TOO LATE?

" THAT fool Twiss!" said the Bounder, between his teeth.

"Eh! What about Twiss?" asked Bob Cherry. "What has Twiss got to do with it?"

"Only that he's dished us!" snapped Vernon-Smith, savagely. "If he hadn't barged in this morning, we should have had it."

They were in the Remove box-room. Smithy's quick brain had jumped to it, that the unknown person who had tried the box-room door while Bunter was there was the mysterious "snooper" —coming there to visit the hidden packet; and it seemed very likely to the Famous Five. If that was so, the hide-out was, after all, in that very box-room. Eagerly they searched. If indeed the bundle of notes had been there the previous day, there was no reason, so far as they could see, why it should not still be there, in its hiding-place: and they were going to root it out.

But they did not root it out. Every foot, or rather every inch, of the box-room was scanned, and scrutinized—every box looked into and over and under and round about. An empty chocolate-box rewarded the eager seekers—but nothing else. Of a packet of notes there was no sign.

"No luck!" said Frank Nugent, at last.

"Smithy isn't quite such a Sherlock Holmes as he fancied!" remarked Johnny Bull, sarcastically.

"Well, it looked jolly likely," said Harry Wharton. "Still, there's nothing here."

They were still looking about the room. **But**

they no longer expected to find anything. Herbert
Vernon-Smith, his hands in his pockets, a scowl
on his face, stood staring at a little ventilator in
the wall—a little rusty iron grid about the size of
a brick. Bob Cherry had jerked at it, to see
whether it could be moved—and found that it
could. But there was nothing in the orifice behind
it but dust and cobwebs. There seemed no other
possible hide-out in the room, unless under or in
one of the many boxes—but every box had now
been explored inside and out by the Famous Five.
They were disappointed—but not so bitterly as the
Bounder. All the fellows were keen to discover
the "treasure," but with Smithy it was a personal
matter—as a hit back at the unknown "snooper"
who had knocked him out in the dark.

"That fool Twiss!" he repeated. "The
meddlin' little ass! He had to barge in and queer
the pitch! If he hadn't meddled this morning, we
should have got in at the window——."

"What good would it have done, as the thing
isn't here after all?" asked Johnny Bull.

"Fathead!"

"Thanks!" said Johnny, drily.

"I don't quite see, Smithy——!" said Harry.

"You wouldn't!" snapped the Bounder.

"The seefulness of my esteemed self is not
terrific," remarked Hurree Jamset Ram Singh.
"The absurd packet is not here——."

"Not now!" snarled Smithy.

"Oh!" exclaimed Harry Wharton. "You
think——?"

"I don't think—I know! Gosling came up on
his ladder and got in, and unbolted the door, while
we were in third school. Well, after that, the
snooper could walk in when he liked, and there
was nobody about during class. He came here and
took it away, to put in a safer place. He wasn't

going to risk being bolted out a second time."

Harry Wharton and Co. looked at the Bounder, and looked at one another. Bob Cherry winked at his comrades, and they smiled. What the Bounder stated was probable enough, in itself: but they could see no evidence of it. If the packet had ever been there, certainly it had been taken away—but had it ever been there?

"That fool Twiss has dished the whole thing," growled Vernon-Smith. "But for him and his meddling, we should have found it here in break."

"No doubt about that, I suppose, Mr. Sherlock Holmes?" asked Johnny Bull, still sarcastic.

"No, ass."

"Well, Smithy knows all about it, I see!" grinned Bob Cherry. "Go it, Smithy—you can look on us as a lot of Dr. Watsons, and explain the jolly old mystery like Mr. Holmes. Where was it hidden?"

"Yes, do tell us that!" said the sarcastic Johnny. "I suppose you know just where the snooper parked it?"

"So would you, if you used your eyes," snapped the Bounder. He pointed to the little ventilator in the wall. "There!"

"Nothing there but dust and cobwebs," said Bob. "I've looked."

"If you looked again, you might notice that the dust has been disturbed, and the cobwebs torn," sneered Smithy. "Think some fellow came up here and shoved his paw into that hole in the wall just to rake up the dust and set the spiders running?"

"Oh!" exclaimed Bob.

Harry Wharton and Co. gathered under the ventilator, Bob jerked out the little iron grid again, and they stared into the dusty cobwebby opening, Wharton turning on the light of a flashlamp. Now that they examined it more closely, they could see the traces the Bounder's keen eye had detected. The dust undoubtedly had been disturbed, and several long trails of broken cobweb hung about. Most certainly it looked as if that dusty recess had been recently groped into.

"By gum!" said Bob. "It looks——."

"Um!" said Johnny Bull. Johnny seemed unconvinced: perhaps because he did not like being called a fathead and an ass.

"Well, if it was here, it's gone," said Nugent.

"No 'if' about it," snapped the Bounder. "It was there, and we should have had it in break but for that rabbit-faced idiot Twiss. Now it's been removed, and goodness knows where it's parked now—outside the House, most likely. I wish I'd landed out with my boot when that interferin' tick grabbed me on the rain-pipe this mornin'."

"Well, we can't be sure——!" said Harry.

"You can't, I daresay," snapped Smithy. "They seem to have forgotten you and your pals when brains were served out."

With that polite rejoinder, Herbert Vernon-Smith walked, or rather stamped, out of the box-room, and tramped away down the stairs.

The chums of the Remove smiled at one another. Smithy was disappointed and angry: and in such a mood, his manners were never very polished.

"Smithy may be right," said Harry. "It does certainly look as if somebody has been groping in that ventilator."

"But it doesn't get us any forrarder!" remarked Bob.

"No! Let's get out."

"Might draw the old Cloisters," said Nugent.

" Lots of nooks and crannies there where a packet might be hidden."

" Yes: let's," said Bob.

In the quad, on their way to the Cloisters, they passed Herbert Vernon-Smith, but he did not join them. For which they were not exactly sorry, for the Bounder looked in one of his worst tempers. He scowled after them, as they went, but took no other heed of their existence.

A glitter came into Vernon-Smith's eyes, as he glanced at little Mr. Twiss, walking in the quad with Hacker, the master of the Shell.

Twiss, if the Bounder was right, had spoiled the whole thing by his interference. Smithy would have been glad to tell Mr. Twiss exactly what he thought of him.

He watched the Head's secretary, as the little man trotted by the side of the long, lean Hacker, with a black scowl. That tame little rabbit—that footling little bunny—couldn't mind his own business, the Bounder savagely reflected—he had to barge in where he was not wanted, and give the " snooper " a chance to remove the hidden packet before it could be found—just as if he had done it on purpose! And as that phrase formed itself in the Bounder's mind, he caught his breath, with a sudden start.

" Oh! " muttered Smithy, his heart beating.

Hardly breathing in his sudden excitement, he stood watching Mr. Twiss—intently, intensely. Strange and startling thoughts were working in his mind.

Chapter XXX

MR. GRIMES HEARS BUNTER'S OPINION

" MY postal-order hasn't come! "

Five fellows chuckled.

Billy Bunter made that announcement after class. He made it with a serious fat face, blinking very seriously at Harry Wharton and Co. through his big spectacles.

After class, the " treasure-hunt " had been resumed, and had gone on merrily. Fellows searched and quested and rooted in every possible and impossible corner for the hidden packet. Nobody, so far, had had any luck. Really, it was rather like looking for a needle in a haystack— there were so many nooks and crannies where a small packet might be put out of sight. The Famous Five were now taking a rest: sitting in a cheery row on one of the old oaken benches under the elms, with a massive trunk behind them and shady branches overhead. As it was getting near tea-time, they were, as a matter of fact, thinking more of tea than of treasure, when Bunter rolled up, and made his announcement respecting the celebrated postal-order which he had been so long expecting. At which the chums of the Remove chuckled.

Billy Bunter, perhaps, expected the arrival of that postal-order. Nobody else did—and perhaps even Bunter had his doubts.

" Well, you can cackle," said Bunter morosely. " But it's a bit awkward. At the present moment I'm actually stony."

"Wet prospect!" said Bob Cherry, sympathetically.

"The wetfulness is terrific."

"What does it feel like to be stony for the first time in your life, Bunter?" asked Frank Nugent, gravely.

"Well, it's pretty rotten," said Bunter. "I wrote the pater a special letter last week, taking no end of trouble about the spelling, because he's jawed me about it. I thought he'd be pleased to see that my orthology was all right——."

"Your whatter?" ejaculated Bob.

"Orthography, perhaps!" suggested Harry Wharton.

"I said orthology, and I mean orthology," retorted Bunter. "That means spelling, if you don't happen to know. And I mentioned that Quelch had a very high opinion of me this term— that ought to have pleased him."

"Perhaps he guessed that it was bunkum!" suggested Johnny Bull.

"Well, I don't see how he can know what Quelch really thinks, till he gets my next report!" argued Bunter. "Anyhow it's done no good. It's a bit thick, too, now the pater's making tons of money. He's a bear, you know, and it's a bear market, and when you're a bear in a bear market, you just rake it in. I rather fancied it might mean a fiver. And I haven't even had a postal-order for five bob!" added Bunter, sorrowfully. "I was expecting another postal-order, too, from one of my titled relations, but—it hasn't come."

"The nobility are a bit forgetful at times," said Bob Cherry, shaking his head. "Why not ask Quelch to let you use his phone, and ring up the Duke de Bunter, or the Marquis de Grunter——?"

"Ha, ha, ha!"

"Oh, really, Cherry! What I mean is this,"

said Bunter. "One of you fellows lend me ten bob, and I'll let you have it back out of my postal-order, or out of my fiver if the pater shells out— whichever comes first. See? Now, which of you fellows is lending me ten bob?"

"The whichfulness is terrific."

"What about you, Bob, old chap?"

"Nothing about me, Billy, old chap."

"What about you, Nugent? You're not so jolly mean as Cherry."

"I am!" contradicted Nugent. "Worse, in fact."

"What about you, Inky?"

"The worsefulness of my esteemed self is terrific."

"Well, you fellows are a stingy lot here," said Bunter, in disgust. "Toddy had half-a-crown to-day, and I asked him to lend it to me, and he said he wanted it himself. Selfishness all round! I wonder sometimes that I don't grow selfish myself, mixing with such a lot."

"Oh, my hat!"

"And I haven't been able to find that beastly packet yet," went on Bunter, "I've hunted everywhere. The Head would be bound to stand a fellow something out of it, if he found it. Don't you fellows think so? Do you fellows think that if a fellow found the packet, he might borrow one of the pound notes——?"

"What?"

"Temporarily, of course," said Bunter, hastily. "Only temporarily. What do you think, Wharton?"

"I think you'd better not look for that packet any more, old fat man, if you don't want to put in next term at Borstal."

"If you think I'd touch it, Wharton, it only

shows that you've got a rotten suspicious mind like Smithy."

"Why, you fat villain——."

"You needn't call me names, Wharton, because I'm too honourable to touch the tin in that packet if I found it. But I don't feel so jolly sure it's hidden about Greyfriars at all—I've looked all over the shop. Grimey's an old donkey, isn't he?" Bunter sniffed, "I don't think much of Grimey. A real detective would have spotted it long ago— he would have found some cigarette-ash or some- thing, and then just pounced on it. Grimey's rooting about the place now—but he won't find anything."

"Is Grimey here?" asked Bob.

"Skinner said he saw him, leaning up against one of the elms," answered Bunter. "Fat lot of good he is. He doesn't even know what Smithy found out in our box-room."

"Smithy ought to tell him, if he really thinks there's anything in it," said Bob.

"Well, I expect it's only Smithy's rot," said Bunter. "Smithy's too clever by half. Skinner said so, when he heard about it. Not that it would be much good telling Grimey. Never saw such an old donkey. That's my opinion of him."

"Thank you, Master Bunter," said an unex- pected voice.

Billy Bunter jumped almost clear of the ground. Harry Wharton and Co. all stared round. From behind the massive elm, at the back of the bench, a plump red face looked, and Billy Bunter blinked at it in great dismay. Skinner had told him that he had seen Inspector Grimes leaning up against one of the elms, but it had not occured to Bunter that it might be that particular elm. Evidently, it was!

"Oh!" gasped Bunter. "Is—is—is that you,

sir? I—I wasn't calling you an old donkey, Mr. Grimes."

"Oh, you fat chump!" breathed Bob Cherry.

There was a grim frown on Mr. Grimes's plump face. Perhaps he had not been pleased by Billy Bunter's remarks! He glared at the fat Owl.

"I heard what you said!" he rapped.

"I—I didn't mean you," gasped Bunter. "I— I was speaking of another old donkey! Not you at all."

"Shut up, you fathead!" breathed Wharton.

"Oh, really, Wharton! I tell you I didn't mean Grimey, but another old donkey altogether ——."

If Billy Bunter expected that to placate Mr. Grimes, he was disappointed. The plump inspector came round the elm, and his look, as he came, was so grim that Billy Bunter backed away in alarm, revolved upon his axis, and departed hurriedly for the open spaces.

Inspector Grimes glared after him, and grunted.

"Don't mind Bunter, Mr. Grimes," ventured Bob. "He can't help being a silly ass."

Grunt!

"The apologize for the preposterous manners of the idiotic Bunter is terrific, esteemed Mr. Grimes," murmured Hurree Jamset Ram Singh.

Grunt!

The Famous Five exchanged glances, rose from the old bench, and walked away to the House to tea. Inspector Grimes dropped on the bench they had vacated, and another expressive grunt followed them as they went.

Chapter XXXI

WHAT SMITHY SUSPECTED

"BUT——!" said Tom Redwing, dubiously.

The Bounder laughed.

"I've told you," he said. "You think there's nothin' in it, what?"

"Well, it's all pretty vague," said Tom, slowly, "and—and you dislike the man, Smithy, and that might make you think——."

"Quite!" said Smithy, with a grin. "Meddlin' little beast, if he's nothing worse. Anyhow, I'm goin' to pass it on to Grimey."

"Is he here?" asked Tom.

"Look under the elms—that object on the bench isn't a sack of coke, though it looks like one."

"If you think you've got it right, Smithy, I suppose you ought to pass it on to him. But——."

"I'm goin' to, anyhow."

The Bounder left his chum, and walked across to the elms, leaving Tom Redwing looking, and feeling, very dubious. But what Redwing thought mattered little to the Bounder: he was sure in his own mind. He had taken plenty of time to think over the sudden and startling suspicion that had shot into his mind that morning, and the more he pondered over it, the more assured he felt that he had put his finger on the facts.

Inspector Grimes glanced at Vernon-Smith as he came, and raised his eyebrows, as Smithy dropped on the bench beside him. Mr. Grimes was not, as a matter of fact, in the best of tempers. The discovery that the story of the hidden loot was all over the school, and that "treasure-hunting" was going on far and wide, had deeply displeased and disgruntled Mr. Grimes. How it had got out he did not know, but it was out: and the inspector's task, already far from easy, seemed doubly difficult now that the mysterious "snooper" was put so thoroughly upon his guard. He was in no mood for a schoolboy's company or conversation: and his look at Vernon-Smith told as much. That did not disconcert Smithy in any way.

"Excuse me, Mr. Grimes." The Bounder spoke quietly, "I suppose if a fellow hit on something that looked suspicious, he ought to mention it to you."

"Oh, quite!" said Mr. Grimes, with heavy sarcasm. "I have already had an offer of assistance from Master Bunter."

"I'm not a goat like Bunter, I hope," said Smithy. "I can show you the place, if you like, where the packet was hidden, though it's been taken away since. And I believe I can point out the man who snooped it on Tuesday night."

Inspector Grimes's keen eyes fixed on his face. He gave Herbert Vernon-Smith a long, long look, and then answered.

"If anything has come to your knowledge, Master Vernon-Smith, it is of course your duty to report it to me, as the officer in charge of the case. Certainly I will hear what you have to say."

He listened with attention, while the Bounder, in a few succinct words, told him of the search in the Remove box-room, and his reasons for believing that the packet had been concealed in the ventilator.

"I shall examine the spot," said Mr. Grimes. "Is that all?"

"Not quite! Suppose," said the Bounder,

slowly, weighing his words as he spoke, "suppose that the packet was there, and that we should have found it in break this morning by getting in at the window—only we were interrupted, and stopped, by a man who is not a master, and had no right to interfere. A mere coincidence, perhaps, that it gave the snooper an opportunity of getting the packet away to a safer place."

"Quite possibly, I should think," said the inspector, drily.

"And suppose," said the Bounder, in the same slow way, "that it happened to be the same man who was up late one night, after everybody else was in bed, and into whom I ran in the dark when I left my dormitory for my own reasons."

Mr. Grimes's eyes narrowed.

"Did the man explain why he was up late that night?" he asked.

"Oh, yes," said the Bounder, with a sneer. "He couldn't sleep, and was going down for a book. I believed it at the time."

"Quite a natural proceeding," said Mr. Grimes.

"Not quite so natural to go down in the dark, keeping so quiet that a fellow butted into him. Why couldn't he have switched on the light?"

Mr. Grimes made no rejoinder to that.

"Several fellows remarked that it was queer he was going down in the dark. I know why now, I think. There was a row when I barged him on the stairs, and my beak came out. He had to leave the job till the following night!" sneered the Bounder, "and left it till midnight to make it safer."

"Is that all?"

"Not quite all yet. A week or two ago, some fellows in my form took a short cut at the 'Three Fishers.' You know the place—rather juicy: out of bounds for Greyfriars men, of course. They put on speed, and ran into this same man—coming in at the gate. They expected him to report them to Quelch."

" And——? "

" I told them he wouldn't, if they'd really seen him going into the ' Three Fishers.' He wouldn't want that talked about among the beaks," sneered Smithy. " Well, he didn't."

Mr. Grimes sat silent. He had listened attentively and patiently to the Bounder. But his stolid plump face gave no clue to what impression might have been made on him.

" That's all," said Vernon-Smith. " A man has connections at a den of racing men—he goes down in the dark when he wants a book, instead of switching on a light—and he barges in when the hidden loot's just going to be found, and the snooper moves it to a safe place." The Bounder's eyes glinted, and he passed his hand over the dark bruise on his forehead. " I know now who gave me this—I've been thinking it over ever since this morning, and I've got it clear—it all fits in. That's all I had to tell you."

Mr. Grimes did not speak.

" We know all about the ' inside job,' since the story got out," went on Smithy. " Somebody was hard pushed for cash—and knew where to lay his hands on it. The man I'm speaking of would know better than anyone else. Perhaps he hadn't had luck on a horse," added the Bounder, his lip curling. " Joe Banks at the ' Three Fishers ' would know! Just the silly ass to fancy he could spot winners, and pick out a horse that came in eleventh. Anyhow, he dabbles in it—or those fellows wouldn't have seen him where they saw him."

Still no rejoinder from Mr. Grimes.

Herbert Vernon-Smith gave him a hard look.

" You think it's all moonshine, and that I've let my fancy run away with me, because the man's meddled with me and I don't like him? " he snapped.

" Not at all unlikely, Master Vernon-Smith."

" O.K." The Bounder set his lips, and rose from the bench, " I thought you ought to know, and I've told you. If it's all moonshine, forget it." Vernon-Smith moved away.

" One moment, please," said Mr. Grimes, quietly.

" Well? "

" Have you told this to anyone else? "

" Only my pal Redwing. He's mum. I'm not a fool."

" Certainly it would be very inadvisable to spread such a story about the school," said Mr. Grimes, drily.

" Especially if it's all moonshine," sneered the Bounder.

" Precisely."

" Leave it at that, then." Smithy turned away again.

" One moment, please," repeated Mr. Grimes. " You have not told me the name of the man you have referred to."

" Oh, you don't want any more moonshine," said the Bounder. " I've wasted too much of your time already." There was a mocking glimmer in his eyes. " You can't have it both ways, Mr. Grimes."

" What? "

" If I'm a silly schoolboy fancying things, you don't want to hear any more of my fancies. If you think there's something in it, you can say so, and I'll give you the name."

Mr. Grimes breathed very hard through his stubby nose. He looked very long and very hard

at the Bounder. Official reticence was strong with
Mr. Grimes. Obviously he did not wish to utter
a single word that might reveal his thoughts on
the subject. But he did want to know that name.

"I think what you have told me may be worth
investigating," he said, at last, slowly and
reluctantly.

The Bounder laughed.

"That's good enough," he said. "The name's
Twiss."

Inspector Grimes almost jumped off the bench.

"Your head-master's secretary!" he stuttered.
For once, Mr. Grimes was startled out of his stolid
official calm. No doubt he had pondered long and
deeply over the mystery of the identity of the
unknown "snooper" who had performed that
"inside job." But plainly little Mr. Twiss had
never entered his thoughts. "Did—did—did you
say Twiss?"

"T-W-I-S-S." The Bounder spelt it out, "T
for Thomas—W for Walter—I for Isaac——."

"That will do," said Mr. Grimes, gruffly.

The Bounder laughed again, and walked away.
Mr. Grimes looked after him with a grim
disapproving stare.

Then Mr. Grimes's eyes fixed on a dapper
figure at a distance. Little Mr. Twiss was taking a
walk in the quad, his rimless pince-nez gleaming
back the sunshine. He looked, in the eyes of all
Greyfriars fellows, a harmless rabbit of a little
man. Was there more in little Mr. Twiss than met
the eye? Long and keenly the inspector's
scrutinizing eyes dwelt on him, and he wondered.

Chapter XXXII

WHOSE TENNER ?

" I SAY, you fellows! Can you change a tenner for me? "

Billy Bunter liked to attract attention when he spoke. He liked to make fellows sit up and take notice. Never had he had so much success as now.

That question seemed to electrify every fellow in the Rag.

Bunter's stony state was well known. That stony state, which he had confided to the Famous Five under the elms the previous day, continued. The sun had gone down on a stony Bunter, and risen again to find him still in quest of a little loan to tide him over till his postal-order came.

That morning Bunter had been trying to borrow any little sum from threepence to half-a-crown, up and down the Remove. In break he had blinked in vain for a letter in the rack—his celebrated postal-order seemed to be still delayed in transit. In break he had succeeded in extracting a half-crown from Lord Mauleverer, which disappeared at once in the tuck-shop.

After third school, Bunter was as hard up as ever—going to and fro, like the lion of old, seeking what he might devour. In class that afternoon the fat Owl, thinking less of his lessons than of methods of raising the wind, had had the acid edge of Mr. Quelch's tongue several times. After class, he had wandered forth on his own, once more treasure-hunting, and had not been seen for some time. And now——!

Now he rolled into the Rag, a cheery grin on

his fat face, and propounded that startling question that caused every eye in the junior day-room to turn upon him.

Often, only too often, did fellows turn a deaf ear to Billy Bunter, passing by his remarks like the idle wind which they regarded not. Now all was changed—Bunter was the cynosure of all eyes.

The Famous Five, chatting by the window, spun round. Peter Todd jumped, or rather bounded. Fisher T. Fish ejaculated " Gee-whizz!" Russell and Ogilvy, who were playing chess, forgot all about chess and stared at Bunter. Skinner winked at Snoop and Stott, who giggled. Tom Redwing caught his breath, and the Bounder burst into a scoffing laugh. Bolsover major, Hazel, Wibley, Morgan, Micky Desmond, Squiff, Tom Brown, and a dozen other fellows, all suspended conversation, or their various occupations, to gaze at the fat Owl. Even Lord Mauleverer sat upright in his armchair, and opened his eyes wide. Bunter had the house!

He did not seem to mind. Bunter liked the spot-light. He blinked cheerily at a sea of staring faces through his big spectacles.

" Did—did you say a tenner, Bunter? " gasped Bob Cherry.

" Yes, old chap! Got some change? "

" You've got a ten-pound note! " exclaimed Harry Wharton.

" Eh! I shouldn't ask you to change it, if I hadn't, should I? " asked Bunter. " Nothing wonderful in having a tenner, is there—for me, I mean? I know you fellows never have tenners—your people ain't rich like mine. At Bunter Court ——."

" This beats the band," said Harold Skinner, with a whistle. " The whole school's been hunting for those banknotes—and the biggest idiot at

Greyfriars is the lucky man! Can you beat it?"

"It's the cat's whiskers," said Fisher T. Fish. "I guess I've given every pesky spot in the whole shebang the once-over, and then some, but did I spot the spondulics? And that fat piecan has worked the riffle! I'll say it's sure the elephant's hind leg."

"Where did you find the packet, Bunter?" asked Hazel.

Bunter blinked at him.

"Eh! I haven't found any packet, Hazel!"

"You haven't?" roared Bolsover major.

"Of course not! I've been looking for it, but I haven't found it. It wasn't in the Cloisters, at least where I looked. Wharrer you mean?"

"You haven't found the packet—but you've got a tenner!" exclaimed Frank Nugent.

"Exactly, old chap. Can you change it for me?"

"Isn't he the jolly old limit!" said Bob Cherry. "Doesn't he take the biscuit? Doesn't he prance off with the Huntley and Palmer, and waltz away with the Peek Frean?"

"What did I tell you?" sneered Vernon-Smith. "Bunter's found it—and findings are keepings with Bunter."

"Oh, really, Smithy——."

"Has he really got a tenner, or is he pulling our leg?" grunted Johnny Bull. "If he has, we know where he got it. But has he?"

"Oh, really, Bull——."

That Bunter had a tenner was soon demonstrated, for he drew it from his tattered wallet: which seldom had a ten-shilling note in it, let alone a ten-pound one.

But there it was! Tenners were seldom seen in the Remove—but they knew one when they saw it! And here was one.

Bunter held it out to the Bounder.

" You've got tons of oof, Smithy. You can change it for me. I'd rather not take it to the tuck-shop."

" Why not? " grinned the Bounder.

" Well, Mrs. Mimble might be inquisitive about it. It might get to Quelch, and he would ask questions, you see."

" Bank on that! " chuckled Smithy. He stared at the banknote, but did not offer to take it. Smithy was one of the few fellows in the Remove who might have had change for a tenner. But he would hardly have been prepared to give six-pence for that particular tenner.

" You unutterable idiot, Bunter," said Harry Wharton. The captain of the Remove was looking, and feeling, quite aghast. " If you found that banknote in the packet, take it to Quelch at once."

" I didn't! " roared Bunter, indignantly.

" Then where did you get it? "

" Like your cheek to ask a fellow where he gets a tip," retorted Bunter. " I don't ask you where you get a ten-bob note, when you have one. Not that you have one very often—he, he, he! Tenners aren't so much to my people as they may be to yours."

" You howling ass! " hooted Bob Cherry. " If you don't say where you got it, do you think any-body will believe it's yours? "

" It's mine! I've got it, haven't I? "

" Bunter's got it," grinned Smithy. " And as soon as Grimey hears of it, he will get Bunter."

" Borstal for Bunter! " said Snoop.

" Oh, they won't send him there," said Skinner. " Home for idiots is more likely."

" Why, you beasts, are you making out that

this tenner ain't mine?" demanded Bunter. " Why, you awful beasts——."

" It can't be yours, you fat chump," said Peter Todd, "and you've jolly well got to tell us where you got it."

" I'll jolly well please myself about that! " retorted Bunter.

" You jolly well won't, unless you want me to take a stump to you," said Peter. " Ain't I your keeper, you potty porpoise? Now, cough it up."

" Yah! "

" For goodness' sake, Bunter! " exclaimed Harry Wharton.

" You can mind your own business," said Bunter, independently. " Anybody would think that I don't get lots of remittances, from the way you fellows stare. Haven't you ever seen a tenner before? Why, at Bunter Court——."

" Cough it up! " roared Peter.

" Beast! " retorted Bunter.

Most of the fellows had been down on the Bounder's suggestion that if Bunter found the " treasure," it would not be safe from his fat fingers. But they could hardly help agreeing with the Bounder now. There were ten-pound notes in the missing packet. Bunter had been hunting for the packet. A few hours ago he had been trying to borrow sixpences. Now he had a tenner. The thing really spoke for itself—especially as everyone knew how very vague were Billy Bunter's ideas on the subject of " meum and tuum." That that ten-pound note came from the missing packet could hardly be doubted by any fellow present. The Bounder was scoffing, Skinner cynically amused: but most of the fellows were alarmed and concerned for the fat and fatuous Owl. Peter Todd's concern went to the length of taking Bunter by a fat ear—eliciting a howl of anguish from the proprietor thereof.

"Ow! Leggo! Beast!" howled Bunter.

He jerked his fat ear away and rubbed it, glaring at Peter with a glare that almost cracked his spectacles.

"Keep off, Toddy, you beast! I was going to lend you something out of this—and now I jolly well won't, so yah!"

"Where did you get it?" shrieked Peter.

"Find out! Look here, Smithy, are you going to change this tenner for me or not?"

"Not!" grinned Smithy. "I don't want to go to chokey with you, old fat man."

"Take it to Quelch, and ask him to change it!" suggested Skinner. "Quelch would be frightfully interested in that tenner."

"Well, I can't," said Bunter. "We ain't allowed to have tenners in the Remove, as you jolly well know. Quelch would be down like a ton of bricks on a man who had ten pounds, if he knew it. I don't want Quelch to know anything about it."

"I guess you sure do not!" chuckled Fisher T. Fish. "Say, what have you done with the rest, big boy?"

"Eh! The rest of what?"

"Aw, I guess you cinched the whole packet? That tenner wasn't lying around on its lonesome."

"I tell you I never——."

"Will you tell us where you got that bank-note?" hooted Peter Todd.

"No, I jolly well won't! It's my business, not yours, ain't it? I daresay you wouldn't believe me, if I did—you've doubted my word before, Peter Todd. You needn't deny it—you have!"

"Guilty, my lord!" said Peter. "I have—many

a time and oft. But get it off your chest, all the
same."

"Shan't!" retorted Bunter. He blinked
indignantly round the Rag, "I say, you fellows,
this is pretty thick. Making out a fellow snooped
a tenner—a tenner ain't so much to me as it is to
you. At Bunter Court——."

"Where did you get that tenner?" yelled
Peter.

"Find out! If you won't change it for me,
Smithy——."

"Not in these trousers!" said Smithy.

"I'll ask a Fourth Form man, then—Temple's
got lots of dough. And you can jolly well go and
eat coke!" hooted Bunter.

And with that, the fat Owl of the Remove,
dodging Peter's hand as it reached for a fat ear
again, rolled out of the Rag—leaving that apartment in a buzz behind him.

Chapter XXXIII

NO CHANGE !

" HALLO, hallo, hallo! Roll in, barrel! "

It was rather unusual for William George Bunter to receive so cordial an invitation when he presented his fat person in a study doorway at tea-time. But on this occasion, No. 1 Study seemed actually glad to see him.

Harry Wharton and Co. had gathered there for tea—rather a frugal tea. Funds were a little low, as may occasionally happen in the best-regulated study. The chums of the Remove had pooled their resources—like the Early Christians, they had most things in common, especially in times of dearth. Wharton and Nugent provided toast, and a ghost of butter thereon: Johnny Bull brought along a cake from his study, No. 14: and from No. 13, Bob Cherry brought a tin of sardines, and Hurree Jamset Ram Singh a bag of biscuits. It was not exactly a festive board for five schoolboys blessed with healthy, youthful appetites: and certainly an energetic trencherman like Bunter was likely to make short work of it.

Nevertheless, Bob Cherry cordially invited him to roll in, and the other four all nodded assent.

The fact was that Harry Wharton and his friends were anxious about Bunter. That tenner had alarmed them. It was practically impossible to believe that it belonged to the impecunious Owl —how could it, when only that day he had been scrounging up and down the Remove for a humble " tanner." The obvious explanation was that he had chanced upon the hidden packet, and helped himself to one of the banknotes—especially as he had been known to be looking for the " treasure " just before he walked in with the banknote. Bunter was just the fellow to persuade himself, by some fatuous mental process, that there would be no great harm in accommodating himself temporarily in that way — Bunter's fat brain moved in mysterious ways its wonders to perform. But the view that would be taken of such a proceeding by the head-master, or a police-inspector, was quite alarming to think of.

So for once the Famous Five were glad to see Bunter roll in, hoping to be able to save himself from himself, as it were.

Bunter seemed surprised by that cordial welcome. He blinked a little suspiciously at the juniors in No. 1 Study.

" I say, you fellows, no larks," he said.

" The larkfulness is not terrific, my esteemed fat Bunter," assured Hurree Jamset Ram Singh. " Your honorific presence is a boonful blessing."

" Oh ! " ejaculated Bunter. He grinned. " I see." Bunter thought he saw. " You ain't so jolly civil when a fellow's been disappointed about a postal-order ! You can be civil to a fellow when he's got a tenner in his pocket ! He, he, he ! "

" Why, you bloated bloater ! " roared Johnny Bull.

" Oh, really, Bull——."

" Look here, boot him out ! " snorted Johnny. " If he wants to go to chokey, let him go, and be blowed to him."

" Steady the Buffs ! " said Bob Cherry, cheerfully. " That's the sort of thing the benighted chump would think. He can't help Buntering."

" The Bunterfulness is truly terrific," murmured Hurree Jamset Ram Singh. " But the bootfulness is not the proper caper, my esteemed Johnny."

"I say, you fellows, you needn't get your rag out, because I know your game," said Bunter, brightly. "The fact is, I intend to treat you fellows generously now that I'm in funds. Only yesterday you refused to lend me ten bob. You know you did! Well, I ain't the man to owe a grudge. Kindest friend and noblest foe, you know —that's me."

"You unspeakable idiot——!" said Harry Wharton.

"Oh, draw it mild! If that's the way you talk, you won't see much of my tenner, I promise you. I say, what have you got for tea?" Bunter blinked at the frugal tea-table, with a blink of ineffable scorn. "Is that all you've got? Hard up, what? Well, I've been hard up occasionally——."

"Only occasionally?" remarked Frank Nugent.

"Yes—it's happened at times," said Bunter. "O.K. now, though. Look here, I'm going to stand you fellows a spread—best you can get at the tuck-shop. Nothing mean about me, I hope. You'll have to change the tenner for me, of course. Mind, I'm not doing this simply because I can't get the tenner changed—I'm doing it because I'm a generous chap, as you know."

"Oh! You can't get the tenner changed?" asked Bob.

"Didn't Temple of the Fourth jump at it?" inquired Johnny Bull sarcastically.

"I don't want to have anything to do with Temple—too much of a supersquilious ass for me."

"Too much of a whatter?" gurgled Bob.

"Putting on airs," said Bunter. "Super-squilious means putting on airs, Bob Cherry, if you don't happen to know."

"I don't!" admitted Bob.

"Well, you know now I've told you. I say, you fellows, that cad Temple said he wouldn't touch my tenner with a barge-pole," said Bunter. "He said I'd better take it back where it belonged! Fancy that!"

"Jolly good advice!" grunted Johnny Bull.

"I'd have punched his head for his cheek," said Bunter. "But I wouldn't soil my hands on the fellow."

"You've soiled them on something," remarked Johnny.

"Yah! Then I asked Hobson of the Shell," went on Bunter, "and instead of changing the tenner, he asked me where I'd found the packet— as if I know anything about the packet. It's a queer thing, you fellows, but everybody who hears that I've got a tenner, thinks at once that I've found that packet. As if I'd touch it if I had!"

"Only yesterday you were talking about borrowing a pound note from it if you found it!" hooted the captain of the Remove.

"That was only—only—only a figure of speech, you know. What I meant was that I wouldn't!" explained Bunter. "Besides, this ain't a pound note! It's a tenner. Talk sense."

"From what we've heard, there were a lot of pound notes in the packet," said Johnny Bull. "Looks as if the snooper may have blued the pound notes, and left only the banknotes."

"Eh! How do you make that out?" asked Bunter.

"Because you've got a banknote."

"Why, you beast——."

"Is it possible that that banknote does belong to Bunter?" asked Bob Cherry, gazing at the fat Owl in wonder. "Look here, Bunter, just try hard not to be such a benighted ass. If that tenner's yours, you can say how you came by it. If you don't, it will be all over the school soon that you've found that packet, and the beaks will get wise to it before long, and then where will you be?"

Bunter blinked at him.

"Well, if I tell you, will you fellows change it for me?" he asked.

"If it's yours, we'll get it changed all right," said Harry Wharton.

"Well, I don't mind telling pals like you fellows. It's a tip from my pater," explained Bunter. "I told you fellows he had been a bear and was raking it in. When you're a bear in a bear market, all you've got to do is to sell shares you haven't got, and the oof rolls in in oodles. But I don't suppose you fellows know much about the City."

"Not much more than you do," agreed Bob Cherry. "So that tenner's a tip from your pater, is it?"

"That's it," said Bunter, with a nod. "I wrote him a very special letter more than a week ago, as I told you—well, he's coughed up a tip. Here you are, Wharton—you get it changed for me, old chap, now I've told you where it came from."

Billy Bunter held out the ten-pound note to the captain of the Remove. The Famous Five gazed at him. Bunter, apparently, supposed that it was all plain sailing now. To judge by the looks of the Co. it wasn't!

Chapter XXXIV

BUNTER EXPLAINS !

THERE was silence in No. 1 Study as the Famous Five gazed at Bunter.

That Bunter was not telling the truth was, of course, apparent to all.

If Billy Bunter had come by that tenner honestly he did not choose, for some mysterious reason, to explain precisely how. That alone was enough to banish any doubts the juniors might have had as to the source of the fat Owl's new-found wealth.

Bunter was holding out the ten-pound note. But there were no takers. He blinked impatiently at staring faces.

" Look here, are you going to get this changed for me? " he demanded. " I'm going to stand a spread in this study when it's changed. Mauly would change it for you, Wharton, if you asked him. He won't for me. What about it? "

" Where did you get it? "

" Haven't I told you? " hooted Bunter. " It's a pip from my tater—I mean, a tip from my pater. Tenners ain't so jolly scarce at Bunter Court as they are at Wharton Lodge, I can tell you."

" And how did it get here from your pater? "

" Eh! In a letter, of course. Think it walked? "

" And when did the letter come? "

" I got it in the rack this morning, of course ——."

" You never had a letter this morning."

" Eh? "

" You nosed over the rack as usual, and asked

Bob to look, to make sure, and there was no letter
for you."

"Oh!" stammered Bunter. "I—I mean——."

Billy Bunter belonged to the class that should,
proverbially, have good memories. But Bunter
had a bad one!

"Well, what do you mean?"

"I—I mean, now I come to think of it, it wasn't
in the rack this morning. You see, it was a—a
registered letter. The pater's careful with tenners
—of course, he registered the letter. See?"

"So you had a registered letter?"

"That's it, old chap! Now you take this tenner
to Mauly——."

"Did Quelch hand it to you?"

"Yes, of—of course. He sent for me to his
study, you know, and said, 'Here's a registered
letter for you, Bunter!' Those very words."

"You've still got the registered envelope?"

"Eh! Yes! No! I chucked it into the waste-
paper basket in my study. What's the good of the
envelope?"

"All clear, then," said Harry. "I'll cut along
to No. 7 and get that registered envelope out of
the waste-paper basket, and that will settle it."

"Oh!" gasped Bunter. "I—I—I mean—the—
the fact is——." Bunter paused, evidently cudgel-
ling his fat brain for a fact that would do.

"Go it!" said Bob. "Let's have the fact!
Facts from Bunter are worth hearing—we don't
get many."

"I mean, I didn't chuck it into the waste-
paper basket in my study," explained Bunter.
"What I meant was, that I should have chucked
it into the waste-paper basket if I'd been in
my study. Only I—I wasn't, see?"

"Oh, crumbs!" said Bob.

" I was in the Rag, I remember now. I chucked the envelope into the fire."

" There wasn't a fire in the Rag to-day."

" I—I mean, into the grate. You keep on taking a fellow up."

" Then it's still there," said Bob. " We'll rouse it out of the grate in the Rag instead of the waste-paper basket in No. 7."

" Oh! I—I mean, I—I chucked it out of the window," gasped Bunter. " That's what I really meant to say."

" We're getting it clear," said Bob. " When Bunter says the fire, he means the grate, and when he says the grate, he means the window. One of us had better cut down and pick up that jolly old registered envelope that's lying around under the Rag window."

" It—it blew away!" gasped Bunter. " There was a—a sudden gust of—of wind, and it—it blew right away! I—I don't think you fellows could find it."

" Bank on that!" said Johnny Bull.

" The bankfulness is terrific."

" Well, now I've told you all about it, are you going to take this banknote to Mauly and get it changed, Wharton?"

" I think you'd better tell us a little more first," said the captain of the Remove. " You fat fraud, you never had a registered letter."

" Oh, really, Wharton! I hope you can take my word."

" I can take Quelchy's, at any rate. Do you mind if I ask Quelch whether you had a registered letter to-day?"

Billy Bunter's plump jaw dropped.

" Oh, crikey! Don't you go saying anything to Quelch!" he stuttered. " I—I say, now I—I come to think of it, it wasn't a registered letter."

" What? " yelled the Famous Five, all together.

" Not—not exactly a registered letter," stammered Bunter. " The—the posts are so slow now, you know, the—the pater decided to send it by— by messenger. That's how it was."

" Great pip! "

" So—so Quelch doesn't know anything about it," explained Bunter. " It's no good asking Quelch anything, as—as he doesn't know."

" I'll ask Gosling instead," said Harry.

" Gig-gog-Gosling? " stuttered Bunter.

" Yes. Gosling must have let the messenger in."

" Oh! " gasped Bunter.

His fat face was a study.

" Try again! " said Bob Cherry, encouragingly. " You can see for yourself that the messenger won't wash. Have another go! "

" Ha, ha, ha! "

" Look here, you fellows, if you don't believe me——! "

" Oh, crumbs! "

" I wonder if that chap could tell the truth if he tried! " said Johnny Bull, staring at the fat Owl.

" Goodness knows! It's not on record that he's ever tried," said Bob.

" Look here," roared Bunter. " Are you going to get this banknote changed for me, Wharton? "

" Not unless I know where it came from."

" I've told you," howled Bunter. " And if you can't take a fellow's word you can go and eat coke, so yah! "

Bunter revolved in the doorway.

" Hold on, you fat ass! " exclaimed Harry Wharton.

Bunter blinked round again. He grinned.

" You're going to take it to Mauly? " he asked. " He, he, he! I rather thought you'd come round as I'm going to stand a spread in the study. Now just get on with it, and not so much jaw. You fellows are like a sheep's head—all jaw! You needn't tell Mauly it's my banknote, as he's a suspicious beast—you can tell him your uncle sent it to you——."

"Oh!" gasped Wharton. "Can I?"

"Well, that might be best," said Bunter. "Still, tell him anything you like—I don't mind what you tell him, so long as you get it changed. That's the point really—get it changed—it doesn't matter much what you tell Mauly, so long as he shells out the change."

"Slaughter him," said Johnny Bull.

"Oh, really, Bull——."

"You fat chump!" roared Wharton. "I'm not taking that banknote to Mauly! You're taking it to Quelch!"

"I'll watch it!"

"Can't you understand, you blithering bandersnatch, that it will soon be all over the school that you've got a tenner, and that everybody will know where you got it!"

"I don't mind——."

"What?"

"It's mine, ain't it?"

"Oh, suffering cats and crocodiles!" exclaimed Bob Cherry. "It's no good talking to him. What about bagging that tenner and taking it to Quelch ourselves?"

"Good!" said Johnny Bull. "Let's!"

"Why, you cheeky beast!" gasped Bunter.

He flew.

The study door banged behind Bunter and his banknote.

Chapter XXXV

NO TAKERS !

" BEEN to Quelch with that tenner? "

"Beast!"

Peter Todd asked the question: Bunter made the reply.

Billy Bunter was peeved.

His position was, indeed, enough to peeve anyone. Generally the most impecunious fellow at Greyfriars School, hoping against hope for the arrival of a postal-order that never seemed to materialise, Bunter was now in possession of a tenner—such a sum as was seldom seen in the Lower Fourth. And for all the use it was to him, he might as well have been tenner-less. Not a man in the Remove would have given him so much as a threepenny-bit for that tenner!

The amount of tuck that could be obtained for a tenner, even in times of dearth, dazzled Bunter. The mere thought made his capacious mouth water. But that tenner seemed as unchangeable as the laws of the Medes and Persians.

After his rapid exodus from No. 1 Study, the fat Owl, with a frowning brow, pondered over that peculiar position. He wanted his tea. He had had tea in Hall—provisionally, as it were, to make sure of something to go on with. Now he was ready—more than ready—for tea in a study. There was nothing doing in No. 7, his own study. Peter Todd was teaing with the Bounder, Dutton with Squiff in No. 14. When Toddy and Dutton tea'd out, they seemed to forget that Bunter wanted his

tea, with the selfishness to which Bunter was so
sadly accustomed.

Bunter rolled along to No. 4 at last, where he
found Peter at tea with Smithy and Tom Redwing.
The three juniors looked at him as he blinked in—
Tom Redwing very grave, the Bounder with a
cynical grin, and Peter Todd with a question to
which Bunter could only reply " Beast."

" You've still got it? " asked Smithy.

" Yes, old chap. I say, Smithy, I owe you five
bob. I—I've come here to settle up—I'm not the
fellow to owe money, as you know."

" Ye gods! " said Peter.

" You can dry up, Toddy. If you can give me
nine pounds fifteen change, Smithy——."

" Ha, ha, ha! " roared the Bounder.

" Blessed if I see anything to cackle at! Don't
you want me to square that five bob you lent me? "

" Not particularly! I shouldn't have lent it to
you if I did."

" Oh, really, Smithy——."

" You ass, Bunter," said Redwing. " For goodness' sake, stop trying to change that banknote,
and take it where it belongs."

" Think it doesn't belong to me? " hooted
Bunter.

" Every man in the Remove knows that it
doesn't," said Peter Todd. " Where did you get
it, if it does? "

" I told you my pater had been a bear, and
——."

" Your pater may have been a bear, or a bull,
or a wolf, or a rhinoceros, but that tenner never
came from your pater. Chuck it."

Billy Bunter paused. Bunter was not bright:
but he was bright enough to realise that it was useless to tell over again the story of the letter, the
registered letter, or the special messenger. They

hadn't believed him in No. 1 Study, and they wouldn't in No. 4. But he was not at the end of his resources.

" Well, it wasn't exactly from my pater, Toddy,'' he said. " I don't mind telling a pal like you where I got this banknote. You know I've got a rich uncle at Folkestone——.''

" I know you've said so."

" Beast! I mean, that's how it was, old chap. It never came in a letter—my Uncle William gave it to me."

" You've had a trip to Folkestone since class? " grinned the Bounder.

" Oh! No! I—I met my Uncle George——.''

" As well as your Uncle William? "

" I—I mean my Uncle William. I—I was taking a walk after class, and all of a sudden, who should I see but my Uncle George—I mean William— coming along the road from Courtfield. He—he was coming to see me, but—but as he met me on the road, he didn't come here after all—see? He said, ' Hallo, is that you, Billy? I've got a tenner for you.' Those very words."

" Oh, my only hat and umbrella! " said Peter Todd.

" It was quite simple," explained Bunter. " My uncle tipped me this tenner. A tenner's nothing to my Uncle George. He's rich."

" As rich as your Uncle William? " asked the Bounder.

" Eh? Yes—I—I mean my Uncle William. A tenner's a trifle to him, Toddy. I've told you often enough that my uncle's rolling in money."

" Too often! " agreed Peter.

" He gave me this tenner, just as your uncle might give you a bob," said Bunter. " He's got lots. My people ain't poor like yours, old chap. Why, I can jolly well tell you that Uncle Samuel had a dozen more like this in his pocket-book when he gave me this one."

"Uncle which?" gasped Peter.

"I mean George—that is, William! How you keep on taking a fellow up," said Bunter, peevishly. "Think my uncle didn't give me this tenner? Think a perfect stranger would come up to me and give me a tenner?"

"Hardly!" grinned Peter.

"Well, then, it was my uncle," said Bunter. "I shouldn't accept a tip from a man I didn't know, of course. Not Greyfriars style. Besides, who'd believe a chap who said that a perfect stranger gave him a tenner for nothing? You wouldn't believe it, Toddy."

"Well, it's not the sort of thing that often happens, is it?" chuckled Toddy. "It would want some believing. Better stick to the uncle, so far as that goes."

"Only the uncle's like Bunter himself," remarked the Bounder. "He won't wash!"

"Ha, ha, ha!"

"Oh, really, Smithy! Look here, will you change this tenner for me, now I've told you all about it?"

"There's one thing you haven't told us yet."

"What's that?"

"Where you got it."

"You silly ass!" roared Bunter. "Haven't I just told you that my Uncle George—I mean Samuel—tipped me this tenner when I met him in Friardale Lane, taking a walk after class?"

"You met him twice?"

"Eh! No! Only once—wharrer you mean?"

"Well, a few minutes ago you met him on the Courtfield Road. Now you've met him in Friardale Lane. Was he in two places at once?"

"I—I—I mean, I—I met him in Courtfield

Lane—I mean Friardale Road—I—I mean, I—I forget exactly where it was—what does it matter, anyhow, as I've got the tenner?" snapped Bunter. "You change it for me, and I'll square that five bob out of it."

"You dithering chump," said Vernon-Smith. "The beaks will hear about this soon. Quelch will want to know. Are you going to tell Quelch, when he asks you, that your Uncle George-William-Samuel tipped you that tenner when you met him in two places at once? Think that would do for Quelch?"

"Beast!"

"Look here, I'll lend you half-a-crown, if you'll take that banknote to Quelch and hand it over," said Smithy.

"Do that at once, Bunter," urged Redwing.

"That's your best guess, old fat man," said Peter.

"Rot!" said Bunter. "Quelch wouldn't change it for me, would he?"

"Oh, scissors! Not likely."

"He wouldn't even let me keep it," argued Bunter. "We ain't allowed to have so much, if the beaks know. Besides, would Quelch believe me if I told him where I got it?" Bunter shook his head, "It's a bit unusual, you know, and Quelch has doubted my word before this."

"Take the whole packet to Quelch, you fathead."

"Eh! What packet?"

"Oh, gad!" said the Bounder. "Have you forgotten already that you snooped that banknote from the packet you've found?"

"I haven't found any packet," howled Bunter. "I tell you my pater—I—I mean my Uncle Samuel—that is, my Uncle Peter—I—I mean

Uncle William—tipped me this tenner. Look here, Smithy, if you won't change it for me——."

"No 'if' about that!"

"I'm stony till I get this banknote changed. I haven't even had my tea yet—only tea in Hall," said Bunter, pathetically.

"You can squat down here to tea——."

"Oh, good!"

"——if you take that banknote to Quelch first."

"Beast! I—I mean, I'll tea with you, Smithy, and we—we'll talk it over," said Bunter.

"We won't," said the Bounder. "Look here, are you taking that banknote to Quelch, or not?"

"No!" roared Bunter.

"Then travel!"

"I say, Smithy, old chap——."

"Hand me that cricket-bat, Toddy!"

"Beast!"

Billy Bunter travelled without waiting for the cricket-bat. The door of No. 4, like that of No. 1, banged behind Bunter and his banknote. Once more the worried fat Owl pondered in the Remove passage: then he headed for No. 12 Study. Twice had Lord Mauleverer refused to touch that tenner: but the Owl of the Remove hoped that it might be "third time lucky."

He blinked into No. 12, where Lord Mauleverer, stretched elegantly on his study sofa, was taking a rest after tea.

Mauly's noble countenance wore its usual placid and cheerful expression. But it looked less cheerful when he saw Bunter. He waved a hand, as if waving away a troublesome bluebottle.

But Billy Bunter was not to be waved away like a bluebottle. He rolled in.

"I say, Mauly, old chap——."

"Oh, dear!" groaned Mauly.

Bunter blinked at him, puzzled.

" I say, what's up, Mauly? You were looking as jolly as anything a minute ago—now you look as if life wasn't worth living. What's the matter? "

" You! "

" Oh! You silly ass! " howled Bunter. " Look here, don't be a goat, Mauly! I only want you to change this tenner for me."

Lord Mauleverer did not reply in words. He rose from the sofa, took Billy Bunter by a fat ear, and by that ear led him out of the study. Bunter went—squeaking. Having landed him in the passage, Mauleverer went back into the study and closed the door.

Billy Bunter rubbed a fat ear and breathed wrath. Third time was not lucky—Mauly, evidently, wasn't going to change that tenner.

" Beast! " yelled Bunter through the keyhole.

Then he rolled dismally down the Remove passage. With ten pounds burning a hole in his pocket, he was still stony—tea as far off as ever. On the Remove landing he encountered Squiff, and paused.

" I say, Field, old fellow———."

" Pack it up! " said the Australian junior, with a chuckle. " I've no use for the Head's tenners, Bunter."

" 'Tain't the Head's," howled Bunter, " it's mine."

" Well, they say possession is nine points of the law," assented Squiff. " But what about the other tenth, old fat man? "

" Look here, if I ask Mrs. Mimble to change it at the tuck-shop, think she'd mention it to Quelch? " asked Bunter.

" Of course she would. She'd have to," answered Squiff. " Look here, Bunter, everybody knows where you got that tenner. Take it to Quelch."

" Yah ! "

Billy Bunter rolled on—his tenner still unchanged. And it remained unchanged. It was really an extraordinary state of affairs, for a whole ten-pound note to be going begging, and finding no takers. But so it was—and when the Remove went to their dormitory that night, Billy Bunter's banknote was still in the state of the Medic and Persian laws—unchanged and unchangeable.

Chapter XXXVI

COKER TAKES A HAND !

" THIS won't do!" said Coker.

Coker of the Fifth spoke with emphasis. He generally did. Being a fellow who knew, and having no use for adverse opinions or arguments, Horace Coker naturally adopted a tone of finality.

His pals, Potter and Greene, didn't ask him what it was that wouldn't do. They didn't want to know. When Coker was talking, his friends were interested in only one question—which was, when would Coker leave off talking?

It was in break the following morning. Coker and Co. were in the quad—Potter and Greene surreptitiously trying to steer Coker in the direction of the tuck-shop. As a conversationalist, Coker had little charm: but as a fellow whose Aunt Judy kept him liberally supplied with pocket-money, he was a useful acquaintance.

But Coker was not to be steered. Potter and Greene might be thinking of elevenses, but Coker had other matters on his mind.

" Look at him!" said Coker, with a nod in the direction of a fat figure and a fat face adorned with a big pair of spectacles.

Potter and Greene saw no reason whatever for looking at Billy Bunter. He was no ornament to the landscape. He did not improve the view. But it seemed that Horace James Coker was interested in the Owl of the Remove.

Bunter, too, seemed interested in Coker. From a little distance, he was blinking at the great man of the Fifth, dubiously.

As a matter of fact, Bunter was debating in his fat mind whether he would ask Coker of the Fifth to change that unchangeable tenner. Coker had plenty of money—that was all right. On the other hand, Coker was the most " Fifth Formy " man in the Fifth and quite likely to kick a junior who had the cheek to come up and speak to him in the quad. So it was rather a problem.

" Look at him! " repeated Coker. " It's going all round the school that Bunter's found the packet of banknotes that was snooped from the Head's study. Everybody knows it. Except the beaks! " added Coker, with sarcasm. " They don't—of course! They never know anything. That young villain has found the packet and helped himself from it. He's been trotting a ten-pound note all over the shop trying to get it changed."

" Young ass! " said Potter. " They'll bunk him for it."

" Well, it won't do," said Coker. " That sort of thing isn't good enough for Greyfriars. Bunter's going to hand that tenner over where it belongs."

" He'll have to, when a pre spots him," said Greene.

" Do the pre's ever spot anything? " said Coker, disdainfully. " From what I hear, Bunter found the banknotes after class yesterday, and he's been hawking that tenner about the school ever since. I'm going to stop him."

" No business of ours," suggested Potter.

" Don't be an ass, Potter.'

" But——! " began Greene.

" Don't be a chump, Greene."

Having thus disposed of argument, Horace Coker lifted his hand, and beckoned to Bunter. Any other Remove man, on beholding that beckoning hand, would probably have stared at Coker and walked off in another direction. Not so

Bunter! Billy Bunter was only too glad of the chance to speak to Horace. This was the opening he wanted. Bunter rolled up promptly.

" I say, Coker, old chap," he began, eagerly.

Coker stared at him.

" Did you call me old chap? " he asked.

" Eh? Yes! I——."

" Well, don't, if you don't want to be kicked across the quad and back again." " Old chap " from a Lower Fourth junior was rather too much for Coker of the Fifth to tolerate.

" Oh, really, Coker——."

" I hear you've been trying to change a ten-pound note," said Coker.

" Yes, old chap—I—I mean old fellow—that is, yes, Coker. I say, will you change it for me? "

" No," said Coker, " I won't change it for you, Bunter. I'm jolly well going to see that nobody else does, either. That tenner isn't yours. You got it out of that lost packet."

" I didn't! " yelled Bunter.

" It's not much use saying you didn't when everybody knows you did. You're going to hand over that tenner at once, and I'm going to see that you do it," said Coker, impressively. " I'm going with you now to your form-master, and I'm going to see you hand it over."

Billy Bunter blinked at him, his eyes almost popping through his spectacles, in wrath and alarm.

" Why, you—you beast! " he gasped. " I'm not going to Quelch, and you jolly well ain't going to make me. Mind your own business, see? Can't you mind your own business, Coker? "

That was a superfluous question. It was really common knowledge that Coker couldn't mind his own business. Coker did not deign to answer such a frivolous question. He dropped a large and heavy hand on a fat shoulder.

"Leggo!" roared Bunter.

"Budge!" snorted Coker, pulling at the fat shoulder.

"Shan't!" yelled Bunter. "Leggo! Beast! Rescue! I say, you fellows, rescue! I say—yaroooh! Leggo, you swob! Yow-ow-ow! Rescue!"

"Hallo, hallo, hallo, what's the row?" Bob Cherry came up at a run, followed by his friends, at the sight of a Remove man wriggling and yelling in the grasp of Coker of the Fifth.

"Chuck that, Coker!" rapped Harry Wharton.

Coker gave the Famous Five a glare.

"Get out of the way!" he snapped. "Here, Potter, Greene—kick those fags out of the way! Come on, Bunter, you little fat scoundrel."

"Leggo!" yelled Bunter. "I say, you fellows, make him leggo!"

"We'll make him let go fast enough," growled Johnny Bull. "Go it, you men—up-end that Fifth Form fathead."

"Clear off!" roared Coker. "Potter—Greene—clear those fags off."

Harry Wharton and Co. surrounded Coker. Coker held on to Bunter's fat shoulder. Potter and Greene exchanged a glance, and faded out of the picture. If Horace Coker chose to mix up in a shindy with a mob of juniors in the quad, Coker was welcome to get on with it, on his own. Potter and Greene did not want any. They disappeared.

Billy Bunter wriggled in one large hand—Horace Coker swayed and staggered in ten smaller but quite energetic hands. All the Famous Five grasped Coker, to drag him away from Bunter. But Coker held on.

"You cheeky little ticks, get out!" he gasped.

" I'm taking Bunter to your beak, to hand over that tenner——."

" No business of yours," answered Bob. " Chuck it—before we chuck you."

" Up-end him ! " growled Johnny Bull.

" The up-endfulness is the proper caper ! " gasped Hurree Jamset Ram Singh. " Now, all togetherfully ! "

" Whooop ! " roared Coker, as he went. There was a heavy bump, as Coker of the Fifth landed on the cold, unsympathetic quad. But he still held on to Bunter, and the fat Owl sprawled, roaring, over Coker's long legs.

Coker struggled. Coker was big and brawny. Even Sixth Form men treated Coker with tact. One or two or three of the juniors Coker could have scattered before him like chaff before the wind. But the five of them were too many for Coker. They rolled him over, and Coker, at last, had to let go his grip on the Owl of the Remove. Bunter, winded, sat and spluttered frantically for breath : Coker, in a foaming state, rolled and roared.

" 'Ware pre's ! " called out Vernon-Smith.

" Here comes Wingate ! " gasped Bob. " Chuck it ! "

And the Famous Five ceased to roll Coker as the Greyfriars captain came striding on the scene.

Chapter XXXVII

BUNTER'S LATEST !

WINGATE of the Sixth stared at five crimson and breathless juniors, at a fat Owl gurgling for breath and at Horace Coker, sprawling and spluttering. Fifty fellows at least gathered round to look on. Wingate frowned.

"Well, what's all this about?" he rapped.

"Urrrgh!" Coker sat up. "I'll smash 'em! Gurrggh! I'll spiflicate 'em! I'—I'll—goooorrggh!"

Coker staggered to his feet. He was wildly dishevelled. His collar hung by a single stud—his tie was at the back of his neck—his hair was like a mop. His rugged face was crimson. He gave the Famous Five a glare. Only the presence of a prefect restrained him from charging.

"What are you ragging Coker for, you young ruffians?" demanded Wingate.

"Not exactly ragging him, Wingate," said Bob. "Only trying to persuade him to mind his own business."

"Ooogh! I say, you fellows, gimme a hand up!" gasped Bunter. "I'm all—groogh—out of breath—oooogh!"

Bob gave the fat Owl a hand up.

"Well, chuck it," said Wingate, "or you'll get six all round. You chuck it too, Coker—you're a Fifth Form man: you ought to have more sense than to rag with juniors in the quad."

"Who's ragging with juniors in the quad?" bawled Coker. "I'm jolly well going to take Bunter to his beak, and those cheeky little swobs aren't going to stop me."

" I'M GOING TO MAKE HIM HAND OVER THAT TENNER! "

" I say, you fellows, keep him off——."

" I'm going to make him hand over that tenner!" vociferated Coker. " See? Everybody knows where he got it, and I'm going to make him cough it up."

" Oh, crikey!" gasped Bunter. He was breathless, but he got into motion. Bunter did not want to discuss that tenner with a Sixth Form prefect. But it was too late.

" Stop!" rapped Wingate.

" Oh, really, Wingate! I—I've got to see Quelch before class——."

" Stop where you are! Now, what's this about a tenner?" asked the Greyfriars captain. " Have you got a tenner?"

" Oh! Yes! I—I mean—no—yes!" stuttered Bunter.

" Everybody knows he's got it, and everybody knows where he got it," snorted Coker. " He's found the packet, and pinched it. And I'm jolly well going to take him to his beak, and——."

" You're going to mind your own business, Coker," said Wingate. " You can leave this to me. Now, Bunter——."

" I—I've got to go to the Head, Wingate——."

" That will do. If you've got a ten-pound note, where did you get it? Lower boys are not allowed to have so much money as that, as you know very well, and your form-master must be told about it. But where did it come from?"

Billy Bunter blinked at the Greyfriars captain. The crowd of fellows gathered round the spot exchanged glances, some of them grinning. There was no choice for Bunter now—he had to explain about that banknote. A prefect was not to be denied. And—interfering ass as Coker of the Fifth was—everyone agreed with Coker's view of the matter—the only possible explanation was that

Bunter had found the "hidden treasure" and helped himself. Where else could the impecunious Owl of the Remove have obtained a tenner? The fibs he had told on the subject, and his obvious unwillingness to answer Wingate, would have banished all doubt, had there been any doubt.

"Well?" rapped Wingate.

"I—I—I——!" stammered Bunter.

Wingate's face grew grimmer. With a packet of banknotes missing, and Bunter in sudden and inexplicable possession of a banknote, the thing really seemed to speak for itself.

"Have you found that packet missing from the Head's study, Bunter?" he rapped.

"Oh! No!" gasped Bunter. "I—I looked for it, Wingate, but I—I couldn't find it. I—I don't know where it is."

"You fat ass," whispered Bob Cherry. "You've got to own up now."

"Oh, really, Cherry——."

"Tell the truth, you awful chump!" hissed Peter Todd.

"Oh, really, Toddy——."

"I'm waiting, Bunter!" said Wingate. "If you haven't found the packet, where did you get a ten-pound note?"

"I—I—I——!" Bunter spluttered helplessly. Even Bunter realised, after his experience with the doubting Thomases in the Remove, that it was no use "telling the tale" to Wingate, as he had told it in his own form. But he was plainly reluctant to state where that banknote had come from. "I—I—it's mine, Wingate."

"Where did you get it?" rapped Wingate, so sharply that Bunter jumped.

"I—I—I—a—a—a man gave it to me!" gasped Bunter.

"What?" almost roared the Greyfriars captain.

"A—a—a man!" gasped Bunter. "He—he came up to me, and—and gave me the tenner, Wingate."

"Great pip!" said the Bounder. "Can you beat that?"

"Bunter, you ass——!" said Bob.

"Bunter, you chump——!" said Harry Wharton.

"I say, you fellows, it's true! I jolly well knew you wouldn't believe it, but it's true!" gasped Bunter.

"True!" murmured Skinner. "Oh, my Aunt Jemima!"

"Ha, ha, ha!"

"That's rich, even from Bunter!" remarked Johnny Bull.

"The richfulness is terrific."

Wingate was staring blankly at the fat Owl. Bunter's remarkable statement seemed to have taken his breath away. Had Bunter told a tale of a tip from his pater, or from his Uncle George or Uncle William, credence might have been at least possible. But a statement that a man had come up to him and given him a ten-pound note was altogether too incredible.

"Has that young ass gone crackers, or what?" said Wingate at last.

"Oh, really, Wingate——."

"Where did you get that banknote?"

"I've told you," groaned Bunter. "That man gave it to me——."

"What man?"

"I—I don't know!"

"You don't know what man gave you a ten-pound note!" stuttered Wingate.

"I—I mean, I'd never seen him before."

"A man you'd never seen before gave you ten pounds?"

"Yes."

"Oh, suffering cats!" murmured Bob Cherry.

The crowd of Greyfriars fellows stared at Bunter. No doubt, had some beneficent stranger presented Bunter with an unexpected tenner, the fat Owl would have preferred to let it be understood in the Remove that he came from some rich relation, which would have accounted for the mixed bag of explanations he had given in the studies. Truth and Bunter had long been strangers: and swank was numbered among Bunter's charming qualities. But nobody, of course, believed for a moment that any beneficent stranger had done anything of the kind. Bunter had said that he knew they wouldn't believe it. He was right! They didn't!

"And where did this happen, and when, Bunter?" asked the Greyfriars captain, staring at the fat Owl in sheer wonder.

"It—it was yesterday afternoon, Wingate. I—I went out after class to look for that packet——"

"And found it!" roared Coker.

"I never found it!" roared back Bunter.

"Shut up, will you, Coker?" exclaimed Wingate, impatiently. "Get on with it, Bunter."

"Well, I couldn't find the packet," said Bunter, "and I got tired, and sat on the Cloister wall. And a man came up in the lane beside the Cloisters and said, 'Is that Mr. Bunter?' So I said, 'Yes,' and he said, 'This ten-pound note is for you.' And —and he gave it to me and—and walked away."

"I can sort of see him doing it!" murmured Skinner.

"Ha, ha, ha!"

"Better have stuck to Uncle William-George-Samuel," remarked the Bounder. "Even that would go down better than this."

" You didn't know the man, Bunter? " asked Wingate.

" I—I'd never seen him before."

" Why did a man you'd never seen before give you ten pounds? "

" I—I don't know."

" Well, I think this beats everything," said Wingate. " Do you think that anybody could possibly believe that, Bunter? "

" I—I know it sounds a bit unusual," stammered Bunter. " I—I rather thought the fellows wouldn't believe it. So—so I never told them."

" A bit unusual! " said Skinner. " Only a bit? "

" Ha, ha, ha! "

" Are you going to spin that yarn to Mr. Quelch? " asked Wingate.

" I—I'd rather not mention it to Quelch! I—I think he mightn't believe it," mumbled Bunter. " He—he might think I'd made it up."

" The mightfulness is terrific."

" Yes, I think he might! " said Wingate, drily. " I advise you, Bunter, when you see your form-master, to tell him the truth. I'm going to report this to your form-master at once, and he will deal with you. And if you've got a spot of sense, you young ass, you'll tell Quelch the truth when he questions you."

" I—I've told the truth, Wingate——."

" That will do! "

Wingate walked away to the House, evidently to make his report to the Remove master without loss of time. Harry Wharton and Co. gathered round Bunter. They were quite alarmed for him. The yarns Bunter had already told about that banknote seemed to the Famous Five as moonlight unto sunlight, as water unto wine, compared with the yarn he had spun Wingate. That really was the limit. The effect of such a yarn on Mr. Quelch was almost unthinkable.

"Bunter, old fat idiot," said Bob, "for goodness' sake cut in at once and hand that tenner to Quelch ——."

"Don't lose a moment, Bunter," urged Harry Wharton.

"Go to it," said Frank Nugent. "Look here, Bunter, we all know what a howling ass you are, and you fancy somehow you've only borrowed that tenner from the packet, but a beak will call it pinching——."

"It's the sack!" said Johnny Bull.

"For the love of esteemed Mike, cut off to Quelch before badfulness becomes worsefulness," urged Hurree Jamset Ram Singh.

"I say, you fellows, don't you believe me?" asked Bunter.

"Believe you! Oh, scissors!"

"I say, that man really gave me the tenner ——."

"He did, did he?" snorted Johnny Bull. "Was that before it came in a registered letter from your pater, or after it came by special messenger?"

"Or was it about the time you met your uncle on the Courtfield Road, and he tipped you a tenner in Friardale Lane?" asked the Bounder.

"Ha, ha, ha!"

"Beast!"

Bunter rolled away. But he did not roll in the direction of Mr. Quelch's study. Friendly counsel seemed a sheer waste on Bunter: and the Removites could only wonder what was going to happen to him when he saw Quelch. There was a thrill of excitement when the bell clanged for third school, and the Remove went to their form-room.

Chapter XXXVIII

WITNESS WANTED !

" HENRY looks grim!" murmured Bob Cherry.

Bob was careful not to let " Henry " hear that murmur.

There was no doubt that Henry Samuel Quelch looked grim, as he rustled to the door of the Remove room to let in his form for third school. Quelch's severe countenance was a little inclined to grimness, anyway. But now it did indubitably look uncommonly grim.

Everybody, of course, knew why. Quelch had heard Wingate's report: and knew, accordingly, that a member of his form had found the missing packet, and helped himself from the contents. That was more than enough to make Mr. Quelch look his very grimmest. Quelch was hardly likely to believe that a man Bunter had never seen before had given him ten pounds for nothing. Such a tale would have taxed his credulity had it come from the member of his form whom he trusted most. And the fat Owl was the member he trusted least!

The Remove fellows filed to their places in suppressed excitement. They knew that the thunder was going to roll before the lesson began. Peter Todd gave his fat study-mate a final whisper of warning as he went to his desk.

" Own up, you fat ass!"

" Beast!"

" Tell Quelch where you found the packet."

" I never found it."

" You benighted chump——!"

" Yah!"

Peter gave it up. Bunter, it seemed, was not to be saved from himself! He was going to repeat his " latest " to Quelch, if Quelch inquired. It was plain that Quelch was going to inquire.

Quelch's eyes fixed on Bunter. Never had they seemed so much like gimlets. They almost bored into the fat junior.

" Bunter! " said Mr. Quelch, in a deep voice.

" Yes, sir! " mumbled Bunter.

" I have heard a most extraordinary report from a prefect—Wingate of the Sixth Form!" said Mr. Quelch. " It appears, Bunter, that you are in possession of a Bank of England note for the sum of ten pounds."

" Oh! Yes, sir! " groaned Bunter. " It—it—it's mine, sir."

" You are aware, Bunter, that a packet is supposed to be hidden somewhere about the school containing a number of notes purloined from the head-master's study, among them ten-pound notes? "

" I—I've heard so, sir! " stammered Bunter.

" You have, I believe, joined with other boys in searching for that packet of banknotes, Bunter."

" Oh! Yes, sir! I—I thought the Head might like me to find it for him, sir, if—if I could."

" Have you found it, Bunter? "

Peter Todd gave the fat Owl an almost beseeching look. Bunter did not add to the joy of existence in No. 7 Study. He was neither useful nor ornamental. Still, Peter did not want to see him sacked. But the Owl of the Remove did not heed that beseeching look. His answer came:

" No, sir! "

" You have not found the packet, Bunter? " asked Mr. Quelch.

" N-no, sir."

" Very well," said the Remove master. " You

will now explain to me how a banknote for ten pounds came into your possession, Bunter."

"It—it's mine, sir," groaned Bunter.

"I trust so," said Mr. Quelch. "If the banknote is yours, Bunter, as I trust, I shall communicate with the relative who sent it to you and explain that junior boys at this school are not permitted to have such large sums of money. Was it a relative who sent you this banknote, Bunter?"

Bunter did not reply at once.

All eyes were on his fat face. As plainly as if he had told them, the Remove fellows could see that he was debating in his fat mind whether a story of a tip from his pater, or a tip from his uncle, would be good enough for Quelch. But it was obvious, even to Bunter, that if he named a relative Quelch would inquire of that relative. And Quelch gave him no time for thinking out new inventions.

"Answer me, Bunter!" he rapped.

"It—it—it wasn't a relative," stammered Bunter.

"Then who was it?"

"A—a—a man, sir!" faltered Bunter.

Mr. Quelch held up his hand.

"Wingate has informed me, Bunter, that you told him that a man with whom you were unacquainted gave you that banknote yesterday, for nothing, and without explanation. Is that what you are about to tell me?"

"Yes, sir!" gasped Bunter.

"Then you need say nothing," said Mr. Quelch. "Bunter, I shall take you to your head-master after third hour, and the matter will pass into Dr. Locke's hands. We shall now commence."

And the Remove commenced: the subject dropping there and then. Which was a sufficient indication of what Mr. Quelch thought of the story of a beneficent stranger with tenners to give away.

Third hour was not a happy hour for Billy Bunter. His fat face was worried and lugubrious. Benevolent old gentleman as Dr. Locke undoubtedly was, no fellow really liked being taken to his study to see him—Bunter least of all. The prospect of that interview with his head-master seemed to weigh on Bunter. He gave no attention whatever to the lesson—he couldn't! But Mr. Quelch considerately passed him over. Perhaps he thought that Bunter had enough coming to him!

Quelch did not, in fact, take any further notice of Billy Bunter's fat existence till the hour of dismissal came. Then he rapped out:

" Bunter! "

" Yes, sir! " groaned Bunter.

" You will wait in the corridor. When I leave this form-room I shall take you to Dr. Locke."

" Oh, lor! "

Bunter rolled dismally into the corridor, leaving Mr. Quelch with papers at his desk. He had to wait in the corridor for Quelch—and then go to the Head—and if he had been going to execution he could hardly have looked more dismal.

Some of the juniors remained with him in the corridor. There was, so far as they could see, only one chance for Bunter: to own up to the truth without telling any more fibs. Matters were bad enough: but obviously, if anything could save Bunter now, it was the truth, the whole truth, and nothing but the truth.

" Bunter, old man," said Harry Wharton, quite gently, " do try to have a little sense——."

" Yah! If you had as much sense in your head, Wharton, as I've got in my little finger, you'd be twice as clever as you are! " yapped Bunter.

" Oh! Well, never mind that," said Harry. " You can see that you're up against it, Bunter.

Tell the Head the truth about that packet and he may go easy with you."

"It's your only chance," urged Frank Nugent.

"I'm going to, of course," said Bunter. "If you fellows are trying to make out that I don't tell the truth——."

"Oh, fan me!" murmured Bob Cherry.

"But very likely the Head won't believe it," said Bunter. "That's what worries me. He may think my banknote came from his packet. See?"

"What else can he think?" gasped Bob.

"Well, it's pretty thick," said Bunter. "Wingate didn't believe me—I could see that! You fellows don't either. You needn't deny it—you jolly well don't."

"Ain't he a cough-drop?" said Bob Cherry. "He's told us that that tenner came in a letter, then in a registered letter, then by special messenger, and then he told Smithy that his Uncle William gave it to him on the Courtfield road, and his Uncle George in Friardale Lane—and then he puts the lid on with a stranger coming up and giving it to him for nothing! Which of the lot do you want us to believe, Bunter?"

"You pays your money and you takes your choice!" remarked the Bounder.

"I—I say, you fellows." Bunter cast an uneasy blink towards the form-room door, but Mr. Quelch had not emerged yet. "I—I say, you stand by a fellow, and back me up. Wharton, old chap, we've always been pals, haven't we? Look here, you're Quelch's Head Boy, and he always takes your word. I don't know why—he hardly ever takes mine. Still, he does take yours, and if you say you saw that man give me the tenner when I was sitting on the Cloister wall——."

"Wha-a-a-t?" stuttered the captain of the Remove.

" I'll do as much for you another time, old chap!" said Bunter, eagerly. " You just tell Quelch you saw the whole thing——."

" But I didn't!" shrieked Wharton.

" I wish you'd keep to the point, Wharton, when Quelch may come out any minute and take me to the Beak," said Bunter, peevishly. " That's the worst of you fellows—you never can keep to the point. You just say you saw——."

" You fat villain!"

" Oh, really, Wharton! Look here, it's only necessary for you to saw you say—I mean, to say you saw——."

" Oh, come on, you men," said Harry, apparently having had enough of Bunter, and the Famous Five went out into the quad.

" Beast!" hissed Bunter. " Letting a chap down, after all I've done for you. I say, Smithy—hold on a minute, Smithy—I say, old chap, will you tell Quelch that you saw that man give me the tenner yesterday——?"

" Will I?" grinned the Bounder.

" I mean to say, you ain't particular about telling whoppers, Smithy——."

" Eh?"

" It's in your line, really," said Bunter, blinking at him. " No good asking a decent chap: but you'll do it, won't you, Smithy?"

Why Herbert Vernon-Smith took him by the collar and banged his head on the passage wall, Bunter did not know. But that was what Smithy did, and he walked away after the rest of the form, leaving the fat Owl yelping and rubbing the fattest head at Greyfriars School. He was still rubbing it when Mr. Quelch came out of the form-room.

" Bunter! Follow me."

In the lowest spirits, Billy Bunter followed Quelch to his head-master's study.

Chapter XXXIX

A PAINFUL PARTING !

DR. LOCKE raised his eyebrows as he listened to what Mr. Quelch had to tell him. Billy Bunter stood uneasily, shifting from one fat leg to the other, and from the other to the one. He gasped as Dr. Locke's eyes turned on him and fixed him with a penetrating gaze.

" Most extraordinary ! " said the Head.

" There seems to me only one conclusion to be drawn, sir," said Mr. Quelch. " Since the story has spread that the packet of banknotes is concealed somewhere about the school, there has been some excitement on the subject, and very many boys have searched for it—including Bunter."

" I—I say, sir——."

" You need not speak, Bunter," said Mr. Quelch. " Bunter certainly has joined in the search for the packet. He now has a ten-pound note, for the possession of which he cannot account. I am reluctant—very reluctant—to believe that any boy in my form could be capable of filching——."

" I—I didn't——! " gasped Bunter.

" ——of filching one of the banknotes, having found the packet," said Mr. Quelch. " But——."

" But——! " said the Head.

" Bunter, sir, has told an absurd story to account for the banknote. He is, I am sorry to say, habitually untruthful, and for this reason I attach no importance to the story he has told— in itself incredible. But the matter is, of course, very simply put to the test by reference to the number of the banknote."

"Oh!" said the Head.

"No doubt, sir, a list of the numbers of the missing banknotes has been supplied to Inspector Grimes," said Mr. Quelch. "Mr. Twiss naturally makes a note of such details."

"Quite so," said Dr. Locke, "but——." He paused.

"Bunter!" snapped Mr. Quelch.

"Oh, lor'! I—I mean, yes, sir."

"Place the banknote on the table."

"It—it's mine, sir——."

"Place it on the table at once," rapped Mr. Quelch, with a look that made Bunter jump.

Bunter's tattered wallet came into view, and the £10 note was extracted therefrom and laid on the head-master's writing-table. Billy Bunter's eyes, and spectacles, lingered on it.

"The number," said Mr. Quelch, glancing at it, "is 000222468, sir. If Mr. Twiss's list is available ——."

Dr. Locke coughed.

"I am afraid, Mr. Quelch, that the matter cannot be put to the test so simply as you have naturally supposed," he said. "In point of fact, sir, the numbers of the missing banknotes are not available."

It was Mr. Quelch's turn to raise his eyebrows.

"It is an awkward circumstance and has, I fear, added somewhat to Inspector Grimes's difficulties," said the Head. "It is, of course, Mr. Twiss's custom to note the numbers of all banknotes passing through his hands as my secretary. But it unfortunately happens that the list was placed in the same drawer as the money, and as it cannot be found, there can be no doubt that it was taken at the same time as the banknotes by the unknown pilferer."

" Oh!" said Mr. Quelch.

It was not for a member of the Staff to reveal annoyance in the presence of his Chief. Mr. Quelch concealed the fact that he was annoyed. But as he had taken it for granted that that simple test would clear up the matter beyond any possible doubt, he was very much annoyed indeed.

" Then it remains only to question Bunter, sir," he said.

" Quite so," said the Head. " Bunter, you will explain to me precisely how this banknote came into your possession."

" Oh! Yes, sir!" groaned Bunter. " I—I—I ——."

" I warn you, Bunter, to tell your head-master the truth," said Mr. Quelch.

" I—I'm going to, sir. A—a man gave it to me, sir!" gasped Bunter. " I—I don't know who he was, or—or why he did—but—but he did, sir."

" Bless my soul!" said the Head, blankly.

" That, sir, is the story Bunter told a prefect and repeated to me," said Mr. Quelch. " Bunter has been in possession of that banknote since some time yesterday, and I gather that the general impression among his schoolfellows is that he has found the missing packet and abstracted a banknote from it. If this be so, perhaps I may be allowed to say, in extenuation of his conduct, that he is a very obtuse boy—extraordinarily obtuse —and may not have fully realised the iniquity of his action."

" I—I didn't—I—I never—I—I wasn't——."

" Bunter!" The Head's voice was very deep. " Tell me at once where you obtained that banknote."

" On—on the Cloister wall, sir."

" What? Do you mean that the missing packet was concealed on the Cloister wall and that you found it there? "

" Oh! No, sir! "

" Then what do you mean? "

" I—I mean, I was sitting on the Cloister wall, sir," gasped Bunter.

" You were sitting on the Cloister wall! " repeated the Head. " I asked you, Bunter, where you obtained the banknote."

" Yes, sir, that's where. You—you see, sir, I—I was sitting on the Cloister wall when that man came up in the lane——."

" What man? "

" The—the man who gave me the banknote, sir."

" Who was he? "

" I—I don't know."

" Bless my soul! " said Dr. Locke. " Are you telling me, Bunter, that a man you do not know came up to you and gave you a banknote for ten pounds? "

" Yes, sir! " groaned Bunter.

Mr. Quelch's lips shut in a tight line. Dr. Locke gazed at Bunter as if the fat junior had hypnotized him.

There was a silence in the study. Then Dr. Locke turned to the Remove master.

" This is extraordinary, Mr. Quelch," he said.

" Very! " said Mr. Quelch.

" Such a story is utterly incredible."

"Utterly! " agreed Mr. Quelch.

" It is, I suppose, within the bounds of possibility," said the Head. " But——."

Mr. Quelch made no rejoinder to that. It did not seem to him even within the bounds of possibility.

" You have nothing more to tell me, Bunter? "

asked the Head, transferring his gaze once more
to the hapless Owl.

" N-n-no, sir."

There was silence again. Dr. Locke gazed at
Bunter. Mr. Quelch waited for Dr. Locke to
speak. Bunter blinked uneasily at the Head's
puzzled, thoughtful face, then at the grim
countenance of his form-master—then at the banknote on the table. His blink at the banknote was
longing—in fact, yearning. It was borne in upon
Billy Bunter's fat mind that his riches were about
to take unto themselves wings and fly away.
There was going to be a painful—a very painful—
parting!

The Head spoke at last.

" Mr. Quelch! Bunter's story is so extraordinary as to seem quite—quite incredible. But
in so serious a matter we must proceed with care.
For the present the boy may go."

" You may go, Bunter," said Mr. Quelch.

" Oh! Yes, sir! C-c-c-can I tut-tut-take my
bub-bub-banknote, sir? " stammered Bunter.

" What! " Quelch almost thundered. " What
did you say, Bunter? "

" Oh! Nothing, sir! N-n-nothing! " gasped
Bunter.

Dr. Locke picked up the £10 note.

" I will take charge of this, for the present,"
he said, "and retain it till the ownership is
established."

He opened his pocket-book, folded the banknote and placed it therein. Billy Bunter's dismayed gaze followed it as it disappeared. He
seemed unable to take his spectacles off it. The
sad eyes of Dido did not follow the departing sails
of Æneas so longingly as Billy Bunter's eyes and
spectacles followed that departing banknote. It
disappeared.

Mr. Quelch pointed to the door.

A dismal Owl rolled out of the Head's study, leaving head-master and form-master in consultation. Sadly and sorrowfully he rolled away. For a brief period the Owl of the Remove had been in possession of a £10 note—unchangeable, it is true, but still a tenner—and now it was gone from his gaze like a beautiful dream. Long and lugubrious was the fat countenance of William George Bunter. Like Lucifer, Son of the Morning, he had fallen from his high estate, and great was the fall thereof.

Chapter XL

BEASTLY FOR BUNTER!

"GERRAWAY!" hissed Billy Bunter.

"Ha, ha, ha!"

"Bunter's got the spot-light!" remarked Bob Cherry.

There was no doubt that Bunter had!

Bunter had tea'd in Hall that day. His ten-pound note was gone, and his postal-order had not come: and his weekly half-crown of pocket-money was safe in the till at Mrs. Mimble's tuck-shop. Once more, like the seed in the parable, Bunter had fallen in a stony place. In Hall, innumerable eyes had turned on Bunter—all the school knew now about that tenner. Everybody, of course, took it for granted that the tenner had come from the lost packet. Bunter was glanced at, stared at, pointed at, as the man who had found the "treasure" and was keeping it dark to help himself from it. Why the Head didn't make him cough up that packet was a puzzle to most fellows —but nobody doubted that Bunter could have coughed it up, had he chosen so to do.

Bunter, as a rule, liked any amount of lime-light that might come his way. But he did not enjoy it now. Gladly he would have swanked as the proprietor of the only ten-pound note in the Lower School. But even Bunter did not enjoy fame as a snapper-up of lost tenners. His fat face wore a frown when he rolled out of Hall—but in the quad he received as much attention, or more. It was not on record that any fellow quite of his own accord had ever sought Billy Bunter's society before. Now all was changed—all sorts and conditions of fellows seemed to haunt him, fairly dogging his footsteps.

When he walked in the quad, he was as good as the head of a procession. Fags of the Second and Third were specially interested in him and they followed wherever Bunter went. On a half-holiday fellows were free to do as they liked—and quite a large number seemed to like to keep an eye on Bunter—the man who knew where the "treasure" was!

In deep ire, Bunter blinked round at his followers. He glared at Tubb and Paget of the Third—he glared at Gatty and Myers of the Second—even at his own minor, Sammy Bunter, did he cast a most unbrotherly glare.

"Will you gerraway?" he howled.

"Well, where's that packet?" asked Tubb.

"You might tell me where it is, Billy!" urged Sammy Bunter.

"I don't know where it is!" shrieked Bunter.

"Well, that's rot," said Sammy. "How could you snoop a tenner out of it if you don't know where it is?"

Bunter, breathing fury, rolled on. Tubb and Co. continued to haunt his footsteps. Obviously they were convinced that Bunter knew where that packet was, and suspected that he might pay it another visit—now that the Head had taken away the tenner. If he did, a whole crowd of fellows were going to be at his heels.

Harry Wharton and Co., when they came out after tea, could not help grinning at the sight of Bunter and his followers—walking like a Highland chief of ancient times followed by his "tail."

Billy Bunter gave them a reproachful blink.

"I say, you fellows, this is too jolly thick!" he said. "Look at those grubby little beasts—

they think they'll find the packet if they keep me in sight. I can't move a step without bumping into a beastly fag. And all you fellows can do is to cackle."

"Well, why not take the packet to the Head and have done with it?" asked Johnny Bull.

"How can I when I don't know where it is, blow you?"

"Forgotten where you left it?" asked Bob.

"I never left it," howled Bunter. "I don't know anything about it. Haven't I told you that a man——?"

"Are you still spinning the same yarn?" asked Bob, with a stare. "Losing your inventive powers, old fat man? It's time you had a new story."

"Beast!"

"Well, be reasonable!" urged Bob. "You don't really expect anyone to believe that somebody's going about giving ten-pound notes away for nothing, do you? You're an old hand—you can make up a better one than that!"

"Ha, ha, ha!"

Billy Bunter snorted and rolled on, disconsolate —Tubb and Co. still on his trail.

He rolled past the big bay window of Common-Room, where a deep booming voice caused him to blink round. Mr. Prout, master of the Fifth, was looking from the window and his eyes fixed on Bunter with disapproval.

"That is the boy!" boomed Prout.

Several other faces joined Prout's in the window. Mr. Capper, Mr. Hacker, Mr. Twiss and Mr. Wiggins, all stared at Bunter.

"Ah!" said Mr. Capper. "That is the boy who has found the packet of banknotes——."

"That is he!" said Prout. "It is common knowledge! Yet he has not produced the packet!"

" Extraordinary ! " said Mr. Wiggins.

" Very extraordinary ! " said Mr. Twiss.

" Amazing ! " said Mr. Hacker.

" Unparalleled ! " boomed Prout.

Billy Bunter's fat ears burned as he rolled on, with Prout's boom echoing behind him. Evidently they had been talking of it in Common-Room—everybody knew about it now and was discussing it.

" Beasts ! " breathed Bunter.

He was getting too much attention in the quad and was more than tired of the attentions of Tubb and Co. He rolled into the House to take refuge in the Rag. If, as Tubb and Co. evidently surmised, he had intended to revisit the hiding-place of the missing packet, he had to give it up. The fags had to give it up also—though some of them continued to keep an eye open for Bunter in case he came out again.

In the Rag a crowd of fellows stared at Bunter as he came in. He was still the cynosure of all eyes.

" Here he is," chuckled Skinner. " Got any more tenners, Bunter ? "

" No ! " howled Bunter.

" Why not ? " asked Snoop. " You know where to find them, don't you ? "

" What I can't make out is why the Head hasn't sacked him already," remarked Vernon-Smith. " He must know that Bunter knows where the packet is."

" There's no proof, Smithy ! " said Redwing, mildly.

The Bounder gave a scoffing laugh.

" Do you believe Bunter's latest ? " he asked. " Think a jolly old philanthropist is wandering about giving away tenners ? "

Redwing made no reply to that. Really, it was not easy to believe.

There was no comfort for Bunter in the Rag. He rolled away again and headed for the Remove studies. The door of No. 2, as he passed it, stood open and within sat Tom Brown and Hazeldene at the study table slicing a pineapple and disposing of the slices. Bunter came to a halt. Bunter liked pineapple.

"I say, you fellows——!" he squeaked. "I say, that pineapple looks all right."

"It is all right!" agreed Tom Brown.

"Well, you might ask a fellow if he'd like a slice, as you've got a lot left," said Bunter warmly.

"None of it left," said Tom Brown, shaking his head. "It's all right! If it's all right, how can any of it be left?"

Hazel chuckled and Bunter stared. It required about a minute for Bunter's powerful brain to assimilate that this was a joke.

"But look here," added the New Zealand junior. "You can have the lot if you like, Bunter ——."

"Yes, rather!" gasped Bunter.

"If you'll tell us where to find that packet ——."

"Oh, really, Browney——."

"We'll take it to the Head without borrowing any of the tenners," added Tom Brown sarcastically.

"Beast!"

Bunter rolled on. He found Peter Todd in No. 7 Study, and Peter gave him a far-from-pally or welcoming look as he deposited his weight in the study armchair. Peter picked up a cushion and eyed the fat Owl.

"Have you taken that packet to the Head, Bunter?" he asked.

"I've never even seen the rotten packet!" yelled Bunter. "Look here, Toddy, you might take a fellow's word, knowing me as you do."

"That's the trouble," said Toddy. "I know you too jolly well, old fat fraud. Now look here, Bunter, I've heard that Grimey is about the school to-day. Everybody's talking about that banknote and Grimey will hear of it sooner or later. Do you want Grimey on your track? Go and get that packet at once——."

"I've told you a man gave me that tenner ——."

"Yes—don't tell me again. Go and get the packet——."

"I tell you the man came up to me and said— Beast! Don't you chuck that cushion at me! If you chuck that cushion at me I'll jolly well— yarooop!"

Bunter rolled out of No. 7 Study again!

Chapter XLI

CAUGHT !

MR. GRIMES hardly breathed.

It was nearly midnight and all Greyfriars was sunk in silence and slumber. On the landing it was densely dark. Mr. Grimes could see nothing —but his ears were keen: and faintly, barely audible, he heard in the silence the sound of a softly-opening door.

Some of the Greyfriars fellows had heard that the Courtfield inspector was about the school again. But nobody, certainly, supposed or dreamed that Mr. Grimes was there now, still less that he was keeping silent and vigilant watch on the dark landing. But there was Mr. Grimes: noiseless, invisible, with red plump ears cocked to listen.

A door had opened—and closed again. Someone unseen had emerged and, with hardly the faintest sound, was crossing to the stairs. Cautious feet in socks were almost noiseless. Mr. Grimes's feet were of substantial size and weight —but in rubber shoes they made no sound at all.

Certainly the unseen man who was stepping so stealthily down the stairs did not dream that a portly figure was behind him in the dark.

On the lower landing there was a gleam of starlight from the big window. Black against the starlight was the silhouette of a man stopping at the window.

For a full minute it stood there—silent, motionless, listening. Then came a faint creak. A casement was being opened.

Outside was a faint stirring of the thick ivy that clustered round the window—tough old ivy, almost as old as Greyfriars itself. An arm was stretched from the window and a hand was groping in the ivy.

The hand came back with something in it.

Then the tiny beam of a small torch was flashed on. Inspector Grimes, from the darkness, watched a strange sight. With a packet in one hand, the flash-light in the other, the stealthy man was peering through rimless pince-nez—examining the packet.

"Thank you, Mr. Twiss!" said Inspector Grimes.

The torch and the packet fell to the floor together: the man spun round with a startled squeal. A hand, plump but with a grip like steel, fastened on his shoulder.

Chapter XLII

MR. GRIMES EXPLAINS

"BUT—— " stammered Dr. Locke.

The morning sunlight falling in at the study window showed his face clouded and troubled. In Inspector Grimes's plump, solid countenance it revealed a quiet stolid satisfaction. Mr. Grimes had "got his man," which was naturally very satisfactory to Mr. Grimes.

"A shock to you, no doubt, sir," said Mr. Grimes. "But it was to be expected when it turned out to be an inside job, sir."

"But Mr. Twiss——!" murmured the Head. "I should never have dreamed——. He has not been long in my service, but—but——."

"From information received, sir, my attention was directed to Mr. Twiss," said Inspector Grimes.

Dr. Locke certainly did not guess or dream that that "information" had been "received" from a Greyfriars junior. Mr. Grimes had no intention of mentioning Herbert Vernon-Smith.

"For that reason, sir, I asked you for a key so that I could, when necessary, keep watch inside the House," said Mr. Grimes.

"I understand that, Mr. Grimes. But I do not understand why you should have expected the wretched man to visit the hiding place of the packet last night and thus fall into your hands."

Mr. Grimes smiled—a smile of satisfaction— almost fatuous self-satisfaction. Undoubtedly Mr. Grimes was very pleased with himself.

"That, sir, was the outcome of measures I had taken," he said. "The man was led to believe

that the packet had been discovered and a part of
its contents abstracted by a schoolboy. Naturally
he was very much alarmed. Yesterday the whole
school, including Mr. Twiss, knew of this supposed
discovery. One can imagine his feelings—his fear
and his anxiety. His impulse would be to revisit
the hide-out and ascertain whether the packet was
safe, to examine it and to remove it to yet another
hiding-place if he found that it had been tampered
with."

"Oh!" exclaimed the Head.

"On a previous occasion, I have reason to
believe, he did actually change the hiding-place of
the packet in fear of its discovery by some junior
schoolboys, and this was done during morning
school," said Mr. Grimes. "Yesterday, however,
he did not venture to act in the daytime—no doubt
because he was aware that I was about the school
and because I made it a point to contact him
several times during the day. Had he done so, I
have no doubt that I should have detected him—
but it was obviously safer to leave it till a late
hour. This he did—and when he made his move
I was prepared for it."

"I understand. But——." The Head looked
perplexed. "Now that the packet has been
examined it has been ascertained that only a
number of the one-pound notes are missing from
it——."

"Twenty-five, sir, doubtless expended by the
man on some of his miserable racing speculations.
The banknotes are intact."

"Then the banknote in the possession of the
boy Bunter did not, after all, belong to the
packet."

"It did not, sir."

"I am glad of that, at least—it is a great
relief," said Dr. Locke. "The story told by the

boy to account for its possession was extraordinary—indeed incredible. Can it have been
true?"

"Quite so, sir."

"It is amazing," said the Head. "According
to the boy, a stranger whom he had never seen
before sought him out and handed him a £10
note. And it was this· extraordinary circumstance
that gave the alarm to the pilferer and caused him
to revisit the hiding-place of the packet and thus
betray himself——."

"The pilferer, sir, was no more likely to believe
Bunter's strange story than anyone else. He, like
all others, took it for granted that Bunter had discovered the packet and helped himself from it.
That, sir, is why the stranger gave Bunter the
£10 note—in order to give Mr. Twiss exactly that
impression."

"Eh?"

Inspector Grimes's stolid face melted into a
grin. But that grin vanished under the surprised
stare of the Head. Mr. Grimes coughed.

"I must explain, sir. The stranger who sought
out Master Bunter and handed him the £10 note
was a plain-clothes officer acting under my
instructions."

"Bless my soul!" ejaculated the Head.

"You will realise, sir, that the pilferer's
identity was unknown—that even had the lost
packet been found and the money recovered, the
pilferer would still have remained unknown—still
here, sir, and enjoying undeserved confidence,
with opportunities for repeating his action at
another time. There was only one way to nail
him—ahem! I should say, only one way to
establish the facts—and that was by taking him in
the very act of handling the packet he had hidden.
For this purpose it was necessary to alarm him

with the impression that the hiding-place of the packet had become known to another person——."

" Mr. Grimes! "

" I have some acquaintance with Master Bunter, sir," continued the inspector stolidly, " and I did not doubt that a banknote in his possession would soon become known to every one and that it would be attributed to what would seem the only possible source—the hidden packet. The matter, in fact, worked out exactly as I had anticipated."

Dr. Locke gazed fixedly at Mr. Grimes.

Mr. Grimes seemed to have taken his breath away.

" Obviously, sir," continued Mr. Grimes, " the boy would not be able to change the banknote acquired in such dubious circumstances and no harm would be done. Now that the matter has come to a satisfactory conclusion it can, of course, be explained——."

" Upon my word! " said the Head. " Then—then the banknote I have taken charge of is your property, Mr. Grimes? "

" Precisely, sir." Mr. Grimes coughed again. " But as it was given to the boy, and as he may be considered perhaps entitled to some reward for his unconscious and inadvertent assistance to the law—hem——."

" Had you consulted me in the matter, Mr. Grimes, I could never have approved of this—this —this most extraordinary proceeding——," said Dr. Locke.

Mr. Grimes did not explain that that was precisely why he hadn't consulted him in the matter! He merely gave a propitiatory murmur.

" However——! " said the Head.

" However——! " agreed Mr. Grimes.

" Your banknote will be returned to you, Mr.

Grimes. But in the circumstances I feel that the boy ought not to be the loser."

"Quite so, sir!" agreed Mr. Grimes.

"But really——!" said the Head. "Really ——!"

He left it at that!

Chapter XLIII

WANTED BY THE BEAK !

" BUNTER ! "

" It—it wasn't me, sir ! " stammered Bunter.

Mr. Quelch was addressing William George Bunter in form on Monday morning. Bunter blinked at him uneasily. What Quelch was going to say Bunter did not know—but he denied it provisionally as it were.

Quelch gave him a look.

" I was about to say, Bunter, that your head-master desires to see you in his study after third school ! " he rapped.

" Oh, crikey ! " moaned Bunter.

Skinner winked at Snoop. The Bounder shrugged his shoulders. Harry Wharton and Co. exchanged glances. Peter Todd knitted his brows. All the Remove took note of Quelch's words, in one way or another. From those words they could draw only one conclusion—that the game was up for Billy Bunter.

The lesson proceeded, Bunter sitting with a worried fat face.

Bunter did not want to pay that call on his head-master. Very much indeed he did not. He dreaded it with a deep dread. When he blinked at the other fellows he could read in their faces the general opinion—that he was " for it." He could not help sharing that opinion. It was a dismaying prospect.

In that worried frame of mind Bunter was not likely to shine in class. He gave even less attention than usual to Quelch's valuable instruction. But

Quelch was unusually patient with him that morning.

The lesson was English Literature: and Bunter gave Shakespeare as the author of the " Elegy in a Country Churchyard ": then, seeing in Quelch's face that that wouldn't do, hastily amended it to Milton: and discerning that this was not a winner, desperately made it Tennyson. But the thunder did not roll—Quelch merely gave him an expressive glance.

Bunter rolled out in break with an expression on his fat face which indicated that all the troubles in the universe, and a few over, had landed on his plump shoulders.

" I say, you fellows, you heard what Quelch said!—I've got to see the Beak after third school!" Bunter blinked dolorously at a crowd of more or less sympathetic faces, " I say, what do you think's up?"

" Your number!" said Skinner.

" Beast!" groaned Bunter.

" You fat chump," said Peter Todd. " Why didn't you take that packet to the Head while there was time? I did my best to make you. I kicked you on Saturday—a fellow couldn't do more."

" I tell you I never——."

" Take the packet with you after third school, Bunter," said Harry Wharton. " That's the best thing you can do now."

" How can I when I don't know where it is? " wailed Bunter. " I keep on telling you that a man gave me that tenner and that I never found the packet at all, and if I had I'd no more have touched it than I'd touch a fellow's cake——."

" Oh, my hat! "

" Ha, ha, ha! "

" A man came up and gave me that tenner

while I was sitting on the Cloister wall——."

"Let's all go and sit on the Cloister wall!" suggested Skinner. "Perhaps a man will come up and give us a tenner each."

"The perhapsfulness is terrific," chuckled Hurree Jamset Ram Singh.

"Go and get the packet now and for goodness' sake don't spin that yarn again," said Bob Cherry. "Can't you see it won't wash?"

"Tain't fair!" wailed Bunter. "The Head would believe you if you told him. So would Quelch."

"Well, it would be true if I told him. But——." Bob looked hard at Bunter's worried fat face, quite a new idea coming into his mind. "I—I wonder——. Is it possible, you men, that Bunter's told the truth and that it did happen?"

"How could anything have happened if Bunter said it did?" inquired Johnny Bull.

"Ha, ha, ha!"

"It's all Wharton's fault!" groaned Bunter.

"Mine!" exclaimed the captain of the Remove in astonishment. "How is it my fault, you fat duffer?"

"I asked you to tell Quelch you saw that man give me the tenner. You jolly well know I did," said Bunter warmly.

"Why, you—you—you!" gasped Wharton, while the other fellows yelled with laughter.

"Blessed if I see anything to cackle at when a fellow's going up to the Head," snorted Bunter. "I say, Bob, old chap, you'll back up a pal, if Wharton won't. You'll come with me to the Head."

"What would be the good of that?" asked Bob.

"I—I mean, you can tell him you saw it all ——."

" What? "

" And—and look here, old chap, if you think it will go down better with the Head. I'll say it was my Uncle William after all——."

" Oh, crumbs! "

" And you'll say that you saw Uncle William hand me the tenner that that man gave me on the Cloister wall——."

" Ha, ha, ha! "

Bob Cherry stared blankly at the Owl of the Remove. He seemed dumbfounded. Apparently taking silence for consent, Bunter rattled on eagerly:

" Only, of course, we shall have to fix up what we're going to say. It doesn't matter what, really, so long as we say the same thing. You see that? You can't be too careful with a beak. You come with me to the Head and say—Leggo my neck! "

" Ha, ha, ha! "

Bob Cherry did not let go the fat neck. He shook and shook and shook again, and finally sat Bunter down on the hard, unsympathetic earth with a resounding bump. Then he stalked away, leaving the crowd of juniors yelling with merriment, and Billy Bunter yelling, too—though not with merriment.

Third school that morning was not a happy hour for Billy Bunter. For the first time in his fat career Bunter would have been glad had the lesson lasted longer. He watched the form-room clock: the hand, which usually seemed to Bunter's eyes to crawl, now seemed to race. Every tick of the clock brought nearer that dreaded visit to the dreaded study.

He would even have been glad to have been kept in when the hour was up. But Quelch, who sometimes kept him in for inattention or careless-ness or laziness, did not seem to think of it on this particular morning. He merely glanced at Bunter when the Remove were dismissed and said:

"You will now go to your head-master's study, Bunter."

"Yes, sir!" groaned Bunter.

He went out with the Remove, but did not head for Dr. Locke's study. It seemed as if his fat little legs refused to carry him thither. He rolled out into the quad after the Famous Five.

"I say, you fellows——."

"Go to the Head, you fat ass," said Johnny Bull.

"I—I ain't going," said Bunter, desperately. "I—I say, think the Head will forget about it if —if I don't go?"

"Fathead!"

"Well, he might forget," argued Bunter. "He's rather an old donkey, you know. I—I jolly well ain't going. I say, you fellows, don't walk away while a chap's talking to you——. Beasts!" hooted Bunter at five departing backs.

An angular figure appeared in the doorway of the House, looking out. Bunter could guess for whom Quelch was looking and he made a strategic movement to screen himself behind Vernon-Smith, who, heedless of Bunter, was speaking to Tom Redwing.

"I hear that Twiss is gone, Reddy."

"Is he?" said Redwing.

"Yes—and Grimey seems to be finished here. It looks to me——."

"I say, Smithy, keep in front of me!" gasped Bunter. "I say, keep just in front, so that Quelch won't see me——."

"Ha, ha, ha!" yelled the Bounder. Keeping in front of Bunter would have left a considerable portion of that plump youth visible on either side

of Smithy, though that circumstance did not seem
to occur to the fat Owl.

"Bunter!"

"Oh, lor'! Now he's seen me——."

"Bunter!"

"Oh, dear! Yes, sir."

"Why have you not gone to your head-master?
Go at once!" rapped Mr. Quelch.

There was no help for it. In the lowest of
spirits, Billy Bunter rolled into the House, and
with reluctant feet trod the corridor to his head-
master's study. And a crowd of Remove fellows
and fellows of other Forms, wondering what was
going to happen to the fat Owl, waited for him to
emerge, to hear the verdict.

Chapter XLIV

ALL RIGHT FOR BUNTER !

" HALLO, hallo, hallo! "
  " Here he is! "
  " Bunked? "
  " Sacked? "
  " Whopped? "
  " What's the jolly old verdict? "
Billy Bunter rolled out of the House. Scores of
fellows stared at him as he reappeared—dozens of
voices hailed him.

Bunter was grinning!

He had gone into the House looking as if he
found life at Greyfriars barely worth living. In
less than ten minutes he came out again with a
wide grin on his fat countenance—a grin so wide
that it almost looked like meeting round the back
of his neck. It was quite a startling change in
Bunter.

Certainly he did not look like a fellow who was
bunked, or sacked, or whopped. He looked happy
and glorious. He almost strutted into the quad.
And the Greyfriars fellows stared at him in
astonishment. Every fellow—including Bunter
himself—had taken it for granted that the fat Owl
was " for it." And now——!

" You've seen the Head? " asked Harry
Wharton, quite puzzled.

Bunter nodded carelessly.

" Oh, yes, I've seen the old boy."

" And what did he say? " demanded Bob.

" Oh, we had a chat," said Bunter.

" You're not sacked? " exclaimed the Bounder.

"He, he, he! Do I look sacked?"

"Or whopped?" asked Johnny Bull.

"Do I look whopped?" asked Bunter, derisively.

"The whopfulness does not seem to have been terrific," remarked Hurree Jamset Ram Singh. "But what——?"

"Didn't the Head want that packet?" demanded Vernon-Smith. "Isn't that why he sent for you?"

"He, he, he!" cachinnated Bunter. "No, he didn't want the packet, Smithy! You see, he's got it."

"What!" exclaimed a dozen fellows.

Billy Bunter's grin became, if possible, wider still. Bunter was enjoying this. Undoubtedly he was the fellow with the news!

"Has that packet been found, then?" exclaimed Bob Cherry.

"So the Head said, and I suppose he knows," grinned Bunter. "He didn't go into particulars, but he told me that the packet has been found and that the banknotes in it were tacked—I think he said tacked——."

"Intact, perhaps!" suggested Nugent.

"Yes, that was it," agreed Bunter. "Anyhow, he meant that they were all there. If he said intact he meant they were all there—I expect that's what 'intact' means. Anyhow, that was what the Head meant."

"Ha, ha, ha!"

"Is he pulling our leg, or what?" asked Johnny Bull. "If the packet's been found with the banknotes intact, where did Bunter's banknote come from?"

"The wherefulness is terrific."

"I say, you fellows, I told you where it came from," hooted Bunter. "A man came up to me when I was sitting on the Cloister wall——."

"Gammon!"

"Don't tell us that one again!" implored Skinner.

"You fellows never believed me," said Bunter, blinking reproachfully at the Famous Five through his big spectacles. "You needn't deny it—you didn't!"

"We jolly well didn't!" agreed Bob.

"Well, the Head knows me better than you fellows do," said Bunter. "The Head takes my word, if you fellows don't. He knows a fellow who would scorn to tell a lie."

"Oh, great pip!"

"And I believe he jolly well knows who the man was," said Bunter. "He said that he was now acquainted with all the circumstances—that's the way he talks, of course—but he meant that he knew all about it. And he jolly well said that in the circumstances I could retain possession of the ten-pound note—which means that I can keep it."

"What?" came a general gasp.

"That's what he said!" trilled Bunter. "He said, 'That tenner's yours and you can stick to it.' See?"

"Oh, my hat!" gasped Bob, "I can sort of hear the Head saying that!"

"Ha, ha, ha!"

"Well, not those exact words!" yapped Bunter. "Of course, he was long-winded. What he actually said was that, being acquainted with all the circumstances, he approved of my keeping the banknote. And I'm jolly well going to."

The juniors gazed at Bunter. It was clear from his looks that his interview with the Head had gone off satisfactorily. But this was the limit!

"Mean to say you've got the banknote, then?" demanded Smithy.

"Well, I haven't exactly got the banknote," admitted Bunter.

"I fancied not!" grinned Skinner.

"Pulling our leg all the time," said the Bounder.

"Oh, really, Smithy——."

"Well, why didn't the Head hand it to you, if he said you could keep it?" demanded half-a-dozen fellows.

"He would have, only——."

"Only!" grinned Skinner.

"Only I asked him to give me pound notes instead——."

"Oh!"

"And he jolly well did!" said Bunter, triumphantly. "He said something about being careful in the explenditure of so much money——."

"In the whatter?"

"Expenditure, perhaps," said Harry Wharton, laughing.

"Well, I think the Head said explenditure," said Bunter. "He said it was a large sum for a junior to have. Of course, he doesn't know about the whopping remittances I get from Bunter Court——."

"Ha, ha, ha!"

"No more than we do!" agreed Bob.

"Yah! Anyhow, the Head gave me the quids, and that's jolly well that!"

"Got 'em about you?" asked Skinner, still sceptical.

"Look!" chirruped Bunter.

A fat hand went into a sticky pocket. It emerged with a wad of pound notes in it, a fragment of an ancient bullseye adhering to one of them.

"What about that?" trilled Bunter.

It was the climax!

Billy Bunter enjoyed that climax. But he did not linger. Greater enjoyments were in store. The tuck-shop called—a call irresistible to Bunter. With that windfall in his sticky fingers, Bunter had no time to waste. He headed for the place where there were foodstuffs, like a homing pigeon. Evidently there was going to be a sticky end for Billy Bunter's Banknote.

THE END